Still Candy Shopping

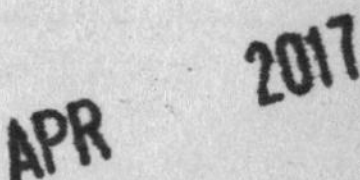

Also by Kiki Swinson

Wifey

I'm Still Wifey

Life After Wifey

The Candy Shop

A Sticky Situation

Still Wifey Material

Playing Dirty

Notorious

Sleeping with the Enemy (with Wahida Clark)

Heist (with De'nesha Diamond)

Lifestyles of the Rich and Shameless (with Noire)

A Gangster and a Gentleman
(with De'nesha Diamond)

Most Wanted (with Nikki Turner)

Published by Kensington Publishing Corp.

Still Candy Shopping

Kiki Swinson

Amaleka McCall

Kensington Publishing Corp.
http://www.kensingtonbooks.com

DAFINA BOOKS are published by

Kensington Publishing Corp.
119 West 40th Street
New York, NY 10018

Published by arrangement with K.S. Publications, PO Box 68878, Virginia Beach, VA, 23471.

Website: www.kikiswinson.net
Email: KS.publications@yahoo.com

All Kensington Titles, Imprints, and Distributed Lines are available at special quantity discounts for bulk purchases for sales promotions, premiums, fund-raising, and educational or institutional use. Special book excerpts or customized printings can also be created to fit specific needs. For details, write or phone the office of the Kensington special sales manager: Kensington Publishing Corp., 119 West 40th Street, New York, NY 10018, attn: Special Sales Department, Phone: 1-800-221-2647.

Dafina and the Dafina logo Reg. U.S. Pat. & TM Off.

ISBN-13: 978-0-7582-9377-0
ISBN-10: 0-7582-9377-1
First Kensington Mass Market Edition: February 2014

10 9 8 7 6 5 4 3 2 1

Printed in the United States of America

The Candy Shop 2

Kiki Swinson

My Epiphany

I'd been out on these streets for two years now, and I realized that shit had only gotten worse for me. The money I got from my divorce settlement went up in smoke quicker than I could blink my eyes. And everybody I'd met on my journey had either gone back to prison or overdosed. I'd seen more body bags dragged out of shooting galleries and abandoned houses than I'd seen children playing on the streets. It was a whole new world out here. And every day it was changing for the worse.

I figured I could stay out here on these streets and die, or get myself some help so I could go back to living a normal life. Shit, there was not a day that went by that I didn't think about how happy my life would've been if I had not started getting high. I would've still had my family, my home, my career, and my sanity. Now I knew I couldn't harp on the what-ifs, but I could do something about my addiction this very day. Thank God for that cat named Seth. If it weren't for him dropping me off in front of this detox center, I would still be running the dope man down to get my next fix.

As I walked toward the brick building, I saw this short black guy force the glass door open with his red Adidas duffel bag thrown across his shoulder.

"You think I give a fuck!" I heard him yell. "I ain't wanna be in this motherfucking place anyway!"

I didn't know whom he was talking to until this tall Hispanic-looking guy walked up to the glass door and pulled it shut. He stood there for just a brief second and then he walked away. Shocked by the actions of this guy, I hesitated for a brief moment. I began to have second thoughts about whether to seek help from this place.

I turned toward the guy and said, "Hey, excuse me." And then I started walking in his direction. He stopped in his tracks and turned around. When I got within two feet of him I stopped and took a deep breath. "Excuse me, but can I ask you something?" I finally asked after I caught my breath.

"If it's about that place, you asking the wrong nigga," he didn't hesitate to say.

"Well, um," I said, and then I paused to gather my thoughts. And before I could utter another word, he beat me to the punch.

"Look, whatcha need? 'Cause I gotta go catch the bus uptown," he said, and then he swayed his body back and forth. I knew this movement as the sign of an impatient addict. And when he said he was going uptown, I knew that only meant he was trying to catch the dope man. I looked into his mouth and noticed how rotten his teeth were, which was a sure sign that he was a heavy crack user. His skin was ashy too.

"How long were you in the program?" I finally asked.

"A week. Why?"

"Because I'm trying to get clean, and I heard that this was the place to come."

The guy spit on the ground, and then wiped his mouth with the back of his hand. "That place ain't shit!" he said. "They just put me out 'cause I cursed out my counselor. They are crazy as a motherfucka! They don't let you do shit up in there. They talk shit to you like you a fucking kid or something. You'll see if you go up in there."

"I ain't got no choice. I'm trying to get off the street," I told him.

"A'ight. Well, that's on you," he replied, and then he turned and began to jog away. I watched him as he jogged up Virginia Beach Boulevard toward the Newtown Road bus stop.

Not knowing whether to follow him uptown or go inside this building to get the treatment I needed, I stood there and wondered what to do. It only took me about ten seconds to realize that I didn't have any other options, so I turned my butt back toward that brick building and took the first step forward. I couldn't tell you what that guy's problem was, but I knew what my problem was, and I needed a lot of help to fix it.

When I approached the front of the glass door,

I pressed down on the gray button near the door handle. Immediately after the bell rang, a voice came through the intercom. "Can I help you?" a man's voice asked.

"I need to talk to someone because I'm trying to get clean," I got up the gumption to say.

"I'm sorry, ma'am, but you just can't walk into the center without making an appointment with the intake counselor," he replied.

"Can I make the appointment now?"

"I'm sorry, but she's seeing another client right now."

"Can I wait until she's done?"

"No, I'm sorry, ma'am. It doesn't work that way. You're going to have to call to speak with her, and then she'll schedule you an appointment to do a screening."

"Listen, sir, I know you guys have a protocol to follow. But I'm begging you to let me in," I said, my voice cracking as tears began to fall from my eyes. "I'm tired of getting high. And I want to get clean really bad, so if I walk away from this door right now, I may not make it back."

I stood there as the tears continued to fall down my face and waited for the man to respond, but he remained silent. He didn't utter another word through the intercom. Immediately my heart sank. All the hope I harbored on my way to this center dissipated instantly. I was doomed and I knew it.

I took a step backward to turn around and leave, but was stopped in my tracks by a voice coming through the intercom. "Ma'am, do you have a valid ID and your Social Security card on you?" the guy asked.

In that instant it felt like a load had been lifted off my heart. I could literally see a light at the end of my dark tunnel, and that alone made me hopeful again.

"I don't have my Social Security card, but I have my ID," I quickly responded.

"Do you know your social?"

"Yes, I know it."

"All right. Well I'm going to buzz you in. When you come in I want you to come up that first flight of steps and turn right, and I will meet you at the entryway."

I exhaled and smiled into the camera that hung over the door. A couple seconds later I heard the buzzing sound and immediately grabbed the door handle. Within ten seconds flat I was in the building and face to face with the man behind the voice from the intercom. He wasn't that easy on the eyes. But he had a warm spirit and that was all I needed. At first glance his one-hundred-thirty-pound, five-feet-four-inch frame didn't match his husky voice. If I hadn't spoken to him through the intercom system, I would've thought that he was one of the residents of this facility. To put it mildly, he definitely looked like a rehabilitated drug user.

He extended his hand and introduced himself. "Hi, I'm Frank Macer, and I am one of the floor monitors here at the center."

I shook his hand and introduced myself as well. "My name is Faith Simmons."

"Welcome to the Salvation Army Drug Rehabilitation Center."

"I am happy to be here," I told him.

"We're happy to have you," he said, and then he instructed me to follow him. We walked down a short hallway and entered a very small office. I knew this was his office space because it had two TV monitors where he could watch both the front and the back of the center. I took a seat in the chair that sat directly in front of his desk while he grabbed some paperwork from his filing cabinet.

"Here, fill out this paperwork, and while you're doing that, I'll make a copy of your ID," he said as he placed the form down on the desk in front of me. After I handed him my ID card, he made a copy of it and then handed it back to me.

While I filled out the paperwork, which was a basic orientation form, he briefed me about the rules of the program. "Now this is a twelve-step program. We deal with drug and alcohol abuse as a learned behavior. Our intake counselor is Pamela Williams. She will be the one who interviews you and processes you into the program. She will also go over all the rules of the program. I must also inform you that this is a co-ed facility. But the men and women have separate sleeping quarters. The women are on one side of the building and the men are on the other. We have video surveillance cameras on every hall so we can monitor everyone's movements. If at anytime I or any of the other floor monitors see you in an unauthorized area of the facility, you will be given a warning. But the second time around you will get kicked out. Now if we see you in a sexual act with any of the clients here, you will get kicked out of the program immediately. No questions asked."

Shocked by his forwardness, I said, "Wow! Really?"

"Those are the rules. Those who are serious about their recovery shouldn't have a problem adjusting."

After he laid down some more rules, he waited for me to sign the form. "Do you have any questions for me?" he asked as I handed him the completed form.

After telling him no, he asked me to follow him. I followed him back into the hallway and into a lounge area with a forty-two-inch TV that sat on a wooden stand. The lounge area was completely empty. There was no one in sight. "So where is everybody?" I asked.

"They're all in an NA meeting."

"So where are we going?" I asked as he walked from one side of the lounge area to the other to open a door that led to another hallway.

"I'm taking you to see Mrs. Williams so she can do your screening."

"Do you know how long that will take?"

"It shouldn't take more than thirty minutes. And once she's done, she's going to show you around the facility, and then she will show you to your living quarters."

After Mr. Macer gave me the rundown about what to expect, he took me around a corner and walked me straight into the intake counselor's office. She was in the middle of a phone conversation when we entered her office, so Mr. Macer instructed me to sit in the chair next to her desk. After I sat down, he placed my paperwork on her desk and exited the office.

I sat there patiently and watched her while she was on her call. She wasn't like anything I pictured her to be. She was very pretty. In fact, she looked like she could've been my younger sister. She and I had the same light complexion with an hourglass body. Her sense of fashion wasn't quite my taste, but if it worked for her, then I guess it was fine. Her hair was gelled back into a very neat ponytail. The actual ponytail itself hung past her shoulders, so it was a no brainer to determine that it was a hair extension. But I would say that her makeup was flawless. It was just the right amount of everything.

After I took inventory of her overall appearance, I tuned in to her conversation. It was obvious that she was talking about the guy who had just walked out of the program. "I can't tell you where he's on his way to. But I can tell you that he's out of this program for good," she said. "So what I need you to do is contact this PO and let her know exactly what happened. And also let her know that he was discharged at approximately four forty-five."

I couldn't hear what the other caller said, but I could tell by Mrs. Williams's actions that they shared the same sentiments. Thankfully, the conversation with that other caller didn't last long. After Mrs. Williams gave a few more instructions, she thanked the caller and said goodbye.

I smiled at her when she looked at me. She smiled

and immediately got down to business. She picked up my paperwork and looked at it. She sifted through both pages and then she looked back at me. "It's Faith, right?"

I nodded. "Yes, ma'am."

"Well, Faith, I'm sure you were told that we don't normally take clients into the program straight off the street unless they go through a telephone screening first."

"Yes, ma'am, Mr. Macer told me. So I am very grateful. Because if he would've turned me away, I can't say whether I'd be alive to see tomorrow," I replied, and then my eyes became extremely watery. Before I could catch it, a single teardrop fell from my left eye. Mrs. Williams handed me a Kleenex from her tissue box. I thanked her and wiped my eyes.

"When was the last time you got high?" she asked.

"I had a pill of dope about two hours ago."

"You do know that you're going to go through the whole withdrawal thing, right?"

"Yes, I know. But don't you guys give out meth pills to help with the vomiting and the aches and pains?"

"No, I'm sorry. We are not a detox center. Every addict that comes through our doors has to go through the withdrawal process on their own."

Hearing Mrs. Williams tell me that they weren't going to give me any meth pills gave me a really bad taste in my mouth. I started to get up from that chair and get to stepping. I mean, to go through a withdrawal period was very painful. It was not a pretty sight. I sat there in silence for a brief moment and thought about whether I wanted to go through all that excruciating pain and the fucking vomiting. Trying to kick heroin wasn't a fucking joke.

Mrs. Williams looked into my eyes and said, "Are you having second thoughts?"

I hesitated for a second, and then I said, "No, I can do this."

"Good for you." She smiled and then she looked back down to my paperwork. "Oh, yeah, did Mr. Macer tell you that we take you through a twelve-step program?"

"Yes, he did."

"Did he tell you how it works?"

"No. He told me you were going to take me through that."

"OK, well I will explain it to you. But first I need to know if you are serious about getting treatment."

"Yes, I am."

"How serious are you?"

"Mrs. Williams, I used to be an assistant principal at the Performing Arts School in the city of Norfolk. I owned a two-story home in Virginia Beach and had purchased a brand new Jaguar off the showroom floor, and now all of those things are gone. I even had a good husband and a beautiful little girl who both walked away from me after I got hooked on heroin. So to answer your question, Mrs. Williams, I've been ready. I am so tired of the way my life is right now. And not only that, I want my family back. I swear I can't go another day knowing that those drugs are keeping me from being with my family. It's killing me. So I got to get clean," I explained to her as tears continued to fall down my face.

Mrs. Williams sat there and listened to me pour out my heart. When I was done she asked me a series of questions and then she asked me to sign a few documents indicating that she went over the rules and regulations of the program. Soon thereafter she welcomed me into the program and showed me around the facility.

After the tour of the facility was over, she showed me to my room. I noticed immediately that I had a roommate because of the other twin size bed that sat against the wall. Before I could make reference to it, Mrs. Williams said, "You will be room mating with Denise Adams. She's been in the program for a little over sixty days and she's doing great. I'm sure she will be instrumental during your treatment here."

"I'm sure she will too," I said, and then I took a seat on the edge of my bed. I looked at the clock on the wall and noticed that it was a quarter to six. My stomach was rumbling like crazy. "What time is dinner?" I wanted to know.

"Dinner is served in the dining hall every day at six thirty."

"Good, because I am starving."

Mrs. Williams smiled and patted me on the back. "You'll be fine," she told me and then she turned to leave. "See you in the morning."

"OK," I replied, and then I sat there and stared off into space. I started reflecting back on my life.

I remembered the very first day I started snorting coke and how that opened the doors to my heroin addiction. I was just grateful that I didn't lose my life in the process like my friend Teresa did. Luckily, God had other plans for me.

The Battle Just Begun

Shortly after I ate dinner in the dining hall, I went back to my room, got undressed, and took a hot shower. I didn't have a change of clean clothes, so I had to put on my same dirty clothes. It was about ninety degrees outside, and since I had not had on any deodorant, my clothes were pretty smelly, especially underneath my armpits. I wanted to call my in-laws and tell them the good news about my road to recovery, and that I needed them to bring me some clothes, but I decided against it. I figured if I called them now, they wouldn't take me seriously. But if I waited to call them after going through two weeks of recovery, then they'd believe that I wanted to change my life.

As I lay on my bed staring at the ceiling, my roommate entered the room. This was the first time I had laid eyes on her. She said hello as soon as our eyes met.

"Hello," I replied.

She walked by my bed and sat on the edge of

hers. I turned my head toward her. "So, you must be Faith," she said.

"Yep, that's me. And you must be Denise," I chimed in, and then I looked at her from head to toe. Denise wasn't the pretty type you'd see in one of those music videos. OK, well, I didn't look like one of those chicks in the music videos either, but before I became a full fledged heroin junkie, I could've gotten a booty-shaking job at the snap of a finger.

But Denise, on the other hand, wasn't the feminine type. She was an average-looking chick sporting a mohawk haircut. The hair was completely shaved on both sides of her head while the hair in the center of her head was dyed blond. She was also on the chunky side. If I had to guess, I would bet money that she was every bit of two hundred twenty-five pounds, even though her clothes fit kind of baggy. She was definitely your typical man trapped inside a woman's body. But what was so unique about her was that she had positive energy surrounding her, despite the sports bra she was wearing to hide her huge breasts and the body piercings she had in her tongue, the right side of her bottom lip, and over her right eyebrow.

"What's your drug of choice?" she asked me.

"Heroin."

"Welcome to the club. I used to be on heroin too."

"How long?" I wanted to know.

"Twelve years."

"Wow! That's a long time. How old are you?"

"Forty-four. And you?"

"Thirty-five."

"How long you been using?"

"A couple years now."

"Is this your first rehab?"

"Yeah."

Denise sighed heavily. "Get ready, because you're about to go on the rockiest ride of your life."

"Don't mention it," I said.

Denise got up from her bed and walked over to her TV. After she turned it on she looked back at me. "Gotta favorite show you would like to watch?"

"Denise, I can't even tell you the last time I sat down and watched TV."

Denise picked up her remote and started sifting through channels. Then she took a seat back on the edge of her bed. "Are you married?" she asked.

"I used to be. After I got hooked on drugs and started hanging in the Huntersville neighborhood of Norfolk, my husband divorced me and filed for full custody of our daughter."

"Drug addiction will definitely tear a family apart."

"Yeah. But I am going to get my family back. Because as soon as I'm done with my treatment, I'm going back to my husband to see if we can make this thing right."

"What if it's too late?"

"Oh, it's not too late. My ex-husband loves me. And so does my daughter. As soon as he sees that I've gotten my mess together, he's going to welcome me back with open arms."

Denise sighed. "OK. If you say so," she commented and then she changed the subject. "If you need anything, like some soap, deodorant, or just a clean T-shirt, just let me know."

I looked down at the dingy tank top I had on and quickly took Denise up on her offer. "Can I borrow a T-shirt?" I asked.

She smiled and stood. "Sure you can," she told me as she walked over to her locker and grabbed out a few garments. After she finished going through her things she pulled out a couple of shirts and two pairs of men's blue boxer shorts. "Now I know I'm a few pounds heavier than you, so these T-shirts and boxer shorts will be a little baggy on you, but you'll be all right."

I sat up in my bed and took the things she handed to me. I smiled at her and thanked her. "Oh, you don't have to thank me. I'm just doing what my old roommate did for me when I first came into the program," she told me and then she walked back over to her locker.

I got up from the bed and stripped myself of my old, dirty clothing. After I slipped on a pair of Denise's boxer shorts and a T-shirt, I felt really clean. At that moment I wanted to throw my old dingy clothes into the nearest trash can, but Denise told me to throw them in her laundry basket and she would wash them with her clothes in the morning.

Denise and I chatted some more after I changed and got back into my bed. She told me about her life before she came into the program. She told me about the woman she had met out on the streets that introduced her to drugs and how that same woman was still out there using. She also told me that her family accepted the fact that she was gay. They just hated the women she had in her life. All of her women were gutter trash chicks who hung out at gay bars and either had an alcohol addiction or a drug addiction.

"How long you been gay?" I asked her.

"I was always a tomboy, even when I was in middle school. I always played men's sports and ran track while I was in high school. So when my parents sent me off to college, I was able to spread my wings and be myself."

"I take it that's when you came out of the closet."

Denise nodded. "Yep, that's exactly when I came out. My first girlfriend's name was Liz Carter. She stayed off campus but we had two of the same classes, so we saw each other a lot."

"Where did you go to college?"

"I'm originally from northern Virginia, so when my parents sent me down this way to attend Hampton University, I went buck wild. But you want to know something that's so crazy? I didn't start using drugs here. I started drinking like crazy and smoking a little bit of pot here and there, but I didn't start using heroin until I went back home."

"Really?"

"Yeah, really. But you know what?"

"What?"

"This is the fifth rehab center I've been to for treatment, and I can say that I am finally done with using drugs. They were dragging me to my grave very fast, and my parents were being affected by it. I come from a middle class family of college graduates. My mother is a retired high school counselor and my dad is a retired chief of police. So not only was I hurting them, but I was bringing shame to them."

"Wow! So this recovery isn't just for you. It's for your parents too."

"Yep, it sure is," she agreed.

Denise and I continued to chat about our lives and how heroin stripped us of everything that we'd once claimed was ours. After about an hour into our conversation my body started aching really bad. And then the aching pains in my back and stomach made me want to regurgitate the food I'd eaten just a short while ago.

When I felt my stomach muscles rupturing, I jumped up from my bed and ran straight for the trash can near Denise's TV. Without hesitating, I buried my head into the trashcan and regurgitated every single food particle I had inside my stomach. Denise saw how pitiful I looked and rushed over to help me. The only thing she could do for me was massage my back. There was absolutely nothing else she could do. This was the first faze of my heroin withdrawal, and I knew it wasn't going to be easy to get through.

After ten minutes of constant vomiting, I had nothing left in my stomach to regurgitate, so Denise escorted me back to my bed and helped me lie down. Not even an hour later I started experiencing hot flashes and heavy perspiration. The sweat from my glands started filtering from my body very rapidly. Denise stayed up with me part of the night as I rocked my body back and forth. I tried to get out of bed to leave the facility over a dozen times, but Denise wouldn't let me go.

It took me almost seventy-two hours to detox, and I owed it all to Denise. She was the one who talked me into staying. I knew I could not have gone through that ordeal without her. She was a gem in her own right, and I would forever be indebted to her.

Once my detox was complete, I was ready to start the program. We had a morning NA group meeting, an afternoon one-on-one session with our drug counselor, and an AA group meeting with outside volunteers. This was our schedule three days out of the week. The other two days we had to attend substance abuse classes where we talked about drug addictions, took random tests, and watched movies. On the weekend we were allowed to have our family members visit us or we had the option to retire to our rooms. Unfortunately, I didn't have the luxury of having visitors, so I either hung out in my room and watched Denise's television, or I went out in the courtyard, which was located in the back of the facility. It was a place where I could go to sit on the bench and watch the birds fly around in the sky. It was the most peaceful thing in the world for me, and I loved it.

Treading on Thin Ice

One afternoon during group meeting, drama finally unfolded, breaking up the monotony of our days. The room was packed with all the men and women clients in the program. Mrs. Williams was present and so was her husband Mr. Matthew Williams. Mr. Williams was the head drug counselor and he was the acting director of the facility until a new director was appointed.

The way we started our meetings was for everyone to stand up, say their names, and then confess to being an addict. On this day as everyone took their turns talking about their addictions, I noticed how upset Mrs. Williams looked. It was pretty obvious that she was upset with her husband. Every time she looked in his direction, she frowned. The first thing that popped in my head about why she could be upset was the rumor circulating the facility about how her husband was sneaking around behind her back with Pricilla Hilton, who happened to be one of the clients in the program. To make matters even more awkward, Pricilla was in the meeting and she didn't seem too happy herself.

On a scale from one to ten, I gave Pricilla an eight and a half in the looks department. And even though Pricilla was in the process of recovering from her addiction, she had more swagger than Mrs. Williams. Pricilla had pretty brown eyes with long, naturally curly hair. And I knew one thing for sure, she wasn't all black. She could pass for Puerto Rican and black. All the guys in the program were attracted to her because she had a pretty face and curves to die for. The only down side to Pricilla was that she was a drug user. If she could stay off drugs, she'd be a prize to any man. And I sensed that Mr. Williams felt the same way.

As the meeting started, I got fired up. This was my fifth meeting, which meant I'd been in the program for almost a complete week. I looked forward to completing another week. I sat there and listened to Mr. Williams as he explained to everyone in the meeting about the rewards of getting clean. He pointed out how drug addiction not only affected the drug user, but it affected the family and friends of the user as well. While he was telling us the success story of one of his clients who completed the program, I noticed Pricilla sitting in her chair with her arms folded across her chest. She looked really frustrated and kept shifting herself around in her chair and mumbling to herself. She became a distraction to everyone. We tried to ignore her, but it was impossible. A couple times I thought Mr. Williams was going to ask her if she needed to be excused, but for some reason or another he didn't. I found myself on the verge of cursing her ass out because I wanted to hear this story without the distracting noises she was making. But Mrs. Williams beat me to it.

"Excuse me, Pricilla, do you need to be excused?" Mrs. Williams asked.

Pricilla was shocked by Mrs. Williams's outburst and her face showed it. "Now I know you ain't talking to me like that," she replied sarcastically.

Mrs. Williams stood and assured Pricilla in no uncertain terms that she was indeed talking to her. So Pricilla sucked her teeth and said, "You know what, Mrs. Williams, I don't think it would be in your best interest to fuck with me right now!"

"What's in my best interest isn't the issue right now. It's about everyone in this meeting. So if you want to be in this meeting, then you need to act like a respectable adult and talk only when the floor is open."

Before Pricilla could respond to Mrs. Williams's comment, Mr. Williams thought it would be best if he diffused the situation. "Pricilla, could I see you in the hallway please?" he asked her.

"Whatcha want me to go in the hallway for? Whatcha scared that I might tell your wife and everybody in here that we fucking?" she snapped.

With that comment I thought everyone's jaws would fall to the floor, but it didn't happen, because apparently everyone already knew about their affair. Mrs. Williams's jaw was the only one that hit the floor. I could tell in that instant that she was embarrassed because she just sat there frozen. While we waited for Mrs. Williams to react,

Mr. Williams took control of the matter. He politely walked over to where Pricilla was sitting, grabbed her by the arm, and literally escorted her out of the meeting.

As he forced her to leave the room, she started cursing and screaming. "I ain't your wife, so you better get your motherfucking hands off me!" she yelled. But he ignored her and continued to escort her away. "Whatcha don't want your wife knowing how you be eating my pussy on the nights you working late?" she continued to yell.

While Pricilla was airing out all of her and Mr. Williams's dirty laundry, everyone else in the room was whispering and giggling. It was heartbreaking to see Mrs. Williams be hurt in front of all of us. I knew she was humiliated to the tenth power because she still had not moved an inch. I couldn't take it any longer. I knew I had to do something to get her out of this room, because she was becoming the laughingstock of the evening, so I walked over to where she was sitting and convinced her to let me take her out of the room. She listened to me and got up. Everyone got quiet when they saw her and me leave. But as soon as we closed the door behind us, all the clients in the program burst into laughter. I knew Mrs. Williams heard them because they were loud. I vowed to say something to them later in her defense.

She and I walked to her office. She took a seat behind her desk and acted like she was still in shock. I wanted to tell her to snap out of it because she wasn't the first wife of a husband who cheated on her, and she wouldn't be the last. But I knew that wouldn't be the proper thing to say, so I just stood there and told her that everything would be OK. She finally broke down and started crying like her world had fallen apart. I mean I was in a worse situation than her, so why the tears? But who was I to judge? I wasn't in her shoes, so I couldn't measure the severity of her pain. I did listen to her when she finally spoke.

"I knew it all the time," she said. "But he kept denying it." She sobbed.

I handed her a tissue from her box of Kleenex. "Come on now, Mrs. Williams, did you expect him to tell you the truth? I don't know any men that'll confess to infidelity."

"It's not the same, Faith. Pricilla is a recovering addict whose children were taken away from her by child services. So you mean to tell me that you would risk losing your wife and kids for someone like her?"

I sighed because I was just like Pricilla. I was in recovery and my child was taken from me by my ex-husband, but that didn't make me a bad person. Pricilla and I were human just like Mrs. Williams, so who was she to judge us?

"She had the audacity to disrespect me by exposing their relationship in front of everyone in the room," Mrs. Williams continued. "And the crazy part about it is that he stood there and allowed her to do it."

"Look, Mrs. Williams, I know you're upset, but you're gonna have to get yourself together. Right now you're acting like the victim, but you can't continue to let Pricilla hold the power. You're gonna have to take it back."

Mrs. Williams sat there and thought about what I said. And then after a few seconds she said, "Look, I know men cheat. But what would possess them to do it so close to home? He and I both work here. So to have an affair with a woman who's in my immediate circle is bold as hell."

"Mrs. Williams, it happens all the time."

"I know. But I just never thought that it would happen to me."

"Well welcome to the club," I said and gave her a hug.

When I let her go she wiped the tears from her face and said, "You're a good person, Faith."

I smiled at her. "And so are you. I'm just glad that I had the chance to meet you, because you saved my life."

She shook her head. "No, I'm not gonna take the credit for that. You saved your own life when you decided to come here and refused to walk away when you were told."

"I guess that's just the persistent side of me." I chuckled.

"No, that's the smart side of you."

I nodded. She was right. I was smart. And I made the smart decision to come here. I just hoped she'd make the smart decision to take her power back from Pricilla because right now Pricilla was holding the steering wheel. She did what she had set out to do, and that was hurt Mrs. Williams. It was a no-brainer to figure out that Mr. Williams had hurt Pricilla. We could see it in her face. So the only way Pricilla knew to get him back was to attack his wife, and that's what she did. I was no psychologist or anything of that nature, but I knew that hurt women would seek attention from any man who would look their way. And Mr. Williams just got caught up. It happened every day. I hoped Mrs. Williams learned something from our conversation, because I was going to need to learn something from her later, and I needed her to stick around.

Reaching Out To My Family

Today marked my tenth day in the program. It seemed like the longer I was in the facility, the better I felt about being there. I credited Denise for holding me down during my stay. If it wasn't for her, I would have been gone after the first day. The only down side to this whole thing with Denise and all the favors she had done for me was that I knew she wanted to fuck me and maybe engage in some kind of relationship. I was not down for that bumping and grinding on another woman's pussy. That was just not my thing. Now I'd fucked random niggas, I sucked their dicks, and I even fucked two to three niggas at the same time, but I'd never been intimate with a woman. I wouldn't even know how to embrace the idea of it. So the next time she tried to come on to me, I was going to play her ass to the left and act naive as hell.

But I wasn't going to let my potential problem with Denise ruin my outlook. Since I had been clean for ten days, I figured it was a good time for me to reach out to my in-laws and tell them the good news about my recovery. I was sure that they'd be really excited for me. Immediately after our afternoon NA group meeting, I rushed into the hallway to snag one of the payphones before they all became unavailable. Thank God I had a couple quarters in my pocket from the bottled water I bought from the vending machine earlier. After I used the change, I was going to be completely broke again. I needed some cash and a few personal items, but I was certain that after I'd gotten in touch with my ex-husband's parents, they would come to my rescue.

My heart rate sped up a bit while I listened to the phone line ring. When I heard Mrs. Simmons's voice as she answered the phone, I instantly became nervous. "Hello," she said. Her voice sounded faint, but I could still hear her.

"Hi, Mom, how are you?" I asked. I tried to make my voice sound upbeat.

She paused for a second. "Faith, is that you?" she finally asked.

I smiled. It felt great to know that she remembered my voice. "Yeah, Mom, it's me."

"Where are you?" she asked.

"You won't believe it when I tell you. But I'm in a drug rehab," I said with excitement.

"Where?"

"I'm at the Salvation Army in Virginia Beach off Virginia Beach Boulevard."

"My goodness! I didn't know that they had a drug rehabilitation center."

"Yeah, they do, and the staff members that work with us are great people."

"Good for you," Mrs. Simmons replied. Then she fell silent again, which made me feel a little awkward. It was like she didn't know what else to say. I chimed in and asked her about Eric and Kimora.

She cleared her throat and said, "Oh, they're fine. Eric should be here any minute. He called about thirty minutes ago asking me if I'd watch Kimora for about an hour so he can run a couple errands."

"Wow! That's great. Maybe I'll be able to speak to them both before I get off the phone. I mean, it's been almost two years since I've last seen Kimora, so I'm sure she has gotten taller."

"Oh, yeah, she's sprouting up like a bed of flowers."

"How is she doing in school?"

"Oh she's doing great. Eric brought her over here a few days ago so me and her granddaddy could spend some time with her."

"I'm sure she had fun."

"She had a ball. We took her outside in the backyard and let her play on the swing set we bought her. And then we let her ride her new bike up and down the sidewalk in front of the house. She loved every minute of it."

"I'm sure she did," I replied, and then I changed the subject. "Has Eric asked about me?"

"Well, um . . ." Mrs. Simmons began to say, as if she was trying to collect her thoughts. "He brought your name up a couple of times," she finally admitted.

Hearing her say that he had talked about me gave me a sense of hope that we still had a connection. It was like music to my ears. "So what did he say?" I asked, pressing the issue.

"Well, um, the reason he brought up your name a couple of times was because Kimora has been asking her daddy when you were coming home. She doesn't like the fact that Eric went on with his life and got remarried."

Shocked by what Mrs. Simmons had just said, I belted out the word *remarried* like my world was about to fall apart. Mrs. Simmons could tell I was upset, so she tried to calm me down. "Sweetheart, I am so sorry that I had to be the one to tell you this, but I thought he'd already told you."

Instead of responding, I fell silent and thought about what I was going to do from this point forward since there was no chance that my ex-husband and I were going to reconcile. Not only that, the thought of my baby girl asking him when I would be coming home made me feel even worse. It was obvious that Kimora wanted her mommy and daddy back together, but with his new bitch in the way, that would surely pose a problem.

I stood there with my back against the wall while my heart began to crumble. All the hopes of me getting my family back were trickling down the drain, and there was nothing I could do to stop it. He had already moved on with his life and gotten remarried, just like his mother had said. I was just a distant memory.

"Faith, are you there, honey?"

"Yes, ma'am, I'm here," I replied as my voice began to crack.

"Sweetheart, I am so sorry!"

I cleared my throat and wiped the tears from my eyes. "There's no need to be sorry, Mrs. Simmons. I did all this to myself," I said. And at that moment I realized that I had called her Mrs. Simmons instead of Mom. Something inside me clicked and made me realize that she wasn't my mother-in-law anymore. The only ties she and I had were because she was the mother of my ex-husband and the grandmother of my daughter. There was nothing else. I needed to move on and respect the fact that I had no place in her life. Eric moving on with his life and marrying God-knew-who was a sign for me to do the same, even though my heart had begun to ache like hell.

Before I was able to utter another word I heard Kimora's voice in the background. "Hey, Grandma, who are you talking to?" I heard her ask. And the moment my baby opened her mouth, I felt a flutter in my heart. My heart felt somewhat empty, but there was still a spark left inside me. I felt a connection to her immediately and I couldn't get her name out quick enough.

"Is that my baby?" I got excited. "Please, can I talk to her?" I asked.

Mrs. Simmons hesitated. "Well, um, let me ask Eric if it's all right," she finally said.

"Ask Eric?" I snapped. "Why would you need to ask him if I can speak to my daughter?"

"Well, um—" she started to say, but I cut her off.

"Look, Mrs. Simmons, it's been two years since I talked to my baby. Now you've already expressed to me that she keeps asking Eric when I am coming home, so it's apparent that she misses me. If you would kindly put my child on the phone, I would greatly appreciate it," I replied sarcastically.

"Wait, hold on a minute," she said, and then she put down the phone.

While I waited for her to put my baby on the phone, I was thinking about all the fucking names I could've called that lady. I mean, how dare she tell me she had to get permission from Eric so I could talk to my damn child? What fucking planet was she from? Now I knew that I had screwed up my marriage and broke up my family, but don't deny me the right to talk to my only child. That was just not right. What in the hell was she smoking before she got on the damn phone with me?

A couple minutes passed and I didn't hear a damn sound. I thought the crazy lady had hung up the phone on me until I heard some rattling sounds. And then I finally heard a voice, but it wasn't my baby Kimora. It was Eric. "Faith, what do you want?" he didn't hesitate to ask.

Stunned by his candor, I said, "Well, initially I called to talk to your parents to see how they were doing and tell them about my news of being in drug rehab. But then when I heard Kimora's voice, I wanted to speak with her."

"Well, I'm sorry, but that's not going to happen."

Hearing Eric tell me that I wasn't going to speak with Kimora got me really irritated. "Why not?" my voice screeched.

"Because I said so," he snarled back.

"Because you said so!" I mimicked with sarcasm. "You're going to have to give me a better excuse than that."

"Listen, Faith, I am not going to sit on this phone and argue with you. I told you that you are not going to talk to her, and that's final," he roared.

"What you're doing isn't right, Eric, and you know it."

"No, correction, Faith, what you did to me and your daughter wasn't right. You damaged her when you left."

"Do you have to keep reminding me of that? I know I fucked up. And that's why I'm getting help for it now."

"It's a tad bit too late for that, Faith. We don't need you around anymore. Our lives are so much better since you left. I have a new wife, and Kimora has a new mother, so things are perfect for us."

"That bitch is not her mother!" I screamed through the phone.

"Kimberlie may not be her biological mother, but she's a better mother figure than you'd ever be," he snapped back.

"Oh, so that's who you ran off and married, your fucking divorce attorney, Eric? How fucking low could you go?" I screamed.

"Look, Faith, I'm not gonna keep going back and forth with you about the decisions I have made in my life. You did what you felt was best for you, and I did the same. Now as far as our daughter is concerned, she is doing fine. Does she miss you? Yes, she does. Would she like to talk to you? I am sure she would love to. But I don't think that it would be good for either of you."

"Speak for yourself," I replied sarcastically.

Eric sighed heavily. "I've got to go," he said.

"So that's it? I don't get an explanation about why I can't talk to my daughter?"

"Don't play dumb, Faith. And I wish you would stop playing the victim. It's not about you anymore. It's about Kimora. So if I choose to protect her from your empty promises, then deal with it, because there's nothing you can do about it. Remember, I'm the parent with full custody. So whatever I say goes. Now the quicker you understand that, the better off you'll be."

"That's how you're carrying it? It's over just like that?"

"I gotta go, Faith. You take care," he said, and without a moment's notice, he ended the call. The phone line went completely dead. The dial tone blared out into my ears very loud and I immediately became devastated. I almost collapsed to the floor, but Denise came on the scene and helped me contain myself.

"Give me the phone," she instructed as she eased the phone out of my hand. After she placed it back on the hook, she allowed me to put my weight on her as she escorted me back to our room. I felt so weak, like my legs were about to give way from the weight of my body.

As soon as I stepped into my room I took a seat on my bed. My head started aching really badly, so

I lay on my side with my back facing Denise and started bawling my eyes out. She sat on the side of my bed and began massaging my back. "My life is over," I said and sobbed.

"Don't talk like that, Faith, because you know that's not true."

I turned over and sat down on my butt. I looked straight at Denise while the tears kept falling. "Do you know that my ex-husband refused to let me talk to my fucking baby? Talking about how I damaged her. And then on top of that, he had the nerve to tell me that he went off and married his fucking divorce attorney. Now tell me, Denise, who does that? Who marries their fucking divorce lawyer?" I continued to sob.

Denise got up from the bed to get me a couple Kleenex from her box of tissues. When she returned with the box in her hand, she held it out for me to grab a few sheets from the box. After I took a couple and began to wipe my eyes and my face, she started rubbing me across my back. "I know you're hurting right now, Faith, but believe me, you're going to pull through this."

"Denise, Eric and Kimora were all I had, and now they are gone." My cries continued.

"Look, Faith, Eric may have moved on with his life and got himself a new wife, but by law he can't keep you from your daughter. All you got to do is finish this program, get a job, and find yourself a place to call home, and a judge will be glad to give you visitation rights. And then, who knows, six months or even a year later, you could petition the courts for joint custody. So don't count yourself out yet. You still got time because she's still young."

"Denise, I don't have that kind of time. I want to bond with my daughter now, not a year and a half from now. By then Eric will have her brainwashed and hating my guts."

"Even if he did do that, it won't work. Your daughter loves you," Denise said, trying to convince me, but her words basically went in one ear and right out the other. I knew my ex-husband. I knew what he was capable of doing. And manipulating people was a craft that he'd mastered. So I knew getting back into my daughter's life wasn't going to be easy. Nor was it going to be anytime soon, so I figured, why even bother to get myself together?

The reason I had come to this place was so I could get off drugs and go back to living a normal life with Eric and Kimora. And since that was not going to happen, I was not going to sit around here and waste my time at this place. I wiped the last bit of tears from my eyes and then I got up from the bed. Denise sat there and watched me as I went into my locker and grabbed the little bit of items I had acquired during my ten-day stay at the rehab.

When Denise finally realized what I was doing, she stood and rushed to my side. "What are you doing?" she asked.

"I'm getting out of here. I don't have a reason to be here anymore," I told her.

Denise grabbed my things from my hands. "You need to stop talking crazy," she said. "There is no way in the world I am going to let you give up on yourself like this. It took willpower for you to leave those streets to come in here and get treatment. So for you to let all that go because of your ex-husband's actions isn't fair to you. You deserve a better life, Faith. And being here in this place will take you in the right direction."

I really wasn't trying to hear Denise's lectures. The way I was feeling, there was nothing she could possibly tell me that would make me stay. I was over it.

"Denise, I don't care about those things," I said, referring to the items she held in her hands. "You were the one who gave them to me, so you can have them back," I told her, and then I stepped away from my locker. I turned around and started walking toward the door, but she stopped me in my tracks. She grabbed me by the arm and pulled me backward.

"I'm sorry, Faith, but I can't let you do this to yourself." She apologized as she held a tight grip on my arm.

I tried to break away from her, but her grip was too tight. My tiny frame was no match for her two-hundred-twenty-five-pound body. It was obvious that she cared about my well-being and wasn't about to let me go back to the streets. It had been a while since I had been in the company of someone who generally cared about me.

At that moment I caught a lump in my throat

and my knees buckled. Denise pulled me into her arms before my legs gave away. She embraced me like Eric used to do, and in a weird kind of way it was comforting. I leaned into her embrace and laid my face in her neck. The smell of the men's cologne she was wearing was intoxicating. And I can honestly admit that it felt like I was in a man's arms. Not to mention that I did not want her to let me go. I sensed she didn't want to let me go either, because before I could grasp what was going on, she had her tongue stuck down my throat. She tongue kissed me so passionately, my body started yearning for her to touch the rest of me.

"Hold me, please," I begged her. And she did just that. She grabbed me around my waist and embraced me like my ex-husband used to do. Her touch was soft and gentle. As she pressed her pelvic area into mine, heat started pulsating from my vagina. I couldn't explain it, but it felt good, and I wanted more. I wanted to explore this new world.

"Fuck me, please!" I whined. "I want you to make me feel good," I begged her.

So just like that, she turned me around, backed me up against the bed, and made me lie down. Before I could finish enjoying the stimulating feelings engulfing my vagina, she started massaging my breasts, causing my nipples to stand erect. She sucked on them and pulled on them like they were her toys, and I loved every minute of it. But I wanted more. I wanted her to lie on top of me. I wanted to feel her naked body next to mine, so I whispered that request into her ear as I kissed her earlobe. "Denise, please fuck me now," I begged her once again.

And at my request she undressed me while I lay there, and then she spread my legs apart. My pussy was dripping wet, because I knew she would fill it with passion. And just like that, she buried her tongue deep down inside me. She teased me inside and out. My body was quivering. I didn't want her to stop, so I started gyrating my pussy in her face. She didn't have much hair on her head, so I grabbed her face and used it for leverage.

"This pussy is good, girl," Denise said in her somewhat manly voice. "So give it to me so I can eat it up."

Despite the way she was making me feel, I had to block out the fact that she was a woman. I didn't think I could've carried on that long if I had my eyes open. I mean, I was hurt behind that shit my ex-husband told me, so I needed someone to show me some love some kind of way. And since Denise was there, I settled for her.

Before long she had eased out of her clothes and got into the bed with me. Now the bed we were in wasn't large enough for the both of us, but we made due. She positioned me to lie at one end while she did the opposite. She instructed me to lie on my side and open my legs, and that was what I did. She did the same thing, but she came closer by connecting to me like we were interlocking scissors. She pressed her pussy up against mine and started gyrating. It felt so good that I started to pull out my hair. I immediately closed my eyes and let her take control. And in less than ninety seconds, I had released an orgasm. It was the best feeling in the whole world. And when she and I were done, we both lay back and exhaled.

Wake-Up Call

Denise went to take a shower so she could freshen up before we were called to go to the dining hall for dinner. Instead of joining her, I got out of her bed and climbed into my own. All I could do was lie there and think about what I had just done. Guilt began to consume my entire body. And then shame started rearing its ugly head. The first question that popped in my mind was why I did it. What the fuck was wrong with me? Was I that desperate for someone to love me that I would indulge in that type of act? Was my need to feel validated so important that I would allow a woman to make love to me? What was going on in my head? Was I really damaged like Eric said? I needed someone to answer these questions for me, since I obviously couldn't figure it out on my own.

While I lay in my bed, I had my back facing the door, so I couldn't see Denise when she entered the room. But I did hear her as she moved about the room, grabbing clothing articles from her locker.

After she got dressed, she walked over to my bed and leaned over my body so she could see my face. I turned my head around and gave her eye contact. She smiled at me, pulled my hair back from my face, and tucked it behind my ear. "Are you going to get up to take a shower before we go to the dining hall?" she asked me.

I was sick to my stomach, so food was the last thing on my mind. I wanted to stay in bed and hide my face forever because of the shame I felt. "I'm not really hungry," I said. "I'm gonna skip dinner tonight."

"Are you sure?"

"Yeah, I'm sure. I'm just gonna lie here for about an hour and then I'll get up to take a shower."

Denise sighed. "OK. But if you change your mind, you know where I'll be," she told me, and then she leaned in closer to me and kissed me on the forehead.

At that very moment I wanted to crawl underneath a fucking rock. How dare she remind me about our sexual escapade? I was not her fucking woman, so what was up with the kissing thing? A part of me wanted to scream at her and tell her to get away from me, but then the other part of me decided against it because I didn't want to hurt her feelings. Denise had been nice to me from day one. When I started withdrawing from that heroin, she was there. She stayed up half the night with me for the first two nights. Not only that, she even had her family send me a box of clothes so I could have something to wear every day. She had been good to me, so I guess the only way she felt like I could have repaid her was by fucking her. Maybe for her it was a fair exchange.

After she kissed me, she grabbed her iPod from her locker and headed out of the room. Knowing she had left my presence felt like a weight had lifted from my shoulders. And at that moment, a light inside of my head clicked on and told me this was my chance to escape.

I hopped out of my bed and slipped on a pair of blue jean shorts, a white and blue Swarovski crystal beaded T-shirt, and the Adidas flip-flops Denise's parents had bought for me. Once I was fully dressed, I grabbed Denise's duffel bag from her locker and stuffed all my things inside. My heart raced the entire time I packed up my things. The last thing I wanted to do was let Denise catch me while I was trying to pack my things to leave, so I found myself looking over my shoulder every chance I got. When I realized that I had packed all my things into the duffel bag, I let out a sigh of relief.

As I made my way toward the door, I remembered that I was dead broke. I didn't have a dime to my name. But I knew that Denise had a few dollars she kept stashed in her locker. I honestly didn't want to steal anything from her, but I was destitute. And I couldn't leave this facility broke. That wouldn't be a good look at all.

"Screw that!" I mumbled underneath my breath as I turned around and headed toward her locker.

"I don't let niggas fuck me for free, so I am not about to let a bitch fuck me for free either."

In ninety seconds flat, I had gotten back into Denise's locker, taken the one hundred seventy dollars she had tucked away in her sock bag, and was out of our room, closing the door behind me. As I made my exit toward the front of the facility, Mr. Macer met me at the end of the hall. He looked very puzzled, but quickly caught on to why I was carrying a duffel bag in my hand.

"Going somewhere?" he asked.

"Mr. Macer, I've got to go. I just found out that my daughter was rushed to King's Daughters Hospital, so I got to be by her side," I lied.

Mr. Macer stepped to the side, and as soon as he cleared the way for me to walk, I put one foot in front of the other and started making my way toward the front door.

"Did you tell anyone on the staff about this?" he asked as he walked alongside me. He acted as if he was going to stop me from leaving at any given second. But I wasn't going to have that.

"No, I haven't spoken to anyone about this. I just found out my ex-husband was on his way to the hospital like ten minutes ago." I continued to lie as I headed toward the exit. Mr. Macer kept walking on my heels.

"You might want to talk to your counselor before you leave," he suggested.

"He's not here."

"I know. So we're gonna have to go to the office and give him a call." He pressed the issue.

Frustrated with Mr. Macer, I stopped in my

tracks and stood in front of him. "Look, I don't have time to be making calls. I've got to leave now," I snapped, because he was holding me up. I was trying to get out of there before Denise realized I was gone and had run off with her money.

"You know if you leave out of here without talking to your counselor, you won't be allowed to come back to this program."

"Right now, Mr. Macer, this program is like the furthest thing from my mind."

"Remember you begged me to let you in the front door," he reminded me.

After he reminded me of the day I cried to come through these doors, I knew I could no longer stand there and look at him. Shame was beginning to consume me all over again. I turned my head and looked toward the end of the hall where the exit was located.

"So, you're leaving just like that?" he asked.

"I'm sorry, but I've gotta go," I said and continued toward the front door of the facility.

"Faith, you're making a big mistake!" I heard him yell from behind me.

I didn't look back. I kept walking until I exited the building. And when I got outside, it felt like I was free. I thought back to the day that I first arrived here and witnessed the man walk out that very same front door. He had the biggest smile on his face. And today I had to admit that I shared his sentiments.

I walked away from the drug rehab with a couple changes of clothes and one hundred seventy dollars. It wasn't a lot of money, but it was enough for me to get some food and a place to stay for the night. I hopped on the HRT and took the city bus uptown. I got off at the Virginia Beach Boulevard and Tidewater Drive stop and strolled into Burger King for a bite to eat since I was in walking distance of the restaurant. I ordered the big fish combo with cheese and a diet Coke and took a seat in the lobby area of the restaurant to eat.

While I devoured my fish sandwich and the fries, I watched the patrons come in and out of the restaurant. I saw the typical young girls who lived in the Kerry Park projects across the street as they came in with their home girls or their boyfriends to order their food. Every last one of them was loud and ghetto as hell. It wouldn't have surprised me if I got high with their mother or daddy, or copped a couple pills of dope from their brother or their boyfriend. This area we lived in was small and everybody knew everybody.

After I ate my food and gulped down my drink, I left the restaurant and headed to the hotel next to Burger King. Everybody who frequented this low budget, roach infested hole in the wall was either a dope fiend or a dealer. Personally I didn't want to see either one of them. All I wanted was a place where I could rest my head and think about what I was going to do next. But unfortunately, that wasn't about to happen, because as soon as I walked to the front desk of the hotel to pay for my room, I ran into this clown named Bee.

Bee was a small time dope hustler from Tidewater Park. He had to be in his early twenties because he didn't have a speck of facial hair, but he carried himself like he was an old G who had plenty of weight and plenty of connections. I couldn't tell you what he was really working with because I'd never been in the company of a man who actually had it going on like that, but I had seen enough TV to know that he was our local block hustler who wished he was big time like Scarface. I was sure every cat in the state of Virginia wished they had the money and the power Scarface had in that movie. But since there were a lot of snitches floating around here, no one would ever be able to rise up and gain that much power.

As I stood in front of this average looking, tall, dark, lanky, young guy, he smiled at me with a mouthful of gold teeth and asked, "Where you been at, stranger? You look like you been getting you some sleep."

"I was in a drug rehab center in Virginia Beach for ten days. I just got out today."

"Oh, so that's why ain't nobody seen you." And then he changed his tone. "Hey, wait a minute. Don't you have something for me?"

When he asked me if I had something for him, I knew he was talking about the twenty dollars I owed him. I got two ten-dollar bags of dope from him the day I checked myself into rehab. He gave me the dope to deliver to this guy who was sitting in his car that was parked around the corner from Bee's dope spot. I was what you would call a runner. Runners were more or less crackheads and dope fiends who ran up and down the block for the dealers. Our job was to deliver the drugs to the addict and collect the money from them. In most cases, dope hustlers tried not to have any one-on-one contact with other dope fiends or crackheads because sometimes that dope fiend or crackhead could be a snitch for the narcotics police, or even worse, the drug addict could be an undercover narcotics detective.

So the runners put their lives at risk and were not even compensated for it, which was why I never took the dope to that car. As soon as Bee gave me those two bags of that lethal white powder, I made a detour and kept going until I found a quiet place to get my high on. So being reminded of that day now immediately brought me back to reality. I was back on the streets and I had no one to protect me. Instead of playing games with this guy, I reached inside my pocket and handed him the twenty dollars I owed him.

He took the money from me and smiled. "Now, see, that's what I'm talking about. Overnight express."

"You're really funny," I replied, and then I turned around to walk up to the desk.

"I gotta new batch if you looking to jump over the moon," he commented and smiled.

Hearing Bee tell me he had a fresh new batch of heroin was like music to my ears. I needed something really potent to take my mind off all the shit I'd experienced today. The bullshit Eric told me over the phone and letting Denise fuck me was a lot of shit to handle in one day. So Bee could not have come at a better time.

"Let me get a room first and then I'll holla at you," I said.

"You ain't gotta get a room. You can come chill with me in my room," he told me.

"All right, well let's do it," I replied and followed him from the front desk.

Back Where I Belong

The Economy Lodge hotel was a low-budget, roach infested fixer upper. The exterior of the hotel looked like it needed to be condemned, so when I entered Bee's hotel room it was no surprise to me that the conditions of it were wretched and sordid. In my former years, I would not have stepped foot in a place like this, much less looked at it. I was too high class. But now I'd take what I could get.

"Come on over here and sit down," Bee instructed me as he pointed to the queen-sized bed with a worn down headboard. The comforter on the bed was an old wool blanket with piles of lint on it. The pillows had no cushioning in them, and the pillowcases that covered them were in even worse condition. They were filthy. But that was what you got in a one-star resort like this. So I took a seat on the edge of the bed and waited for Bee to pull out his dope so I could get my first fix of the day. I wanted to ease my mind and forget about everything that had happened today.

And as soon as Bee gave me a taste of his dope, I'd be able to do just that.

"You got any needles?" I asked him.

He walked up to me and stood directly in front of me. "You know I do," he replied and then he reached inside his front jean pocket and pulled out about five syringes and a couple of ten-dollar bags of heroin. Bee's bags were always black. He called his dope black widow, and it was good, so I couldn't wait to get my hands on it.

I reached for one of the syringes. "Give me one of them," I said.

Bee closed his hand and pulled it back. "Slow down. I ain't going nowhere," he said.

I sighed. "Look, Bee, you need to stop playing games and hand that shit over to me so I can get busy. I told you I was in rehab for ten whole days and just got out today, so you know I'm trying to get high really bad."

Bee shoved the syringes and the dope back into his pockets and walked closer to me. "If you give me some head, I'll give you two bags of dope for free," he offered. But I wasn't in the mood to suck his dick. I had my own resources to get what I needed, so there was no need for me to trick with him in exchange for a couple bags of his dope. And I had to let him know that too.

"Look Bee, I had a rough day, and I am not in the mood to give you or anybody else some head. All I want to do is shoot some of that good shit you got into my veins. That's it."

Bee looked at me like I had just disrespected him. Apparently he wasn't used to a woman telling him no. But, hell, I was a fucking dope fiend. I wasn't pretty like I used to be, and I'd lost over twenty pounds. I still had my curves, but I was working with a smaller frame. Not to mention that I'd been with over one hundred men. What man in his right mind would proposition a chick like me? Under normal circumstances, the drug addicts were the ones that propositioned the dealer in exchange for a few dollars. Not the other way around.

"Look, bitch, you better be glad I came at you with this offer!" he replied, clearly offended.

This guy was not too happy with me. And since I wasn't in a position or in the mood to go back and forth with him on this matter, I got up from the bed and walked toward the door of the hotel room.

My actions must have really made him mad. "Yeah, bitch! Get the fuck out of here before I spit on you!" he roared.

I wanted to curse that bastard out so bad. But I kept my cool because I knew firsthand how these young guys were out here. They would kick your ass if you looked at them the wrong way. It was their way of proving to those around them that they demanded respect and they would stop at nothing to get it. So after I walked out of Bee's hotel room without a scratch on me, I ran all the way up Tidewater Drive and didn't look back.

I started to head out to Kerry Park projects, but if you didn't live out there or have a family member who resided out there, then you were bound to get a trespassing charge by the local police officers. So I headed back out to Huntersville, which was my old stomping grounds. Not to mention, I wouldn't get a fucking trespassing charge since the Redevelopment Housing Authority had no authority over this neighborhood. Quiet as it was kept, Huntersville was paradise for dope fiends like myself, and it would take an act of God to get all of us out of there.

I had my duffel bag thrown across my shoulders as I walked into the neighborhood. As usual the entire block was packed. I saw a couple of familiar faces as I walked down Washington Street. But the face that stood out the most was this cat named Ty. Tyrone was his real name, and he was the man to go to if you needed to know who had the best heroin in the neighborhood. He was an unattractive man, but he was kind. He'd always wear his dingy red baseball cap turned backward, so you could see him from a mile away.

As I approached him, I could tell that he was very happy to see me. He smiled at me, revealing that he had at least ten missing teeth in his mouth. He was indeed a good guy, in spite of being a drug user.

"What's up, Ty?" I asked.

"Ain't nothing, baby girl. Where you been at?" he asked me as he scratched the open sores on his left arm.

"I was in the Salvation Army rehab center on Virginia Beach Boulevard, but got tired of that shit and decided to check out today."

Ty found what I said very funny and he laughed.

"I know so many people who went in there and left without finishing the program."

"Well, I count as one of them. Now tell me who has the good stuff around here." I didn't waste any time asking what I needed to know.

Ty turned around and looked over his right shoulder. "That nigga Duke got dem half caps, but his shit is fire. That chick named Mary that lives on C Avenue by Shop & Go almost ODed off it this morning. So you know everybody 'round here has been scoring from him because they said his dope is mixed with horse tranquilizers."

"Shit! If his dope is that potent, then I need to cop me four of 'em."

"You gotcha money ready?"

I reached into my pocket and pulled out all the money I stole from Denise. After I separated forty dollars from the rest of the money, I stuffed the wad back into my pockets. "Are you gonna take the money to him?" I asked.

"Nah, Faith, baby, you know I don't get into that hand to hand shit. A nigga 'round here won't ever say that I dipped into their shit," he replied.

I smiled at him, tapped him on his shoulder, and told him to come on. The cat Duke was less than two hundred feet away from us, so it took me and Ty a matter of ninety seconds to get to him. There was a crowd of dope fiends around him trying to get his product, so I got in what appeared to be the line and waited for him to serve everyone before me. And then all of a sudden the guy Duke announced that he only had five caps left. Now, again, he had a crowd of people around him. I saw at least eight junkies surrounding him, so that meant if he passed every one of them a cap of dope, I would be ass out. And I couldn't have that. So I bum-rushed everybody and slid my ass through the crowd. I held my money up high, literally trying to force it into his hands.

He looked at me and said, "Hold on, shorty. I'ma get to you."

Right after he assured me that I was next, he handed three dope fiends a cap each and then he handed me the last two caps he had. Instead of spending forty dollars with him, I handed him twenty. I was somewhat disappointed, but I figured I'd be all right since I had two caps with which to start off the night.

As I headed away from the crowd, Ty followed on my heels. It was no secret he wanted to get a hit of my dope since he was the one who hooked me up with it, so I allowed him to tag along.

It was his idea to take me to the new candy shop on the corner of Washington and Okeefe Streets. The entire house was painted a soft pink color and it stood out among all the houses on the block. I wasn't too keen on going inside, but I didn't have anywhere else to go, so I had to get with the program.

As we approached the house, Ty insisted that we enter through the back door. It was dark as hell traveling down the side of this house. Ty didn't make it any better by having me walk through a bunch of fucking bushes. But this was the only way to get to the back door, so I had to go through the motions.

The lady of the house met us at the back door. "Hey, Brenda, this is my girl, Faith. We just trying to get a little shelter for a few minutes," he told her, which meant we needed a spot where we could get high.

She stepped to the side and allowed us to come in. "What y'all got?" she wanted to know.

"We picked some of that fire up from that nigga Duke," Ty replied.

"Oh, shit! He's back out there?"

"He was, but he just left to go re-up. Me and Faith got the last two caps."

Brenda nodded and started smiling like she'd just struck gold or something. I looked at her troll-looking ass like she was crazy. There was no way in the world I was going to share my dope with her and Ty. Both caps were only filled halfway, so they needed to get the fuck back.

From what I could see, the house was packed with all the neighborhood crackheads and junkies. It never ceased to amaze me how every drug addict migrated to the same spot. When the narcotics police detectives shut down one spot, junkies like Ty and me always found another one. Candy shops were all over the fucking place.

"You got a needle?" I asked Brenda.

"I don't have any new ones, but you can use this one," she said and handed me a needle from her pocket. I took it from her and entered into the living room area of the house. There were two other people in there nodding their asses off. Both of them were men and they looked like they were in a zone. I figured they must've gotten their dope from Duke too, because they were laid out across the floor.

Now of course there was nowhere for any of us to sit, so we got down on the floor and got into a small circle. Brenda pulled out a spoon and a lighter so we could get the party started. "I ain't got no filter," she informed us.

Ty looked around the room and noticed that one of the other junkies had an old cigarette butt lying next to his needle. Some of the filter material was already hanging out of the butt of the cigarette, so Ty grabbed what was left of it. I was sure that junkie didn't mind, since he was already in la-la land.

"Come on and get this show on the road," I said as I watched Ty pulling the rest of the filter from the cigarette. Seconds later the dope was mixed in with a teaspoon of water and it was sitting over an open flame from Ty's cigarette lighter. When the dope started boiling, I took it out of Ty's hand and stuck the filter in it to keep the garbage from being sucked up into the syringe. And then I pushed that bad boy right into that fat ass vein I had poking out in the crease of my left arm. If Ty and Brenda weren't there, I would've emptied the entire needle into my arm. But he and Brenda both watched me closely, and when it looked like I was about to empty all the heroin into my vein, Brenda snatched the fucking needle from my arm.

"What the fuck are you doing?" I snapped as I

watched blood drip from my arm. I started to back hand slap the bitch, but the heroin started taking effect immediately. Instead of going off on Brenda's ass, I laid my head back against the wall and mellowed out. I was feeling so good that I just closed my eyes and enjoyed the ride.

Popping Shit

I wasn't quite knocked out, so I was fully aware of what was going on around me. I opened my eyes a little bit and saw Brenda going off on Ty. "How the fuck you think you gon' hit that shit before me? I'm the fucking lady of the house, and I'm supposed to get some of that shit before you," she screamed.

"I was the one who took her to score," he explained as he shoved the needle down into his vein.

"I don't give a fuck! It's my motherfucking needle, and y'all are in my house," Brenda roared as she watched Ty inject the heroin into his arm.

Being fair to all parties, he only injected half of what was left in the syringe. And as soon as he pulled the needle out of his arm, he handed it to Brenda. Without hesitation Brenda snatched the syringe from Ty's hand and looked at it. Frustrated, she said, "There ain't shit in this damn thing."

Ty ignored her and leaned his head against the wall. He went straight into a zone. Instead of Brenda relaxing and trying to get a buzz off the rest of the dope in the syringe, she stormed out of the room and slammed the door behind her. We heard her talking shit about us as she walked down the hallway, but we didn't entertain it.

After fifteen minutes passed I stood up from the floor and got the hell out of there. That chick Brenda was insane. And I was not in the mood to go upside her fucking head behind pills of dope that I bought. That was really not how I rolled.

On my way out of Brenda's spot, I looked back a couple times to see if Ty would follow me, but he didn't, so I headed down Washington Street toward Church Street. Ty wasn't lying when he said that this was some good ass dope. It was probably a good thing that I didn't shoot the whole thing into my vein, because I probably would've expired like that chick Mary. And that wouldn't be a good look for me, especially when I'd just come out of rehab.

As I traveled down Washington I crossed over Proscher Street, and as soon as I hit the next block this guy approached me. Now I was already fucked up and didn't feel like being bothered, so I tried to pass him, but he stood directly in the path I was walking.

"Do you know me?" I asked him.

"Nah, I don't know you, but if you tell me your name, then we can start from there," he replied. His voice was deep and masculine.

I looked at him from head to toe and noticed

how much taller he was than me. He had to be about six feet one, weighing every bit of one hundred ninety pounds. He was a skinny guy for his height. At first glance he looked to be in his late twenties, but something inside me told me he was older. He was wearing jean shorts, sneakers, and a white T-shirt. He looked like he had just left the barbershop because his hairlines were razor sharp. The only jewelry he had on was a gold watch, so to me that meant that he wasn't the flashy type, and whatever he was doing out in these streets wasn't anything to call home to mama about.

"So are you gon' tell me your name or what?" he asked, pressing the issue.

I was too fucked up to be holding a conversation with this cat, but I stood there and tried my best. "It's Faith," I finally told him.

"So, where you going, Faith?"

"I can't tell you right now, because I'm not sure myself."

"Where is your man?" His questions continued as he folded his arms across his chest.

"I don't have one."

"Why not?"

"Hey, look, you are asking me too many questions for me not to know who you are."

He smiled. "Oh, I'm sorry. My name is Slim," he replied, and then he extended his hand for me to shake.

I shook his hand. "Nice meeting you," I told him and then I tried to step off.

He moved in front of me once again to block

me from walking away. I looked up at him and asked, "Are you lonely? Need some companionship?"

He chuckled. "That's funny. I like that."

"Listen, Slim, I gotta go."

"What's the rush? You just said you didn't know where you were going. I mean, if you like, you can come hang out with me."

"If you're looking for me to give you some pussy, then you're talking to the wrong chick. I'm buzzing right now off this good ass dope I got. And all I want right now is a place I can chill without a whole lot of fucking drama."

"Well, if that's the case, then you can come to my spot and chill."

"Didn't you just hear me when I said that if you was looking for some pussy, I was the wrong chick?"

"Look, shorty, I ain't trying to fuck you. If I wanted some pussy, I could make a phone call right now."

"So what is it that you want from me?"

"Look, Faith, I was just standing out here and saw you walking up the street and decided to pull you to the side so I could talk to you. That was it."

Before I took Slim up on his offer, I looked into his eyes to see if I could see through all his nice gestures. Normally cats from this part of town didn't have a nice bone in their bodies. They were full of ulterior motives. But for some reason, I couldn't see any bullshit from this guy. If he was hiding something, then he was doing a damn good job of it.

I let down my guard. "Where you live at?" I asked him.

He turned around and faced the Okeefe Apartments. "I stay right there," he told me.

"Do you live alone?" I asked.

"I got a couple of roommates. But they're out right now."

I sighed. "Well all right. I guess I can chill at your place until your roommates come back."

"A'ight, well let's go then," he said and escorted me toward the apartment building.

I followed him to the second floor of the apartment building. He lived in apartment 2-C. All the lights were on in the apartment, so I could see everything from the front door. I immediately took inventory of the entire living room and noticed that everyone who lived there seemed to have problems with tidiness. I set my duffel bag on the floor next to the couch while Slim started cleaning up. Plates, cups, forks, women's clothing, and shoes were all over the living room. There was barely any space for me to sit on the sofa, but I made the best of it. The main thing was that I was out of that hot night air and inside soaking up some good AC that was pumping through the vents.

Before I could fully relax in the coolness, I heard a knock on Slim's front door. I sat up on the sofa while Slim answered the door. He looked through the peephole and then he opened the door. Two young girls walked into the apartment dressed in short, skimpy dresses and high-heeled sandals. Their hairdos were jacked up. One of the girls wore red extensions hanging down her back while the other girl had purple fucking hair extensions pulled back into a ponytail. I assumed that they were in their early twenties because their immaturity showed big time.

As soon as they stepped into the apartment, Slim closed the door behind them. The girl with the red hair spoke first.

"Slim, me and Jennifer ain't getting no play on Goff Street. So can we go on Church Street down there by C Avenue with Sabrina and Tacora?"

"Yeah, go 'head. But don't come back here an hour from now talking about y'all ain't getting no play down there either, because there's gonna be some consequences," he threatened.

My eyes popped when I heard this young girl ask this cat's permission for her and the other young girl to go down on Church Street. The cat was out of the bag. These chicks were fucking prostitutes. And Slim was their pimp. Now all the clutter of women's clothing and shoes made sense.

As the girls were about to head back out onto the streets, I politely got up from the couch, grabbed my duffel bag, and walked toward the door to leave. "Hey, Slim, I gotta make a run," I told him as I began to leave.

Slim turned around. "Where you going?" he asked.

"I gotta make a run," I said again.

"You ain't going nowhere, so sit your ass down!" he roared.

I looked at Slim's face and could see that his whole demeanor had changed. He literally looked like he was possessed with a demon. I couldn't fucking believe my eyes. I tried to run for the door, but he reached over and grabbed me by my hair. If I'd moved one more inch, he would have snatched every strand of hair from my head. That was how tight his grip was.

Caught completely off guard, I screamed, "Get off me!" Both girls looked at me as I struggled to get him to loosen his grip.

"Shut the fuck up, bitch!" he snapped and yanked me backward, causing me to lose my balance and fall to the floor.

Lying on my back, I looked up at Slim, who by this time was standing over me. "What is wrong with you?" I screamed. "Are you crazy or something?"

I had to let this bastard know that I wasn't his fucking property, so he needed to recognize that. Unfortunately he had some other shit on his mind, because as soon as I expressed how I felt about him putting his hands on me, he reached down and wrapped his entire hand around my throat. I tried to prevent him from choking me, but everything I tried just would not work. I thought that maybe one of the young girls would get up the nerve to help me, but I found out the hard way that I had to deal with this psycho on my own.

While I gasped for air and struggled to get his hand from around my neck, he started lifting me up from the floor. Where in the hell was he getting his strength from? I tried to cry out, but the only sound I could belt out was a choking sound. And from the looks of things, my situation did not look like it was going to get any better unless I stopped resisting. So that was what I did. And guess what? The asshole loosened his grip and eventually released his hand from my neck altogether.

When Slim let me go, I fell back onto the sofa. I sat there and tried to re-group. The high from the dope I had just injected into my arm was long gone and replaced by a feeling of fear. While I was coughing and massaging my throat, Slim grabbed my duffel bag from the floor and threw it down the hallway toward the back of the apartment. His actions immediately told me that he had no intention of letting me go anywhere. Both girls must've known that too, because after they witnessed him toss my bag, they turned around and quickly made their exit.

After they left the apartment, a million things ran through my mind. Watching Slim walk back and forth from the kitchen area to where I was made me feel really uneasy. I knew that it was only a matter of time before he tried to rape me. I didn't know whether to play his game or go against the grain. But I did know that I didn't want to be there, and if I didn't think of an escape plan really soon, then I was going to end up being one of his bitches just like those young girls.

"You know you made me do that to you, right?" Slim asked as he continued to pace from the kitchen to the living room. "I was trying to warn you, but you didn't wanna listen."

I just sat there and looked at him. I couldn't believe what the fuck I had just gotten myself into.

Not even thirty minutes ago I was walking down Washington minding my own business. And then Slim approached me and convinced me to come and chill with him at this apartment. I realized too late that he was a fucking pimp and I was his next recruit. How was I going to get out of there without him ripping me to shreds?

I sat there clueless. I finally decided to strike up a conversation with him. I needed to get inside his head so I could figure out what kind of cat I was really dealing with.

Still massaging my neck to ease the pain, I asked, "Slim, did I do something to upset you?"

He stopped pacing and stood directly in the middle of the floor. "What the fuck you think?" he roared. "When I tell you to do something, you do it!"

The more this guy spoke, the more afraid I got. All I could think about was why me? But then I had to remind myself how karma worked. I had just left the rehab center with money I stole from Denise. And on top of that, I hadn't wanted to share my dope with Brenda. So was I now being punished for being selfish?

"Look, Slim, I don't know you, and you don't know me. I see that all of this is just a big misunderstanding. Now if you let me get my bag and leave, I will forget all about this whole incident."

Slim took a couple steps toward me. The closer he got, the scarier he looked. "What the fuck is wrong with you?" he yelled. "Are you retarded? You are my bitch now! You chose me by coming into my house. Now you gon' go out there on them streets and get me some money. So that means you ain't going nowhere. And if you ever try to run away, I'm gon' kill your motherfucking ass! Do you understand me?"

I tried to digest what he'd just said, but I couldn't swallow it. How the fuck could he tell me that I was his bitch and that I wasn't going anywhere? What part of the game was this? Now for the life of me, I knew I'd done some fucked up shit to people, but I'd be damned if I was going to sit there and take this shit from him.

I stood from the sofa, but before I could utter one word from my mouth, Slim took another step toward me. "What the fuck you gon' do?" he asked, his teeth grinding together like he was waiting for me to make the first move. His voice intimidated me to the point that I reconsidered busting my way out of there.

"I need to use the bathroom," I lied.

"It's down at the end of the hall." He pointed out as he looked down the hall.

I stepped by him very casually and made my way down the hall. Once I was in the bathroom, I looked for a window and was truly devastated when I realized that this bathroom did not have one. "I don't hear you using the bathroom," I heard him yell from the other side of the door.

Knowing that he was standing on the outside of the bathroom door listening to me got me spooked. I immediately pulled down my shorts, slid down my panties, and sat on the toilet seat. My bladder wasn't that full, but there was enough for me to let off that tinkle sound. Afterward I wiped myself and flushed the toilet.

As soon as Slim heard the toilet flush, he opened the bathroom door. He stood at the entryway and instructed me to wash my hands. "Hurry up! 'Cause I got some rules I need to lay down for you," he told me.

I had no idea what rules he had for me, but I was certain that whatever they were, he was going to shove them down my throat, and it didn't matter to him if I liked them or not. I was in his world, and it was going to take an act of God to get me out.

Tricking 4 Nothing

Slim made me strip down to nothing so he could take inventory of my body. I stood there in front of him stark naked. Despite all the tricking I'd done since I'd been on drugs, I'd never felt so violated. Once he got an eyeful, he made me get into the shower. Immediately after I finished showering, he pushed me down on the edge of his bed and forced his dick into my face.

"Show me how you suck dick," he demanded.

The only dick I'd ever sucked for free was my ex-husband's, so I hesitated. I had to get my mind right. Every man I'd encountered since I'd been on drugs paid me at least five dollars to get some head. I couldn't fathom why I would give it up for free now.

"Whatcha think I'm playing with you?" he snapped and grabbed me by the back of my hair. He literally shoved his dick into my mouth. I was half an inch from scraping the skin off his penis with my teeth.

I immediately gained control of the situation since I knew my life depended on it. I repositioned my mouth so I wouldn't gag, and I quickly tightened my mouth around the base of the head and began to take his entire dick in and out of my mouth. Instead of holding a tight grip on my hair, he loosened up a bit, which gave me more leverage to move my head back and forth.

"Yeah, suck this dick, bitch!" he instructed as he joined in the rhythm of my strokes.

Although I was not enjoying this at all, it seemed to please him, so I was all for it.

"Ahh, shit, girl! You got my dick rock hard," he commented as he pumped his dick into my mouth even harder. It seemed like the further we got into the rhythm, the harder and faster his strokes got. Unfortunately for me I couldn't control this situation because he wouldn't give me any room to hold the shaft of his dick. He just wanted me to sit down and hold my mouth open just enough so he could push his penis back and forth into my mouth. So I had to go through the motions and keep my teeth as far away from his dick as possible. I found myself gagging a couple of times, but I held it together.

"Yeah, bitch! You better suck daddy's dick!" he said. The only sound I could make as a response was a slurping sound. Saliva from a mouth and a man's dick were the ingredients for some loud slurping noises. And I was sucking on him for dear life.

"Umm, man! Please don't stop! Suck faster! I'm about to cum!" he yelled. And then he moaned with passion. He grabbed the back of my head really tightly as he exploded every drop of his warm juices into my mouth. Under normal circumstances, meaning like if I was getting paid for my services, I would have swallowed every ounce of his cum. But not this time around. I spit every bit of it onto the floor of his bedroom the moment he turned his head.

"You did good, girl." He complimented me as he wiped off his dick with an old shirt.

Instead of acknowledging that he said something to me, I got up from the bed and grabbed my duffel bag so I could find some clothing. While I searched my bag, he walked up behind me and said, "Hurry up and put on something so you can take your ass out on the street and get me some money."

Again I refused to acknowledge that he was talking to me and continued to search for something to wear. But then he mentioned to me that he'd taken the money and the half pill of dope I had tucked away in the pockets of my shorts. I was furious. I knew I was going to need that pill in the next couple of hours. Not only that, but I had plans for that fucking money. I'd earned it, so how dare he take it from me?

Ten minutes after I got dressed, Slim handed me a small makeup bag filled with foundation, eyeliner, mascara, and several shades of lipstick. He stood over me while I made up my face. He stressed to me the importance of looking good enough for a man to approach me.

"You can't go out there looking how you looked

when you walked up to me. Ain't no nigga gon' pay you top dollar for your pussy if you walk around here looking like a fucking drug addict! You gotta fix yourself up. And you gotta look like something for them to even stop their car. Shit, I know because I'm a man," he said.

He continued to give me the spiel about what he expected from me. Half of that crap he was talking about didn't make any sense. But I listened to him anyway. I mean, what else did I have to do? I knew one thing, I was rusty as hell when it came to applying makeup to my face. I remembered I used to be a pro, but now I was just feeling my way through by applying a dab of foundation to cover up all the battle scars I'd gotten since I'd been in these streets. I also touched up my eyes with a little bit of eyeliner and mascara. And then I finished things off by applying bright red lipstick. When I looked in the mirror to check out my overall look, I didn't look half bad. I really did clean up well.

As soon as I was done Slim grabbed me by the arm and escorted me outside. He made me leave my duffel bag behind at the apartment. But I didn't care. It had no use for it anyway. My main concern was my dope and my money, and since both of these were gone, I was out of fucking luck.

I walked side by side with Slim as we made our way down Okeefe Street. We walked past a dozen people as we strolled through Huntersville. But it didn't matter, because when people saw you with your pimp, or saw him beating your ass, they would do absolutely nothing to help you. That was just how the game was played. If I'd known that

Slim was a pimp, I never would have crossed the threshold of his house. I fucked up! I made that bad judgment call, and now I had to deal with it and find a way to get away from this psycho.

When we arrived at the spot on Church Street, Slim got everybody's attention. The two young chicks from earlier were there, along with two more. The other two women looked younger than the ones I saw at the house. I stood there in awe as Slim introduced me to his little fucking girls. I already knew that the chick with the purple hair was Jennifer. But the chick with the red hair didn't introduce herself to me because she was so fucking wrapped up in getting permission to change locations. So when Slim spoke, I paid close attention. He turned toward the chick with the red hair and said, "Paris, this is Faith. She's one of my new bitches, so I want you to watch her and make sure she doesn't go anywhere. Now if she tries to run off, I want all of y'all to jump on her and kick her ass. Do you understand me?" he asked.

In unison, everyone said OK and nodded, except for Paris. She asked him if he was going to be close by.

"Don't ask me any stupid questions. Where the hell you think I'm gon' be?"

Paris didn't respond. She took a couple steps backward like she was trying to avoid any conflict. The other two chicks didn't say one word. They stood before Slim and waited for him to dismiss them. But before he did that, he looked at them and asked how much money they had made.

As I mentioned before, the other two chicks

looked younger than Jennifer and Paris, but they looked like they were working with a little more common sense, so I waited to hear their answers.

"I just made seventy-five dollars," one said.

But the other one had a sad song to sing. "Slim, you know it ain't military payday. It's been slow since me and Sabrina been out here," she explained.

Slim wasn't buying her story. He got in her face like he was about to bite off her fucking nose. "Tacora, do you think I give a fuck how slow it is out here? If Sabrina can make it happen, so can you! Now you better get yourself together before I fuck your ass up!" he snarled.

After Slim threatened Tacora, she and Sabrina walked across C Avenue and stood in front of the Shop & Go convenience store. As they walked away, I looked at them from head to toe. Sabrina and Tacora were both every attractive young girls. They had caramel complexions and pretty brown eyes. And even though they looked like they were still in high school, they had the bodies of grown women. They wore their tiny skirts in the sleaziest way possible. These young girls looked way better than I did. And I was sure that they would generate more money than me too. So I couldn't figure out for the life of me why Slim recruited me. Was it because I was older and I probably knew the streets better? I couldn't call it, but whatever it was, I was sure he had it all figured out.

Before Paris esorted me to her post, Slim schooled me about how I needed to work the streets. "When you get your first trick, let that nigga know off the top that you ain't about to pull off in his car. You can get inside the passenger seat and take care of his business, and then you get the fuck out. But you gotta make sure he pays you first. Is that understood?" he asked.

I nodded. Then Paris chimed in. "Have you ever been on the strip before?" she asked me.

I nodded once again.

"Do you ask your dates if they the police?" she asked.

"Sometimes," I responded.

"Well you gotta ask that shit 'round here," Slim said. "If you don't, then your ass is liable to get hauled off to jail."

"He ain't lying, because that almost happened to Tacora," Paris said. "So you gotta be careful and make sure you ask him before you even give him your price."

With that warning done, I listened to Slim and Paris tell me what to charge for certain favors. I was told to charge fifty dollars for a dick suck, fifty dollars for a pussy fuck, and seventy-five dollars if the date wanted to fuck me in my ass. If he wanted a dick suck and a pussy fuck, he had to pull one hundred dollars out of his pockets.

When I heard the prices we had to charge, I was blown away. I honestly could not believe that cats were paying that type of money for sex. I couldn't remember the last time I got fifty dollars to suck a man's dick. The most I'd ever gotten was thirty dollars, and that was on a good day. So I figured I might be all right after all. Shit! How hard could it be to be Slim's bitch and get paid decent money to fuck these clowns around here? Plus, I'd have a place to lay my head at night. And if I played my cards right, I would not have to tell him exactly how much money I made out here. That way I could cop me a couple pills of dope when I got ill. Damn right! If all went according to plan, then I'd be sitting pretty.

Once all the cards were laid out on the table, Slim stepped away from me and Paris. As soon as he got far enough away from us where he couldn't hear what we said, Paris leaned toward me and said, "Come on, let's get to work before he starts to flip out."

I followed Paris over to where Jennifer was standing, which was on the side of the Shop & Go convenience store. Slim walked across to the other side of C Avenue and sat on the foot stoop of an abandoned house. I couldn't help but ask Paris how Slim kept any of his women from running off.

"Have you seen that big ass gun he's got?" she asked me.

Stunned by her reply, I said, "No."

"Well, you best believe he has it on him. He uses it to run cats off who ain't trying to pay us our money. But don't get it twisted, because he will use it on us if we try to get out of pocket with him."

"Don't worry about me, because I'm trying to get paid," I told her, and then I turned my back to her so I could get the attention of the next car that drove by.

Twisted Individuals

I hung out on the corner of C Avenue and Church Street for three hours straight and made two hundred twenty-five dollars. I was very happy, but Slim wasn't thrilled. After he collected money from me and all the other girls, he stormed back over to his spot by the abandoned house. But before he left, he screamed at all of us. "If y'all don't want me to go upside y'all fucking heads, then y'all better get me more money than this," he complained.

Of course, no one dared to challenge him, so I left well enough alone. I was, however, upset with myself that I didn't keep a few bucks. It had been a few hours since my last dose of dope and my body was beginning to feel the effects. I knew that I needed to get me a pill sooner rather than later, because if I waited until later, then I wouldn't be any good to Slim or myself.

I tried to hold out at least until after I served up one more date, but the night had slowed down and it seemed like no one was willing to cough up any more money. I stood alongside the Shop & Go for about thirty more minutes, and when I realized that no one was trying to spend their money, I got up the gumption to walk across the street to where Slim was standing.

He looked at me like I stunk when I approached him. "Why the fuck you over here in my face? You know you ain't supposed to leave your post until I say so," he roared.

"I know, but I'm starting to feel really ill. And if I don't get another pill of dope, I'm gonna get sick as hell," I warned him.

"Bitch, don't you think I know about fiends like you? Y'all dopeheads snort that heroin through your nose or shoot that shit in your veins all day long. And as soon as that shit wears off, y'all are 'round here trying to get another fix. I've been 'round that shit all my life. My mama ODed off that shit when I was fifteen, so I know how that shit works."

"Well can I have my pill of dope back?" I asked.

"Whatcha think I was gon' walk around with that shit on me?" he snapped.

"No, but I—" I started to say, but he cut me off in mid sentence.

"But nothing!" he roared. "Now if you think I'm gon' let you close down shop so we can run back to the house and get your dope, then you got me fucked up! I ain't gon' let no bitch stop me from getting my paper. So getcha ass back 'cross that street and get me some more money."

The tone of his voice made it clear that he didn't give a fuck about me getting sick. And the fact that I knew he had a gun on him made it even more clear to me that whatever I decided to do from this point forward would have to be done with caution.

I was beginning to feel really weak. And if I did not get a grip of something from a needle really soon, then I wasn't going to be able to do anything.

As instructed, I walked back across C Avenue and stood beside Paris. "Are you all right?" she asked me.

"Nah, I'm starting to get ill. And if I don't get me a pill of dope soon, then my body is going to start aching and I'm gonna start throwing up all over the place."

"You snort dope?"

"No, I use a needle," I told her.

"Turn your back toward Slim and follow me," she instructed, and I did just as she said.

I had no idea what she was about to do, but I was willing to find out. I followed Paris to the back of the Shop & Go, but before we turned the corner we heard Slim yell at us, "Where the fuck y'all going?"

"We gotta pee," Paris said. "so we're gonna watch each other's backs."

As soon as we turned the corner, she ducked down behind the bush and reached into her purse. Seconds later she pulled out a cap filled with a white substance. My heart fluttered at the sight of it.

"Is that heroin?" I asked in a low whisper.

"Yeah. So take some before you get ill," she insisted.

I couldn't tell you how happy I was to see Paris handing me some of her dope. But there was a problem. I didn't have a needle, nor did I have a spoon and a lighter. I was fucked up and back to square one.

I held the pill of dope in my hand like I didn't know what to do with it. Paris peered around the corner for a brief second, and then she looked back at me. "Look, Faith, we ain't got all day, so you better hurry up and do something. Because if Slim comes over here and catches us fucking around with this shit while we're working, then he's going to bust our asses for sure."

"Fuck it!" I said and unscrewed the top part of the cap. I dumped part of it into my right nostril and snorted it as hard as I could. When it felt like I had gotten all of it in, I wiped my nose with the back of my hand and waited for the drug to take effect.

Paris snorted the other half of the cap of heroin like a pro. She didn't leave behind even a trace of the substance inside the clear medicine capsule. After she wiped the heroin residue from her nose with the palm of her hand, we fixed ourselves up and headed back around the building to our post. When I looked to see what Slim was doing, I noticed that he was preoccupied with Tacora, so we eased back to our spot and chatted for a bit.

"How you feeling now?" Paris wanted to know.

"It's taking its time to work, but I'm feeling better than I did a few minutes ago."

"Just give it another minute or two. You'll be fine."

"Yeah, I know. But let me ask you something."

"What's up?"

"How old are you?"

"Twenty-five."

"How long have you been getting high?"

"A couple years now."

"You've been on heroin for a couple of years?"

"Nah. I just started snorting heroin about six months ago. When I first started working for Slim I was only smoking weed. But then I got introduced to heroin through one of my dates. Slim knows I snort it, but he told me if he caught me using it while I was working then he was gon' fuck me up."

"How long have you been working for him?"

"For about three years now."

"Did he trap you up like he did me?"

"Nah, he didn't pull me in like that. I was already on the streets when I met him. I used to work on the other end of Church Street by Young's Park. And one night he was walking by when I was getting my ass kicked by one of my tricks, so when I saw him I yelled and asked him for his help. He hesitated at first. But when I started begging him, he came to my rescue and told me that if I worked for him then he'd protect me. So that's how our paths crossed."

"Do you know he almost choked me to death back at his apartment?"

"I kind of figured he would do that. He's the type of man that wants all the control. If he feels like you threatening his manhood, then he's gonna come down hard on you."

"Somebody should've warned me," I commented underneath my breath, and then I changed the subject. "So how old are the other girls?"

"Jennifer is twenty-one, and Sabrina and Tacora are nineteen."

"They're fucking babies!" I commented.

"They're grown as far as Slim is concerned."

"How long they've been working for him?"

"Well Jennifer started right after I did. That's why we're always together. And the other two started tricking for him like a couple months ago. I think Sabrina is his favorite, so you better watch her because she's one sneaky bitch!"

"Oh, really?"

"Yeah. Some shit went down the other night with Jennifer while Slim was back at the house. But guess what?"

"Slim found out," I said, answering her question.

"Yep, he sho did. And the only people who was out here when it happened was me, Jennifer, and Sabrina. And Jennifer ain't gonna tell on herself."

"That makes sense."

"I'm glad we're on the same page. So keep your eyes open and your mouth closed," she advised, and then she took her attention off me and turned it toward the streets. She smiled as soon as she saw a small, dark blue pickup truck pull up curbside. "There goes one of my regulars," she said as she walked off in the direction of the truck.

I stood there and watched as Paris opened the passenger side door of the truck and got inside.

"Hey, baby," I heard her say.

And before she had a chance to close the door behind her, I heard a man's voice say, "You gave me herpes, bitch!" And then I saw bright sparks and heard a loud roar like there was an explosion.

I nearly jumped out of my fucking skin as my heart dropped to the pit of my stomach. I knew at that very moment that what I saw and heard was gunfire. And so did everyone else who was standing around, because they scattered like roaches. But I stood there. I was completely frozen. With all the chaos, I couldn't think straight. It seemed like everything was happening so fast.

"Oh my God! Paris got shot!" I heard Sabrina scream. Tacora and Jennifer started screaming for help, but no one listened. And then I saw Slim through my peripheral vision running toward the pickup truck, letting off gunshots. When the driver saw that he was being shot at, he pushed Paris's lifeless body out of his truck and squealed his tires as he sped off. Paris's body fell to the curb.

I freaked out. I mean, she was just standing beside me, giving me a head's up about how to deal with Slim and his girls. But now she was dead. What the fuck was this world coming to?

Unfortunately the guy driving that pickup truck got away before Slim got a chance to get him. Tacora, Sabrina, and Jennifer ran to Paris's limp body and cried over her.

"She's dead!" Sabrina yelled while sobbing.

Jennifer sat down on the curb, lifted Paris's

head, and laid it in her lap. Blood oozed from Paris's head as Jennifer wrapped her arms around her face.

"Somebody call the fucking ambulance!" Jennifer screamed. But there was no one in sight except the four of us.

Slim ran back to where we were standing a few minutes later. He was completely out of breath. "We gotta go before the police come," he told us.

Jennifer looked up at Slim like he was crazy. "We can't just leave her here." She continued to sob.

Slim grabbed Jennifer by her arm and lifted her from the ground. Paris's blood was all over Jennifer's hands and clothes. "Let's go now!" he demanded.

The minute he lifted Jennifer from the ground she became hysterical. She started kicking and screaming. "I can't believe she is dead, Slim. That man killed her just like that."

Slim realized that Jennifer wasn't going to leave Paris's body willingly, so he picked her up and threw her over his shoulders. Before he walked off, he looked at me and instructed me to grab Paris's purse. I looked at him like he was fucking crazy. I mean, who did that? Who tried to rob the dead? I knew I'd done some fucked up shit to people, but I'd never taken anything from a dead person. That was by far the most foul thing any human being could do.

Frustrated with my lack of cooperation, Slim looked like he was about to spit venom out of his mouth. "Faith, why the fuck are you standing there when I told you to get her purse?"

"It's got blood all over it," I said.

"Do you think I give a fuck? Pick that shit up before somebody else gets it," he demanded.

I reached down, grabbed the strap of Paris's purse, and I immediately handed it to Slim so I would not have to carry it. Slim clutched the purse in his right hand while he used his left hand to hold Jennifer's body across his shoulders. Let's go," he roared, and then he walked away.

Sabrina, Tacora, and I walked behind Slim as he led the way back to his apartment. Paris's blood was all over my hand, and I desperately wanted to wash it off. I had not started crying yet. I was more focused on processing what had just happened.

In the distance we all heard paramedics and sirens from several police cars blaring loudly. The louder they got, the closer we knew they were. Slim panicked. He took Jennifer off his shoulder and made her run beside him. As a matter of fact, he instructed all of us to do the same.

We were all out of breath when we arrived back at Slim's apartment. There were a couple of his neighbors standing outside when we ran up to the building. They looked at all of us and I was sure they wondered why we were running, and why Jennifer and Slim were covered in blood. They didn't open their mouths to question us, but they watched until we disappeared behind the door of the apartment.

No Respect 4 Da' Dead

Jennifer tried to collapse on the living room floor when we entered the apartment, but Slim grabbed her and took her into the bathroom while Sabrina and Tacora took a seat on the sofa. I walked into the kitchen to rinse the blood off my hands. When I was done I joined Tacora and Sabrina in the living room.

We heard Jennifer crying in the bathroom while the shower water was running. We knew Slim had stripped her down and made her get in the bathtub to wash off all of Paris's blood.

We sat in complete silence until Sabrina finally opened her mouth to speak. "I can't believe Paris is dead! What the fuck happened? Why did that guy kill her like that?" she asked, I guess hoping that someone in the room could answer those questions for her.

I had to speak up, because I was right there. I heard exactly what the truck driver said. "Right before that man shot her, he yelled at her and told her that she gave him herpes," I said.

Tacora and Sabrina both looked at me like I was crazy. "You sure he said that to her?" Sabrina asked me.

"Yeah, I heard him loud and clear. But then he shot her before I could even absorb it. I mean, it happened so fast."

Sabrina gave me a puzzled look. "He said Paris gave him herpes?" she asked me. Then she looked at Tacora. "But Paris didn't have herpes, did she?"

"If she did, I didn't know shit about it," Tacora replied.

"Know about what?" Slim asked as he walked into the living room.

We all turned our heads in Slim's direction, but Sabrina was the one to repeat the question. "I just asked Tacora if she knew Paris had herpes."

Slim stood next to me and folded his arms. "Why the fuck you wanna know if she had herpes?" he asked.

"Because Faith said she heard the man say that Paris gave him herpes right before he shot her," Sabrina said.

Slim turned his attention toward me. "You heard that motherfucker tell her that?"

"Yeah, I heard him say it right before he shot her."

"Are you sure?"

"Yes, I'm sure."

Slim stood beside me with a bizarre expression on his face. I assumed that he didn't know what to say. Sabrina broke the silence by asking Slim what they were going to do now. I also wanted to know what plans he had for us, so I waited patiently for him to respond. It took him a moment to reply, but he finally had something to say. "We gon' have to lay low from C Avenue and find another spot to work at until all this shit blows over."

"Where we gon' go?" Tacora blurted out.

"I don't know. But I'll figure out something by tomorrow," he told her.

"Do you think the police is gonna catch that guy and charge him with Paris's murder?" Tacora asked.

He gave us this uncertain look. "I don't know," Slim answered.

"Do you think somebody 'round there by the Shop & Go gon' tell the police that Paris stayed with us?" Sabrina asked Slim.

"I hope not. 'Cause I can't handle that type of heat right now."

"They may not be able to identify her body since we took her purse," I said. "I mean, if you wanted her money, all we had to do was take it out and leave her purse behind."

Slim was not at all happy about my comment. He snapped on me as soon as I closed my mouth. "What the fuck you mean, *her* money? Paris worked for me! So whatever she got out there on those streets was *my* money. And for your fucking information, she didn't have shit in her purse for the police to identify her body with."

"I was referring to her ID," I interjected.

Slim leaned toward my face. His face was beet red and so were his eyes. "She didn't have a fucking ID! So mind your motherfucking business!" he yelled, causing spit to come out of his mouth.

I stepped back about two steps. It was apparent that Slim wanted to take my head off because of what I said. I was not in the mood to be his punching bag, so I kept my mouth closed. I decided only to talk when I was spoken to since I was a newcomer in this group.

After Slim let off all his steam on me, he stormed back down the hallway toward the bathroom. We could still hear Jennifer sobbing, but she wasn't as loud as she was before. I ended up sitting down next to Sabrina while she and Tacora buried their faces in the palms of their hands and cried.

When Jennifer was done bathing, she joined us in the living room and crawled on the sofa beside Tacora. Tacora let Jennifer lay her head in her lap. Slim walked into the living room and stormed right by us. We all sat there and watched him as he opened the front door and walked outside without saying a word to any of us. Something inside me told me that he wouldn't be going too far considering what had just happened.

Sabrina confirmed my thoughts when Tacora wondered out loud where Slim was going. "He told me he was just going in the front of the building to find out what's being said about Paris's murder," Sabrina told us.

"Does any of y'all know her family?" I blurted out. I couldn't help it. I had to say something, since it was revealed to me that she didn't have identification on her.

Jennifer lifted her head from Sabrina's lap and said, "I don't know who her parents are, but she did say that they lived out in Suffolk somewhere."

"Do you know if she kept in contact with them? I mean, it would only be right if they knew about what happened to her," I said.

"Since she's been 'round here with us, I don't remember her ever calling them. But I do remember her telling me that her and her mama had a falling out because Paris told her mama that her daddy tried to molest her when she was seventeen, which was why she ran away."

"Damn! That's fucked up!" I said. "You would think that when you're home, you're safe. But then you find out later that you're living amidst a predator. How crazy and screwed up is that? She didn't have a chance in hell, either way you look at it."

"Her daddy ain't the only one who's fucking sick in the head," Tacora said. "My daddy got the chance to molest me over a dozen fucking times and my mama still don't believe me till this day. I hate them both and I wish that they'd get hit by a fucking train and die painful deaths," she said as tears began to fall from her watery eyes.

"Did the police get involved?" I asked.

"Nope."

"Why not?"

"Because he didn't penetrate me."

"Well, how did he molest you?" I asked.

"When I was fourteen that nasty motherfucker

used to make me get undressed in front of him. And while I was naked, he used to make me play with his fucking dick."

"Oh my God, Tacora, did he make you suck it?" Sabrina asked.

Tears falling more rapidly, Tacora said, "No. He just used to make me jerk him off."

"Where was your mother when all of this was happening?" I asked.

"She worked at night so that's when he always came after me."

I shook my head with disgust. I could not imagine a father doing that type of act to his own children. It was so fucking sick. Those guys were mentally fucked up in their heads.

As we continued to chat about what episodes in our lives brought us to this place, Slim burst through the front door. He looked even more worried than when he left the apartment. "The homicide detectives are 'round there on C Avenue asking everybody questions," he said. "Somebody told one of the cops what Paris's name was. And they told the police that she was a prostitute."

"Who told you that?" Jennifer asked Slim.

"That's something you don't need to concern yourself with. All you need to worry about is what to say to the cops if they run up on you and start asking you questions," he replied.

"Do you think the police is gonna come over here and ask us questions?" Sabrina asked.

"I hope not. But if they do, y'all gon' have to be prepared."

"So whatcha want us to say?" Sabrina asked.

Slim stood in the middle of the floor, demanding everyone's attention. "If they come 'round here, they might ask y'all if y'all are prostitutes, and if they do, y'all gotta tell 'em nah. I mean, y'all gon' have to deny it like your life depends on it. And then if they ask y'all if y'all knew Paris, you can tell 'em you knew her, but do not tell them that she stayed here with us. Do I make myself clear?"

Everyone, including myself, agreed to say what Slim had instructed us to say. But Jennifer wasn't quite clear on one thing, so she brought that to Slim's attention. "What should we say if they ask us if we witnessed the shooting?"

"You can tell 'em you were out there, but do not tell 'em you were right there at the scene. Act like you were down the opposite end of C Avenue when she got shot."

"Why you want us to tell 'em we were down the other end of C Avenue? I mean, don't you want them to catch that guy who killed her?" Sabrina asked.

We all looked at Slim and waited for an answer. We could tell that he was extremely irritated by her question. "What kind of fucking question is that? You damn right I want them to get that nigga, but not at our expense. Because as soon as you start talking to them, they're gonna start harassing you every time they see you. And then when that happens, you ain't gon' be able to make my money. And I can't have that happening. Life for us ain't gon' be productive, so it's gon' get really ugly," he replied, and then he stood there to see if anyone else had any questions for him.

I wanted to say something to him in reference to Paris's murder, but I figured he'd snap my fucking head off, so I kept my mouth closed. It was clear that he cared about no one else but himself. It was also clear that he wasn't going to let anyone or anything come between him and his money, so I played it safe and allowed him to run his show.

When he realized that no one wanted to raise another question, Slim raised a question of his own. He turned his attention to Tacora first and asked her where the money that she made tonight was. Apparently she knew the drill because she went into her purse and dug out every dollar she'd earned. I couldn't tell how much money she gave him, but it looked to be around the neighborhood of one hundred dollars. A couple seconds later, Sabrina handed him her profits for the night, and I followed suit and gave him what I made as well.

"Remember you already got mines from earlier," Jennifer told Slim.

"Yeah, I know," he replied, and then he went into the kitchen area of the apartment. He sat down at the table and started counting the money. After he was done, he folded all the bills together and stuck them into his front pocket.

We all watched him in silence as he grabbed a Corona from the refrigerator and opened it. After he threw the bottle top into the kitchen trashcan, he took a swig. He swallowed and let out a loud burp. From the entryway of the kitchen he dropped another bomb on us. “Looks like we gon’ have to go back on the streets tonight,” he announced.

Jennifer and I looked at him like he’d just lost his fucking mind. “I thought we weren’t going back on the streets till tomorrow,” Jennifer said.

“I changed my mind,” he replied. “I need more fucking money because y’all didn’t make y’all goal tonight.”

“You’re acting like it was our fault,” Sabrina commented softly. She knew that if she’d raised her voice, Slim would’ve buried his fist in her left eye.

“Look, don’t back talk me!” he snapped. “Just get your asses up and get ready to head back in the streets.”

“What about the police?” Tacora wondered aloud.

“What about them?” he asked.

“Aren’t you afraid that they may come up on us while we’re on the stroll?”

“Let me make something clear to all of y’all,” he said. “I run a tight ship and I’m about my motherfucking money! So I ain’t gon’ let no one stop me from getting it. Now I know y’all are upset about Paris and shit, but she’s dead. So wipe the fucking tears and getcha asses up so you can get me some more money.”

Everything within me wanted to curse out his insensitive ass. How dare he tell those girls to wipe their fucking tears and get their asses up? Come on, show some respect for the dead. I mean, she did give him every fucking dollar she earned on those streets before she took a bullet in her head. And to add insult to injury, I was sure he fucked Paris at his leisure, so where were his fucking tears? It was bad enough that he was not contributing to her funeral fund or helping the homicide detectives identify her body. If I had my way, I'd tell him to shut the fuck up and then I would bounce on his good for nothing ass. But I was trapped, and for now I had to do what he said so I could keep my life.

Seconds after Slim made his speech, everyone got up and headed back out to the streets. We followed him down to the other end of Huntersville and posted up on the corner of Washington Street and Tidewater Drive. It was a little after midnight so the streets were semi-crowded. A couple of people Slim knew stopped and gave him a bit of information about what they'd heard and what the streets were saying about Paris's murder. None of them mentioned that the cops were looking for him for questioning, so I was sure he felt good about that.

The Lifestyle of a Drug Addict

Slim wasn't aware of this, but one of my dates was with a heroin dealer from around Young's Park. I knew he wasn't a big time hustler, because I copped some heroin from him in the past. When I got into his car on this night he asked me if I'd suck his dick and let him fuck me for fifty dollars. I told him no and ran down the prices. But he made a counter offer and told me he'd give me sixty dollars. So I came back at him and demanded that he give me fifty bucks in cash and two pills of dope. He smiled and agreed. I was so fucking happy. And so was he after I served his young ass up really nice and sent him on about his way.

Thank God Slim didn't make us work the streets all night because I was tired and I needed a pick me up. And these two caps of heroin were definitely right on time.

Back at the apartment Slim collected all of our money and then he retired to the living room sofa. He made sure he slept in the living room so he could keep watch on us to make sure we didn't sneak out of the apartment.

I went into the bathroom and snorted one of the capsules of heroin I got from that guy since I didn't have the required items to shoot the dope into my veins. I figured I'd use this method this one last time, but when I went out on the streets the next night, I would make it my business to get what I needed to shoot up without Slim finding out.

When I exited the bathroom I went into the bedroom where Jennifer slept. Before Paris got killed, she and Jennifer shared this bedroom while Tacora and Sabrina shared the other room. The room was very small. But somehow Slim was able to fit two twin-sized beds in there. Jennifer's bed was only inches from the one I was about to sleep in, so if I wanted to reach over and touch her, I could.

When I first entered the bedroom I thought Jennifer was asleep because her back was turned to me. But as soon as I sat down on Paris's old bed, she turned over to her other side and faced me. I was high and didn't want to make it seem so obvious by nodding my head or scratching any part of my body, so I laid my head on the pillow and tried to play it cool.

"You get high, don'tcha?" she asked.

She totally caught me off guard with her direct question. I didn't know how to answer her at first. But then I looked at her and asked myself what I had to hide, so I came clean and told her the truth.

"How long you been getting high?" she wanted to know.

"A couple years now."

"Where you from?"

"Virginia Beach."

"You got kids?"

"Yeah. One."

"Girl? Boy?"

"A girl."

"Where is she? In a foster home or something?"

"No. She's living with her daddy and her new stepmother."

"Ahhh, shit! I know that sucks!" she said. "So what's your story?"

I really did not feel like rehashing my entire life story with this young girl, so I kept it simple. "I used to have a good job, a beautiful home, a brand new car, and a husband. But I lost it all."

"I used to be a stripper before I got with Slim."

"Do you have any children?"

"Nah. But I've been pregnant twice. Got rid of them through an abortion."

"I take it you don't want any kids."

Jennifer sighed. "Well I didn't at the time because I was fucking with this asshole who worked at the strip club. He was fucking me and a few other chicks there. I didn't know it at the time. But when I found out he was playing me for a joke, that was when I went to the clinic and got rid of it."

"What about the other time? You said you had two abortions."

"I know," she said and sighed once again. "I fucked around and let him talk me into hanging out with him one night after I got the first abortion. He took me to IHOP for breakfast right after we left the strip club and then one thing led to another. And then boom, I gave him the pussy and six weeks later I found out I was pregnant by him again."

"Do you regret having the abortions?" I asked as I began to nod. The heroin had started to take effect, which meant I wasn't going to be in the mood to talk much longer.

"Yeah, sometimes I think back on it and regret that I did what I did. But then when I think about who I was pregnant by, I start to feel a little better about it."

Jennifer continued to harp on her life and how hard it'd been for her. She even shed light on how she had dabbled in marijuana, and now she snorted coke from time to time so she could take her mind off the problems in her life. After she filled me in on the journey of her life that brought her here, she started reminiscing about her relationship with Paris and how close they were.

I kept my mouth closed the entire time because I was high off this dope and I wasn't going to let her fuck it up by talking me to death. I did, however, get an earful of all the drama Paris and Jennifer encountered during their time together. From the looks of things, Paris was a very decent person even though she was a prostitute on heroin. Too bad she and I didn't get to spend more time together, because I was sure we would have made the most of our crappy lives as prostitutes on heroin.

The very next morning I was up at the crack of dawn. It was a little after eight AM and I was beginning to feel that withdrawal sickness coming on. I looked up and noticed that Jennifer was still asleep, so I sat up in the bed very quietly to avoid interrupting her sleep. The moment I retrieved the other capsule of heroin from my purse, I didn't waste any time sniffing the drug up my nostrils. I tried to be as quiet as possible, but unfortunately Jennifer heard me and woke up. I wiped my nose with the back of my hand and said good morning. She gave me a half smile and said good morning to me in an early morning groggy voice.

After I cleared my nose of any visible evidence of my heroin use, I laid my head back against the headboard and waited for the drug to take effect once again since I did not have my needle and other materials to help me inject the dope into my arm.

"Gotta get that early morning kick, huh?" Jennifer asked.

"You know it," I commented and closed my eyes.

"What time is it?" she asked me.

"A little after eight."

She started stretching her legs and her arms and belted out a loud yawn. "I'm hungry as hell."

"Well I'm not."

She sat up in the bed and folded her legs Indian style. "I'ma go in the kitchen and get me a bowl of cereal in a minute," she said.

I kept my eyes closed and didn't respond. I would have preferred complete silence, but I was the one who woke her up, so I knew I had to deal with the consequences of it.

"You know what?" she asked. "I used to ask Paris

how that heroin made her feel, but she couldn't give me a straight answer. All she would say was that it felt good, and that it got her high."

"What did you want her to say?"

"I'm not sure. I mean I guess I wanted her to describe the feeling to me. Or maybe tell me that heroin gave her the same kind of high coke did when she used to use it."

"Well let me be the first to tell you that it isn't the same. As you should already know, coke is an upper."

"Yeah, I know."

"OK, well heroin is a downer. It makes you really mellow and tired. You see me nodding right now?" I asked her.

"Yeah."

"Well that's what heroin does to you. It relaxes you. It makes you tired and it makes you scratch your fucking skin to death."

"I see," she replied as she witnessed me scratch my face. "So how many pulls of heroin you go through in a day?"

"If the dope is good, then I can go through about five to six a day. But if the dope is garbage, then I could go through like ten of them."

"Damn! That sounds like a serious habit."

"It is," I assured her as I pulled the blanket back over my body. I had begun to feel extremely tired, so I wanted to be very comfortable. Once Jennifer noticed how relaxed I had gotten, she got up from the bed and left the room. I was happy to see her worrisome ass leave. I could finally enjoy my high in silence.

Junkies & Cokeheads

I had dozed off for a bit, but that was short lived when I heard Slim screaming at Jennifer in the living room. I lay in the bed and listened to them go back and forth. I really couldn't hear Jennifer all that well because Slim was talking over her, but I could tell that she was saying something.

A few minutes later she stormed back into the bedroom and startled the hell out of me. I didn't say anything about it because Slim was right on her heels. Before she could get in the room good, Slim punched her in the back of her head. And before I could blink my eyes, she was face down on the floor. I sat up in the bed to see if she was all right.

"Bitch, you gon' learn how to shut the fuck up when I tell you to," he yelled.

Tacora and Sabrina both came out of their bedroom to see what had happened. They peered into the bedroom from the hallway. They looked at Jennifer on the floor and then they looked at me. I hoped that they didn't expect me to say something, because I wasn't going to say a word. Slim looked like he was about to kill someone, so I wanted to stay out of his way.

"Get your stupid ass up!" he shouted, but Jennifer didn't move, so he kicked her in her side.

He had on a pair of Air Force One sneakers so I knew the force behind his kick was really painful. I figured Tacora and Sabrina couldn't take seeing Jennifer getting kicked while she was down, so they both started begging Slim to leave her alone. I wasn't going to get in the middle of that shit. I was on his shit list yesterday, so now I was gonna play low-key. And besides, I was high as a kite. I wouldn't be able to help Jennifer even if I wanted to.

"Y'all better shut the fuck up before I jump on y'all asses!" he roared. "I'm not gon' have no bitch of mine talking back to me. That ain't how shit is 'round here. So you better talk some sense into her dumb ass before I kill her," he said and then he walked back out of the room.

After Slim went back into the living room, Tacora and Sabrina helped Jennifer get off the floor and they laid her on the bed. "You need some ice for your head?" Sabrina asked as she took a seat on the edge of Jennifer's bed.

"No, I'm fine," she finally said as she laid her head on the pillow.

Tacora stood there and watched Jennifer from the center of the floor. She didn't say a word.

"What the fuck happened?' Sabrina asked in a low whisper.

Jennifer placed her right hand at the bottom of her tummy. I was sure she was in excruciating pain because Slim kicked her pretty hard in that spot. Before she spoke, she very quietly asked Tacora to close the door since she was the closest to it. Whatever she wanted to tell Tacora and Sabrina, she didn't want Slim to hear it.

Immediately after the door was shut, she started talking. "I was in the kitchen washing dishes. When he heard me putting some of the dishes away he got up from the sofa, walked over to the sink, and started grinding on my ass. I told him to stop and let me finish cleaning up, and he got mad and started cursing me out, telling me I belong to him and I ain't gon' be telling him when he can get some pussy. But I wasn't paying him no attention and kept doing what I was doing. So he started yanking on my shorts, trying to take them off, but I told him to stop and started walking away from him. When I started walking away, he started yelling and telling me to bring my ass back. But I kept ignoring him, and that's when he ran down behind me and hit me in the back of my head."

Sabrina shook her head with disgust. "He hit you because you didn't want to fuck him?" she asked.

Jennifer nodded.

Sabrina continued to shake her head. "That's messed up."

"Yep, it sure is," Tacora agreed and then she walked over to Jennifer and started rubbing her head.

"I'm so tired of him putting his fucking hands on me. I swear, if I had a gun I'd blow his fucking head off," Jennifer said. I knew what Jennifer had just said was heartfelt, because I could see how ice cold her eyes were. I also looked at Sabrina's expression. I remembered when Paris warned me to watch out for her because of her sneaky ways. I hoped Paris had warned Jennifer about Sabrina as well, because I would hate to see another blood bath.

"Stop talking crazy, Jennifer, because you already know how Slim is," Tacora said.

"I'm just so tired of him putting his hands on me," Jennifer replied.

"You don't think we're tired?" Tacora asked.

Sabrina smiled and said, "Yeah, Jennifer, we are all tired of getting our asses kicked, but what can we do?"

Before anyone could comment on Sabrina's question, Slim opened the door and came back into the bedroom. "Y'all in this motherfucker talking about me?" he roared, scaring the hell out of all of us. I wasn't going to open my mouth. I was a newcomer and from day one I found out that when you went toe-to-toe with Slim, no one was going to save you.

Wearing the exact same thing he had on yesterday, he walked to the center of the floor and waited for one of us to answer his question. Sabrina got up the gumption to respond.

"Slim, we ain't talking about you," she began to lie. "We're just sitting here making sure Jennifer is all right."

"Whatcha mean you're making sure she's all right? I ain't did nothing but hit her in the back of her damn head. Shit! She better be glad I didn't hit her in her face," he snapped.

"What time you want us to hit the streets?" Tacora asked, trying to change the subject.

"I don't know," he replied in a somewhat agitated manner. "I'm gon' have to go out there and see what's going on first before I put y'all out there to work."

"You think we might need to go back down to the other spot on Washington Street and Tidewater Drive?" Tacora asked.

"Didn't I just say I don't know, Tacora?" he snapped.

She nodded.

"So why you keep asking me those stupid ass questions? Y'all know it's hot out there, so whatever we do is gon' have to be right."

"Can I ask you something?" Tacora asked.

"I hope it ain't nothing stupid."

Tacora sighed. "Have you thought about what we gon' do with Paris's clothes and stuff?"

"Can any of y'all fit her stuff?" he asked, looking around the room at everyone.

The way I remembered Paris, she was really thick. She definitely had the apple booty of a video vixen with B cup breasts. And no one in this room, including myself, could fit any of her clothing. We all had to be at least ten to twenty pounds lighter than Paris. Tacora and Sabrina had to be a size five or a six. And Jennifer looked like she was a size four. She was the smallest of us all, so I figured the best thing to do with Paris's clothes would be to throw them away or donate them.

"I don't think any of us can fit her clothes," Sabrina said. "You might as well throw them out."

"Well pack up her shit and throw it in a couple garbage bags from the kitchen. I'll put that shit in the Dumpster when it gets dark."

As instructed, all of Paris's things were packed away in huge garbage bags. I saw Jennifer and Tacora keep a few shirts for themselves, but I would be damned if I pocketed a couple of her things. There was just something about inheriting things from dead people. I just couldn't get with that program. I even got an unsettling feeling just thinking about it.

Six hours had passed since my last hit of heroin, and I was starting to feel it. I was completely out of dope, so I was thinking of some clever shit to get my hands on some more. I knew Slim still had the pill of dope he took from me the very night Paris was murdered, so I knew it was still some good. Now if he played Mr. Nice Guy and gave me my shit back, my boat would be smooth sailing.

I was sitting on the sofa in the living room watching TV with Jennifer when my stomach started cramping up. I tried to play it off, but Jennifer knew what time it was. "You're starting to get sick, aren't you?" she asked.

I nodded.

"Whatcha gon' do? I mean, you know Slim ain't gon' let you leave out of the house," she said.

"I know. But he took a pill of dope from me last night, so that's the one I got my mind on."

"Oh, you can fucking forget it. I know for a fact that Slim isn't gonna give it back to you," Jennifer said. "It wouldn't surprise me if he already got rid of it."

My heart sank when Jennifer told me that my chances of getting my pill of dope from Slim were zero to none. I was devastated because I needed something right now, and like Jennifer said, Slim wasn't going to let me leave this place, so what the fuck was I gonna do?

Slim was outside in front of the building talking to a couple of guys he knew who lived in the neighborhood. Now I knew Jennifer informed me that there was a slim chance that Slim still had possession of the dope, but I refused to believe it. I got up the gumption to look for it. If he still had it, I knew it had to be in the house, because he wasn't the type of cat who'd walk around with it in his pocket. He'd be a fool to carry it with him. Narcotics police frequented this area of Huntersville all day long, so I knew he wouldn't risk his freedom to keep me from getting high.

As I slid off the sofa, I looked at Jennifer and said, "If he still had it, where do you think he'd keep it?"

Jennifer looked around the room. The kitchen area was less than five feet away and it was an open space next to the living room, so it wasn't hard to see everything from where she was sitting. "Check the refrigerator," she told me.

"Where in the refrigerator?" I asked as I walked quickly toward the kitchen.

"I don't know," she said in a whisper to keep Tacora and Sabrina from hearing her. They were in the bedroom listening to a rap mixed CD Slim bought from some guy in the neighborhood. The music was fairly loud, so they wouldn't be able to hear us unless we wanted them to.

When I opened the refrigerator I immediately looked inside the butter compartment, but it was empty. Then I searched everything that wasn't nailed down. I went to the extent to search underneath every egg in the egg carton and I dug inside the flour bag. I was beginning to believe that the pill of dope wasn't there after all. I closed the refrigerator and stood there puzzled.

Jennifer looked at me and hunched her shoulders. "If he still had it, it would've definitely been in there," she said.

I sighed heavily and tried to figure out what I was going to do next. And then it struck me. "Where are his shorts?" I asked.

"Which ones?"

"The ones he had on last night."

"They should be in that hall closet," she said as she pointed to the only closet next to the living room. "He's got a dirty clothes hamper in there."

I rushed over to the closet and opened the door. The smell of dirty clothes hit me dead in the face. The stench was horrible, so I held my breath as I looked for the jean shorts he wore yesterday.

"You better hurry up before he comes back in the house."

"Well go and look out the window and let me know when he's coming," I said.

"All right. But you better hurry up. Because I don't want to be a part of this shit if he busts you."

"Don't worry, I'll take all the blame," I assured her.

I searched his dirty clothes and could not find his jean shorts anywhere. I was getting frustrated as hell. I knew that I only had a few minutes to find the pill of dope if it was in this apartment, so I went into detective mode.

"Faith, you better hurry up," Jennifer warned me.

"Is he coming?" I asked.

"No. Not yet. But you gotta also watch out for Sabrina. You can't let her catch you going through his shit."

I didn't respond to Jennifer's warning. My mission was to hurry up and find my pill of heroin, so that was what I concentrated on. Unfortunately my search came up dry. I searched Slim's entire dirty clothes hamper and came up with absolutely nothing. I was frustrated and sick to my stomach all at the same time.

"Did you find it yet?" she asked me.

"No, and I searched the entire hamper."

"Well it's got to be there," she whispered.

I started looking through the items he had on the built in shelves. When I moved his deodorant to the side and saw a vitamin bottle, my heart dropped. I picked up the bottle and opened it, and, bam, there was my pill of heroin wrapped up in a clear plastic sandwich bag. I was excited as hell.

"I found it," I told Jennifer.

"Well hurry and get it before he comes in the fucking house," she replied sarcastically.

I grabbed the pill bottle, closed the closet door, and rushed into the kitchen with it in my hand.

Jennifer turned around and looked at me like I had lost my mind. "What the fuck are you doing? Why didn't you just leave the bottle in the closet?"

"Hurry up and hand me a piece of aluminum foil," I instructed her while I pulled the capsule apart. When Jennifer handed me a piece of the aluminum foil, I immediately dumped the heroin onto it. With empty shells of the capsule in my hands, I reached for the canister filled with flour and dipped it inside. Jennifer watched me as I made a fake dummy of dope. My heart was racing at the speed of lightning. I knew that if Slim caught me stealing my pill of heroin, I'd be in a world of trouble.

Jennifer turned around and looked back out the kitchen window. "Oh, shit! I don't see him," she said.

Hearing those words almost made me want to keel over and die, because that could only mean that he was on his way back into the apartment. Without hesitating, Jennifer left me in the kitchen all by myself and rushed back to the living room sofa. I couldn't blame her, though, because I was treading on some very thin ice. Fortunately I remained calm long enough to close the pill back up and stuff it back into the sandwich bag. Before I stuffed the sandwich bag back into the pill bottle, I folded the aluminum foil with the heroin inside of it and stuck it inside the pockets of my shorts.

One second after I stuffed the aluminum foil into my pocket, Slim walked into the apartment. My heart fell to the pit of my stomach. I had my back turned to him, so I turned on the faucet water and made it seem like I was washing my hands.

"I hope ain't nobody in the bathroom because I gotta piss real bad," he said and walked through the living room area and straight into the bathroom.

I looked back at Jennifer the moment he closed the bathroom door. She gave me a few hand gestures as if to say I better put that pill bottle back in the closet or else. Which was exactly what I did. When Slim's retarded ass came out of the bathroom, I was sitting on the sofa next to Jennifer. We were both acting like we were watching TV on Slim's old, rundown thirty-two inch. The Maury show was on, and he was doing his famous paternity segment.

Slim looked at both of us and said, "Y'all stupid ass hoes would probably be up there too if it wasn't for me taking control of your lives."

"You got that right!" Jennifer commented sarcastically. "My life would've been fucked up if you would not have come along."

Slim must have thought what Jennifer said was funny, because he burst into laughter. I looked at her like she was crazy. She and I both knew that this fool looked for anything to give him a reason to go upside our heads. And I was not in the mood to see any more drama for the day. I was becoming extremely ill and I wanted him to carry his ass wherever he was heading so I could feed my addiction.

Luckily for Jennifer, Slim had to go back outside and brushed off her comment. "I'ma take that little comment as a joke and let you slide this time, since I'm in a rush to go back outside. But you better watch your mouth from now on," he warned her and exited the apartment.

I looked at Jennifer and asked her what her problem was.

"Faith, you just don't know how tired I am of that nigga. If you'd been here as long as I have, then you'd probably try to kill his sorry ass!"

"Look, Jen, I know he's an asshole and you wanna fuck him up, but making trouble for yourself ain't gonna make the situation any better. Right now he has the upper hand. So just deal with it until you're ready to bounce on him."

"How the fuck am I going to do that? Slim got all the niggas in this whole apartment building watching us."

"You bullshitting me!"

"Hell, nah, I'm not bullshitting! Try to leave out of here and see what happens."

"Has somebody already tried to leave?" I wanted to know.

"You damn right. And Slim's friend Bino stopped her ass before she could get around the building."

"What, he got those guys working for him?"

"You damn right! He pays them to keep watch on us every day."

I was stunned when Jennifer told me about Slim's watchdogs. I always wondered how he kept the girls here for as long as he did and no one got away. Now my question was answered.

As bad as I wanted to continue this conversation, my body wouldn't let me. My illness was getting more severe by the minute. I rose from the chair.

"I gotta get this dope in my body before I start throwing up all over the place," I said.

"Whatcha gon' do, snort it again?" Jennifer asked.

"No. I'ma chase the dragon," I told her as I looked around the living room for a cigarette lighter.

"How the fuck do you chase the dragon?" she blurted out. Her voice carried loud enough for me to tell her to lower her voice. "I'm sorry. But what the fuck is that?" She pressed the issue.

I heard Jennifer's question, but I ignored her while I located a lighter. I sensed she knew that I was more focused on what I was doing, because she didn't repeat the question. She waited patiently for me to finish doing what I was doing. After searching the kitchen drawers I finally found a half filled lighter. I rushed out of the kitchen and headed into the bathroom. Jennifer got up from the sofa and followed me. I assumed she wanted to see what I meant about chasing the dragon first hand.

Inside the bathroom, I grabbed the first towel I saw hanging from the hook on the back of the bathroom door. And then I closed the lid of the toilet and sat down on it.

"Close the door before one of them sees me," I told Jennifer. She did as I instructed. Not a minute later, I had the aluminum foil unfolded with the heroin visible. Jennifer stood by the door and watched me closely as I added a couple drops of water from the bathroom faucet to the heroin. Immediately thereafter, I heated the mixture of water and heroin with the cigarette lighter until it started boiling up. While I held the lighter underneath the aluminum foil, I asked Jennifer to put the towel over my head. When the towel was completely over my head, I leaned forward and inhaled all the fumes from the vapor of the heroin liquid. Slowly the vapors from the drug got into my system and I started to feel good.

I guess Jennifer felt like she'd seen enough, because she opened the bathroom door. "I'm going back in the living room before Slim comes back in the house and wonders what the hell we doing in this bathroom," she told me, and then left before I could acknowledge what she'd said.

After she closed the door, I sat back on the seat of the toilet and finished what I had started. I wasn't going to let anyone interrupt what I was doing, because for me it was a matter of battling my sickness. Thank God Tacora and Sabrina stayed in their bedroom the entire time and didn't have a need to use the bathroom. Because if they had, I was sure that would have been a disaster waiting to happen.

An Unpleasant Reminder

Since I had a hit of heroin around eleven AM, I knew I'd be fine for the next six to seven hours. I chilled out in the bedroom so I could bask in the feeling of the drug. Plus I wanted to stay out of Slim's way. The entire day he ran in and out of the apartment. He came in the bedroom to check on me a couple times, and when he realized that I wasn't causing any problems, he left me alone.

Unfortunately I couldn't get the same courtesy from Tacora. She burst into the room about thirty minutes after Slim paid me a visit looking for a pair of her shoes she said walked out of her bedroom. Jennifer walked into the bedroom behind her.

"I don't know why you're looking in here," Jennifer said. "I told you I haven't seen your shoes."

Apparently Tacora didn't take Jennifer at her word, because she got down on the floor and searched underneath both beds. Jennifer stood there with her arms folded and watched Tacora as she searched for her belongings. When Tacora realized that her shoes weren't underneath either of the beds, she got off her knees and headed toward the bedroom closet.

I guess Jennifer got ticked off, because she said, "Whatcha going in there for? I told you your shoes ain't in here."

"I know you're gonna let me find out for myself," Tacora replied sarcastically and flung open the closed door. Inside the closet she started rambling around the floor of the closet in search of her shoes, and in the process making a mess of the items that belonged to Jennifer. So Jennifer walked up to Tacora and warned her that if she didn't straighten her closet, then there would be consequences to pay. Tacora turned around and stepped up to Jennifer's face and dared her to lay a finger on her. I sat up in the bed because I saw a brawl about to go down.

Jennifer looked back at me and chuckled. "Do you see this little bitty ass bitch acting like she's about to beat my ass!"

I got up from the bed because it had become obvious that neither of them was going to back down. And even though Jennifer weighed a couple more pounds than Tacora, I believed that Tacora would have given Jennifer a run for her money. Tacora struck me as a chick with a lot of heart.

I got between them before either of them could throw a blow at each other. They were definitely talking trash to one another, but I made sure it didn't get physical. While I stood between them, Sabrina walked into the room with a bath towel wrapped around her. She was in the shower when this whole thing started, so she only caught the tale end of it.

"What's going on?" Sabrina asked.

"I came in here looking for my silver sling-back sandals and I can't find them. But I know Jennifer had something to do with 'em walking out of our room."

"Bitch, I ain't touched them ugly ass shoes!" Jennifer barked at Tacora while I stood between them.

I looked back at Sabrina. "Can you please help me before they start throwing blows at each other?"

Sabrina walked up to Tacora and grabbed her arm. "Come on, don't go there with her. It ain't even worth it," Sabina said, trying to reason with Tacora.

"Yeah, Sabrina, talk some sense into her narrow ass mind. Tell her all that shit she popping ain't gonna be worth it after I put my foot in her ass!" Jennifer roared as she moved from side to side as if she was getting amped up.

"Well if you think you can beat my ass, bitch, then leap like a motherfucking frog!" Tacora snapped.

"Come on, Tacora and Jennifer, y'all gotta stop this mess," I said. "All this arguing ain't cool. We just lost Paris last night and you two are 'round here acting like damn children. You two need to snap out of this shit! Life is too short for this petty shit you two are arguing about."

"Tell her to give me my shoes and you won't even hear my mouth!" Tacora gritted her teeth like she was at her wits' end.

Sabrina started pulling Tacora in her direction because she saw how angry she was becoming. Jennifer stood there and cracked a huge smile. That did it for Tacora, so she lunged forward and punched Jennifer directly in her left eye. Jennifer must not have seen that blow coming, because after Tacora's fist stung Jennifer's left eye, Jennifer's body staggered a bit.

I think I was more shocked than Jennifer. And now that I was caught in the middle of all this drama, I had one of two things I could do. I could prevent Jennifer from retaliating, or I could let her return a blow. As my mind battled back and forth with the decision, I realized that Jennifer had already figured out what she was going to do. She reached over my shoulders, grabbed Tacora's hair, and commenced to hit her repeatedly in the crown of her head. I was literally stuck in the middle.

Sabrina and I tried every tactic to break them apart, but with Jennifer refusing to let go of Tacora's hair, it was definitely a struggle. Tacora was screaming and Jennifer was talking shit to her while she continued to hit her in her head. I figured Sabrina got tired of Jennifer getting the best of Tacora, because when she realized that she couldn't get Jennifer off Tacora, she started hitting Jennifer in the back of her head. It caught Jennifer completely off guard, and Jennifer started demanding that I help get Sabrina off her back.

"Faith, that bitch is hitting me in my fucking head!" Jennifer yelled.

At that moment I had to switch gears and help

Jennifer by stopping Sabrina from attacking her. Sabrina definitely wasn't playing fair and she knew it. So I removed myself from the middle and focused on stopping Sabrina. I immediately grabbed Sabrina in a bear hug and applied pressure to her stomach. By then her towel had fallen from her body so she was completely exposed. In the beginning I found that my efforts didn't work, but as soon as I applied more pressure to her, she realized that I wasn't going to let up, so she let Jennifer go.

I was exhausted. But Sabrina was pissed off, and I knew that I was now added to her shit list. "Get the fuck off me!" she screeched.

"I'll let you go, but you gotta calm down, Sabrina. I can't let you get cheap shots at Jennifer while her back is turned."

Meanwhile Jennifer and Tacora were still going at it. "Bitch, when you let me go, I'ma show your stinking ass something!" Tacora threatened.

"Bitch, you ain't show me shit witcha punk ass! Got all that mouth and look at you now," Jennifer said.

"What the fuck is going on?" Slim roared. I felt the heat from his mouth hit my neck the moment he opened it, and it startled the hell out of me. I let Sabrina go immediately. But Jennifer continued to whale on Tacora. By this time they were both on Jennifer's bed, but Jennifer remained on top.

Slim stormed by me and Sabrina and put a serious chokehold on Jennifer, causing her to release Tacora's hair immediately. While Slim held Jennifer in that chokehold, she started gasping for air.

I saw her face change to two different colors in a matter of five seconds flat. As he pulled her off Tacora, Tacora managed to kick Jennifer in the stomach in the exact same spot where Slim had kicked her earlier.

"Stupid bitch!" Tacora yelled. But Jennifer wasn't fazed by Tacora's blow. She was more focused on Slim and trying to get out of his death grip.

"Let me go," I heard her say, but it was barely audible. She was kicking too, but it didn't work. Slim was adamant about getting control of this situation.

"You just wanna keep causing me fucking problems, huh?" he asked. He gritted his teeth and applied more and more pressure to her neck.

I could tell her body was giving out because her fight to get him to loosen his hold on her neck became less intense. I knew right then I had to step in and help her or else he was going to hurt her severely. Tacora and Sabrina just stood there watching as Slim slowly crippled Jennifer by applying pressure to her neck, so I jumped on Slim's back and began to tear into the flesh of his shoulder with my teeth. I tried to bury my teeth into him as deep as I could, and he felt it. He belted out a scream like the head of a silver bullet had pierced his skin.

"Owww, you fucking bitch!" he yelled and then let Jennifer go to focus on getting me off him.

Apparently Sabrina felt the need to get in on the situation too, because she started punching me in my back. "Bitch, let him go!" she snapped.

I released my teeth from Slim's back and tried

to shield the blows Sabrina was throwing at me. Slim attacked me as well. He pushed Sabrina away from me and immediately started throwing one punch behind the other at me. He used my face as a punching bag and beat it until the entire right side of my face swelled up. I remember landing on the floor and losing consciousness.

I couldn't tell you how long I was unconscious, but when I opened my eyes I could tell that it was night outside from the darkness in the room. I looked around the bedroom and realized that Jennifer was nowhere in sight. I tried to get up from the bed, but when I lifted my head, it started hurting really badly. I laid my head back down on the pillow and yelled Jennifer's name. But I didn't get an answer. I lay completely still and listened for any movement, but heard none.

I was confused. I knew that I hadn't been with Slim long enough to pinpoint his behavior, but something inside me told me that it wasn't normal for him to leave any of his girls alone. After three minutes passed I called Jennifer's name again, but I still didn't get a response. Something told me that I was alone. But then I figured that Slim wouldn't dare leave me alone. That would be too risky. As I tried to figure out what was going on, I heard footsteps.

"Whoever is in here, can you please come here?" I yelled, and then I fell silent and waited for a response.

Unfortunately the person on the other side of

the bedroom door would not utter one word to me. I heard the footsteps a couple more times and then they stopped altogether. I became really leery. "Who's there?" I yelled.

Yet again, I didn't get a response, and that bothered me. I eased my head up from the pillow and slowly eased myself off the bed. I had to get on the other side of that door to see who was ignoring me and why.

I felt excruciating pains coming from my battered face. There wasn't a mirror in the bedroom, but I knew that my face had been beaten up pretty badly. From the corner of my eye I could see how badly the right side of my face was swollen. And when I tried to touch it, it hurt worse. I tried to deal with the idea that I was banged up while I headed for the door. I grabbed the doorknob and turned it, but it wouldn't open. The fucking door was locked. I started banging on it.

"I gotta use the bathroom!" I yelled. "Please open the door!"

And, again, no one responded. I was now more frustrated than pissed off. But I figured that if I caused another scene, I would be on the receiving end of another beat-down. So I returned to my bed and lay down. Whoever was in the other room knew I needed some attention. But they didn't give a fuck, so I decided to chill out and wait to see what happened next.

Beating a Dead Horse

Sometime later the bedroom door finally opened. Slim stood in the entryway with a grin on his face. I didn't see a fucking thing funny. I was tempted to ask him what the hell he saw that was so amusing, but what the hell was the use. I would've gotten my ass kicked all over again. And with the shape I was in at the moment, I couldn't afford to make things any worse.

"You look like shit!" Slim commented and then he chuckled.

I lay there and tried to block him out, but unfortunately I couldn't.

"I bet you regret sinking your teeth in my back now, huh?" he taunted. "I know you're probably cursing yourself out right now and wondering why you messed with a crazy ass nigga like me. And you're probably mad that you got involved in something that had nothing to do with you. I mean, if it was me standing there watching somebody I only knew for two days getting their ass tore up, I would not have risked getting hurt myself. Are you fucking insane or something? Do you like getting the shit beat out of you?"

I guess he was waiting for me to respond, but I kept my mouth closed. Knowing his dumb ass, it was probably a fucking trick question. So I lay there and let everything he said go in one ear and right out the other.

I assumed it irritated him that I was ignoring him, because he rushed toward me and lunged directly at my face. I threw my arms over my face to block him. But it didn't matter, because he stopped his arm in midair and then he burst into laughter. "Don't be scared now, you little bad bitch!" he yelled.

I continued to shield my face with my arms even though he had not hit me. The fact that he was still within arm's reach kept me alert and instantly reminded me that he could change his mind at any given moment. So to keep an eye out for him, I peeped through my arms.

"How does it feel to be locked up in a fucking room all by yourself like you're a dog?" Slim asked. "You can't leave out of here and roam around the house when you get ready. And you can't go and use the bathroom unless you ask me. I am going to treat you like the dumb dope fiend bitch you are. And if you ever try that bullshit that you did earlier, I swear I am gonna rip your fucking throat out and feed it to the dogs outside!"

Before he walked away from me, he hawked and spit on my arm. Some of it seeped through my arms and onto my face. I guess he wasn't trying to keep it a secret that he hated my fucking guts. In fact, he made it blatantly obvious that I was beneath him. I was a broke down dope fiend with no life. I was also a fucking prostitute, so I was a ho in his eyes. And what man had respect for a woman like that? I was convinced that as long as I dragged myself through the mud, men would continue to treat me like dirt. And since I had no will to pull myself out of this rut, I knew I had to deal with it.

Slim finally left me alone. When he walked back out of the bedroom and locked the door from the other side, I got up from the bed, grabbed one of my dirty shirts from my duffel bag, and wiped his spit off my face and arms.

While I cleaned myself, I figured that there was no way for me to convince him to let me out of the room, so I sat there and prepared to endure whatever type of punishment he sent my way.

Slim was definitely a heartless son of a bitch. And he was a control freak. He prided himself on beating and tearing down the self-esteem of women like me. To see us squirm and beg him for anything made his chest stick out. I hated that bastard for it, but that was the way the ball rolled.

Like clockwork, my body started the withdrawal process. I was getting sicker by the minute. Not only was my head pounding, but my stomach had started aching too. I jumped up from the bed twice to vomit within the same hour. I even begged Slim to let me out of the bedroom to go to the bathroom. Diarrhea had plagued my body as well, and I found myself right back in the same place I was in the day I checked into rehab over two weeks ago. And the worst part of it all was that I had no one to help me through it. When I was in the rehab center Denise coached me through my illness and I would never forget that. I knew I did her wrong in the end, but that was just the life I lived. I was a fucking drug addict, and when on drugs, I was always doing bad things to the people who cared about me. So I guess I was paying for everything I'd done to the good people who had crossed my path.

I lay in the fetal position in the center of the bed and cried out every chance my mouth opened. I didn't have access to a watch, but it seemed like time was moving slowly. Slim poked his head in the room a couple times and laughed at me. He found it amusing that I was dope sick. I ignored his antics and tried to play the cards I was dealt.

It seemed like forever, but Jennifer and the other two hoes were finally allowed to come back to the house. I heard Tacora and Sabrina go into the other room and Jennifer came into the room with me. My body wouldn't allow me to embrace her, but I expressed how excited I was to see her. She rushed to my side.

"Oh my God! Look at you," she said as she sat on the edge of my bed.

I knew she was looking at how badly my face was bruised up, but that was the least of my concerns. My entire body was ill and I had a hard time dealing with it.

"You're sick, aren't you?" she asked.

"Yes, Jennifer, I need some blow really badly to take this pain away. I swear I can't go another minute like this," I whined. And like a guardian angel, she went into her pocket and pulled out two pills of heroin.

If I had the strength, I would have jumped straight up and snatched both capsules from her. That was how happy I was to see them. But instead I began to cry. I was already in severe pain, but I immediately became emotional when I saw that Jennifer cared enough to cop me some dope to get well. I couldn't hold back the tears. "Thank you so much, Jennifer," I said as I sobbed.

"Just be quiet and sit up for me," she instructed.

It took everything within me and the help of Jennifer to get me to sit up, but we managed to do it. Seconds later she unscrewed one of the heroin filled caps and dumped half of it into my right nostril. I snorted every grain of it. And when the first half of the capsule was empty, I begged Jennifer to put the other half up to my left nostril. She did as I asked, and immediately after I snorted every grain of heroin from that one, I laid my head back against the headboard. At this point it didn't matter to me if Slim walked into the room and saw the residue around my nostrils. But Jennifer cared, because while I had my head tilted back, she used my shirt to wipe my nose clean. Somehow I managed to utter the words *thank you.*

Snorting heroin wasn't my favorite method to get high, but at this juncture, I'd drink it if I knew it'd get me the high I so desperately needed. Truth be told, getting high wasn't my main focus. My mission was to prevent myself from getting sick. So if it meant that I had to get that dope through any means necessary and snort it or smoke it, then that was what I'd do.

Not too long after I snorted the heroin Jennifer copped for me, I noticed that my stomach cramps started subsiding and I was beginning to feel some relief. I looked at Jennifer and thanked her at least a dozen times.

She rubbed me on my leg and said, "You don't have to thank me. I owe you. Because if you would not have jumped on Slim's back and bit that fucking plug out of his back, then I'd probably be lying around here bruised up like you are, or maybe even dead."

"It's OK," I said, my voice barely audible.

"No, it's not OK. Faith, you took an ass whooping for me. I mean look at you. Have you seen your fucking face?"

I shook my head.

"Girl, you are a lifesaver. And I owe you dearly."

"It's OK," I repeated.

"Stop saying that, Faith, because it's not OK," she whispered. "That grimy motherfucker beat you like he was beating a man, and that's not how you lash out on a woman. I don't give a fuck what we did, a real man would not have done what he did to us earlier."

"Don't sweat it! Because he's gonna get back everything he did to me, you, and everybody else he put his hands on," I whispered back.

"Yeah, you're right, but I want something to happen to his ass right now."

"Don't worry. It's coming," I told her, and then I took a deep breath and exhaled.

Jennifer massaged my back while she watched the heroin take its effect on me. "How are you feeling now?" she wanted to know.

I cracked a half smile. "I'm feeling better than I did fifteen minutes ago," I assured her.

"Good. I'm glad," she replied and continued to massage my back. She acted like she was my protector and that eased my mind more than I would have imagined. As the drugs took complete effect, I closed my eyes and tried to block out everything around me. Once again I was put out of my misery, and this time it was Jennifer who made it all possible.

Thank God for Jennifer, because I was back in business. I wasn't that appealing on the surface, but I wasn't sick, so I felt great on the inside. While the sun was rising, I was rising too. I looked around the bedroom and noticed that Jennifer wasn't in her bed. I panicked a bit because I knew I would need that other pill of dope she had for me, and if Slim had made her leave the apartment with him, then I would be up shit's creek without a paddle. I didn't want to go through another withdrawal. I wanted to prevent the illness before it had a chance to rear its ugly head, so I immediately got out of bed and rushed toward the door. When I opened it up to look for Jennifer, I found her walking toward me and I exhaled.

"You all right?" she whispered.

I grabbed her right hand and pulled her into the room. "I thought you had left," I replied nervously.

Jennifer closed the door behind us. "Where was I going at eight o'clock in the morning? I only went to the bathroom."

"I thought it was later than that," I said and took a seat back on the edge of my bed.

Jennifer took a seat on her bed and asked me how I was feeling. I sighed and told her that I would need that other pill of heroin very soon because the other dope she gave me was wearing off. Without hesitation she dug inside her purse and handed me the other pill of heroin. I instantly felt like a kid in a candy shop. I took the drug and cupped it in the palm of my hand because I knew I would be using it in the next few minutes.

Jennifer asked me how my face felt. I told her that it felt better today.

She frowned. "Can you see out of your right eye?" she asked.

I cracked a smile. "Yeah, I can see."

"Well, it doesn't look like it."

"Don't worry. I can," I assured her. And when it looked like she was about to open her mouth to make another comment, she paused because we both heard a door open and then it closed. We looked at the bedroom door and then we looked back at each other.

"That's probably Tacora or Sabrina going to the bathroom," she whispered.

"Is Slim in the living room on the couch asleep?" I asked her.

"Yeah, he's in there."

"Boy, I wish I had a gun because I would walk up on him in his sleep and blow his fucking head off," I commented as I kept my volume down to a minimum. I could not afford to let anyone on the outside of that bedroom door hear me talk about anything dealing with Slim. I learned the hard way that Tacora and Sabrina were my worst enemies, and if I wanted to keep my head above water around here, then I was going to have to play it easy until the right opportunity came along.

Jennifer got up from her bed, walked over to my bed, and sat down next to me. "I heard some people talking about Paris's grandparents putting out a reward for information about who murdered her," she said.

Being reminded about Paris's murder was a very sore issue for me. I mean, I was the one who she'd last talked to before she got into her killer's truck. And even though I never had a chance to actually see the man's face, I did get a glimpse of his license plate. I never told anyone this because I didn't think it would matter. Immediately after she was killed Slim made the announcement that he didn't want us to be questioned by the police, and it wasn't like I could approach the police secretly, since Slim watched our every move. But today I had to tell Jennifer what I knew.

I took a deep breath and said, "I saw the guy's license plate number."

Jennifer's eyes grew two inches. It was pretty obvious that she was happy. "Oh my God! Why didn't you tell me?" she asked in a whisper.

"Because I didn't think that it would matter."

"Oh my God, Faith! Do you know what this could mean? We gotta get in touch with the police."

"But how?"

Jennifer's reaction changed. "I don't know. But we're gonna have to figure out something."

"I can tell you right now that it's going to be pretty hard coming up with a plan when we don't have access to a cell phone. And not only that, there is simply no one in this entire neighborhood that will help us because they know we work for Slim."

Jennifer sighed heavily. "I know. But I'm still not giving up. Because when there's a will, there's always a way," she told me and then she fell silent. It was evident that she was in deep thought about ways to get this information to the police.

Looking at it from a clear standpoint, it would be a win-win situation for the both of us. Not only would we be able to break free from that asshole in the next room, we would be collecting a reward and Paris's grandparents could rest knowing that her murderer got what he deserved, no matter what Paris may have given him.

While we were both in deep thought, we heard a little bit of chitchat in the hallway. It was none other than Slim and Sabrina.

"We need some toilet paper in the bathroom," Jennifer and I heard her say.

"I just bought some a couple days ago and you mean to tell me that it's all gone?" he asked.

"There was only a little bit left before I went in

the bathroom. I had to go in the kitchen and get a couple paper towels before I used the bathroom."

"Well that's what y'all better use, because I ain't going out this house until later on," he told her.

Sabrina didn't respond to Slim's unwillingness to make a trip to the neighborhood convenience store. Instead we heard her suck her teeth, walk back into her room, and slam the door.

Jennifer chuckled. "That's what her stupid ass gets. The nigga she's always going to bat for and jumped on your back for won't even go out and get her dumb ass a roll of shit paper. Now ain't that crazy?"

I smiled and nodded.

"You should've seen her last night out on the corner trying to be all up in his face like they were a couple. But he wasn't paying her ass any mind. He kept telling her to get away from him and flag down some cars to get him some money. I just laughed the whole time."

"You gotta be kidding me. He played her like that?"

"Girl, please, he ain't thinking about her ass for real. And she's just too stupid to realize that he don't give a fuck about her. Because if a nigga come on the block and fired a shot at her ass, Slim wouldn't do a damn thing but run down behind the guy and fire a couple shots back at him to prove to everybody on the block that he will shoot his gun."

"So you're basically saying he's a pussy?"

"That's exactly what I'm saying, because if you really think about it, Slim was only a couple feet away from that truck when it sped off. If he really wanted to shoot that guy, he could've. He was right there, so why didn't any of the bullets he fired penetrate the man's truck?" Jennifer asked, and then she fell silent and waited for me to speak.

I was blown away when Jennifer revealed all this information to me. She literally called out this bastard. But as far as her question was concerned, I truly didn't have an explanation or an answer for it. I had not been in Slim's life as long as she had, so I was the wrong person to ask. However, I did think that she had made some damn good points, and I wanted her to know that.

"You damn sure make a person go umm!" I said.

"Faith, I'm telling you some good shit. That nigga that's on the other side of that door is a fucking coward and he preys on women like you and me. And one of these days, I am going to get him back for everything he has done to me."

"To be honest with you, Jennifer, I'm not seeking revenge on that loser. I just want to get out of here and never look back."

Jennifer looked at me and smiled. She had seen how tired I was, and how drained I was about this situation. She rubbed me on my back and said, "Don't worry. We gon' make sure that happens."

Back on the Corner

Slim finally gave me the green light to leave the house once he thought that my bruises had healed enough. But it wasn't to go on a joy ride or a shopping spree. I had to report back to the corner where I belonged, as he so eloquently put it. It had been four days since I had been out of the apartment, so I welcomed the fresh air. We were back on the corner of Washington Street and Tidewater Drive, so we knew exactly where we would stand. Everything was cool and customers rolled in one after the other. But when there was traffic like that, it attracted the police.

While we were standing at our posts Slim spotted a cop car coming toward us and warned us to get behind the building. After the police left the block, Slim ordered us to come back to our posts. While I stood there, I wondered how I would get a chance to talk to the cops about Paris's murder. I knew that they were riding around policing the area, looking for someone who might give them the answers they needed. There was one problem, though. People in this neighborhood didn't like the cops. They hated them to be more frank about it. They looked at the local police department as the enemy because most of the people living in the neighborhood were doing everything illegal under the sun.

Even though I broke a lot of the laws in this city by buying drugs and being a prostitute, I'd welcome the chance to talk to the police. I wasn't afraid of them. I was afraid of the motherfuckers that roamed this neighborhood. Everyone out here cared about no one but themselves. And since the day I'd been out there, I knew that I was on my own.

Slim told us that we had fifteen more minutes before we were going in for the night. To be perfectly honest, I was ready to go a long time ago. When he wasn't looking, Jennifer copped me a couple pills of dope from a guy whose dick she'd sucked earlier. I had ducked behind a building and snorted it in a matter of ten seconds flat, so now I was buzzing and I wanted to relax. I wasn't in the mood to talk, much less fuck somebody. But when this idiot pulled curbside for some pussy, Slim made me hop in the car with him. I wanted to tell this man that I had herpes or the clap so he could carry his ass, but then I thought about what happened to Paris and decided against it. The men around here were crazy and would kill you over the pettiest things. And in spite of my actions, I really did want to live.

Now the guy was a fat ol' black guy with a musty smell. He looked like he was a mechanic or a construction worker because his hands were hard and filthy. The facial hairs on his face looked really bushy and unkempt. I wasn't feeling him one bit. He had on this old, red greasy baseball cap and a plaid flannel shirt while it was eighty degrees outside. He smiled at me and even though it was pitch black outside I could see his stained teeth. There was no question in my mind that he was a tobacco-chewing loser looking for some cheap fun.

After I sat down on the passenger seat of his old, beat-up van and told him the prices of my services, he said, "Come on, little lady, it's a recession out here. Can you give an old man like me a break?"

I gritted my teeth because not only did this asshole want me to fuck his disgusting ass, he wanted me to give him a discount on top of that. How dare him?

"Look, man, don't tell me to give you a break," I said. "You need to give me one and stop hassling me about fifty bucks."

"Goodness gracious, young lady, you sure drive a hard bargain," he said and pulled fifty dollars from his wallet. After he handed me the money, I stuffed it inside my bra and climbed in the back of his van so we could get the show on the road.

In the back of his van this fat fuck instructed me to bend over so he could screw me from the back, and I happily obliged. The less I saw his face, the better off I was. I buried my face into the seat in the rear of his van and allowed that jerk off to do his thing. When I heard him unzip his jeans and slide them down around his ankles, I knew my time was coming and I dreaded it. But I figured the sooner he penetrated me, the sooner he'd be done, and the sooner I could go back to the apartment and finally enjoy the dope I had in my system.

Finally he pushed himself inside me. He was pretty big, but it felt awful. I remembered when I wasn't on heroin and I used to love to have sex with my husband. But now it seemed like a chore and I didn't enjoy it at all. Every junkie around here would say that if sex was banned, they wouldn't give a fuck. All we cared about was getting high and getting a good meal every now and again.

As this old, dirty man pushed himself in and out of me, he became more and more annoying. "Can you hurry the fuck up, please?" I barked.

"Shut up, bitch! I paid you my money. Now be quiet so I can concentrate," he continued and kept boning me.

I sighed and shook my head. I tried to block out all the noises he made while he was banging me, but I found it very hard. The grunts and insane noises were unbearable.

"Uhhh . . ." he growled, and then he started pounding me faster. And I knew right then that his nasty ass was about to get his nut.

"You can't cum inside me," I warned him.

"Shut up, bitch!" he roared as he pounded me a little harder. And after another handful of strokes, he pounded me one last time and then he pulled out his dick and started beating it on the back of my ass. I felt his warm body fluids squirt me on the back of my ass and that truly did it for me. That was the last straw. I abruptly got up.

"Where the fuck you going?" he whined.

"It's over. You're done and I gotta go," I snapped.

After I pulled up my panties and put my skirt back over my ass, I bailed out of that van quicker than he could blink his eyes.

Before I closed the passenger side door, he climbed back to the front of his van and said, "Hey, wait a minute. Your pussy wasn't all that good! So can I get some of my money back?" he asked.

"And your dick wasn't that good either, and I ain't complaining. So fuck off, fat boy!" I yelled, and then I slammed the door in his face.

By the time I got out of the van, everybody was waiting and ready to go. I joined them and we all followed one another back to the apartment.

Tacora and Sabrina walked ahead of me and Jennifer while Slim followed us. We always did this when we headed in for the night. I guess Slim figured if he stayed behind all of us he'd be able to watch us better or prevent any of us from running off. But he just didn't know that Jennifer and I had another plan up our sleeves, and sooner rather than later we were going to implement it.

When we got back inside the apartment, Slim did his normal routine by collecting everyone's money and then going to the kitchen table to count it. I would usually sit in the living room and watch him count the money on the sneak tip, but tonight I wanted to enjoy my buzz, so Jennifer and I headed to our bedroom. Before we closed the door, we heard Sabrina and Tacora whispering and giggling in the living room. Jennifer made the assumption that they were talking about us, but I ignored her and laid my butt down. I was not interested in entertaining that mess at all. All I wanted to do was relax.

It Comes with the Territory

It was a Friday night, a few minutes after midnight, and the streets were jumping. We were getting a ton of business that night, so Slim was very excited. He was even counting the cars we got in, I guess to keep tabs on how much money we raked in. But unbeknownst to him, Jennifer and I still managed to skim some fat from around the edges. Jennifer had a coke habit and I had a heroin addiction, so we refused to let that bastard get all the money we made with our blood, sweat, and tears.

Slim had eased up on us somewhat, and he wouldn't say anything to me or Jennifer about getting high as long as it didn't stop us from making his money. He did question us about how we got the drugs, but of course we lied to him about a lot of our customers being dope boys from other neighborhoods. We didn't say which ones, because we had to keep our lies close to our chests.

On this Friday night while all of us were stacking

our money for Slim to take at the end of the night, a black, late-model 745i BMW drove up and parked on the side of the street where Tacora and Sabrina stood. Jennifer and I had to stay back and let one of the others get the customer, because Slim had made a rule that whatever side of the street a driver parked on, the girls standing on that side of the street got that customer.

As Jennifer and I stood there and admired how nice the car looked, Slim instructed Sabrina to take the customer. Jennifer started talking shit about Sabrina when she approached the car. I knew she was jealous by the comments she was making, but what could I say? Jennifer had become a dear friend to me, so she was entitled to hate if she wanted to. I was there to listen to her, and that was what I did.

"Do you see this shit?" she asked.

"What?" I asked, even though I knew what she meant.

"Do you see that bitch strutting her shit over to that BMW like she's hot?"

I chuckled. "Yeah, I see her."

Jennifer sucked her teeth. "She ain't gon' know what to do with that nigga in that car. That's why he should've pulled up on this side of the street and got with me, because I would've had him begging me to come back out here tomorrow."

"Yeah, you're probably right," I said and smiled. But I was really being sarcastic.

Jennifer was a very sweet young girl, but she took this tricking thing to a whole new level. If she didn't get the guy with the nicest car, she acted like her whole world was going to fall apart. To me it didn't matter what kind of car they drove, because at the end of the day, we were providing a service to these bastards in exchange for money. So we knew what to expect from each other. We were fucking streetwalkers, not wifey material, and they knew it. These guys weren't looking to take us home to meet their parents. I found myself explaining this whole scenario to Jennifer dozens of times, but it just wouldn't sink in.

Slim stood a few feet away from the BMW. I watched him as he admired the car. I assumed he pictured himself in the driver's seat of a vehicle like that one day. And in my opinion, if he kept hustling the way he was, then he'd definitely have the car he wanted.

Jennifer and I couldn't hear what Sabrina was saying to the guy, but we knew she was trying to get his money. Finally she got into the car, and we knew she had her sale.

"That lucky bitch!" Jennifer said. And then before we could blink our eyes, the guy put his car in drive and tried to pull off.

Slim quickly stepped to the car and yelled, "Where the fuck you think you going?"

The guy yelled back, "I'm police! Get back because she's under arrest." And then he sped off.

Jennifer and I looked at each other in disbelief.

"What the fuck just happened?" I asked as I watched the car drive farther and farther away. Watching the car as it got smaller and smaller was like watching my chances of getting out of this situation fade away.

"Yo, Faith and Jennifer, y'all get y'all asses over here right now!" Slim yelled from across the street. He looked like a nervous wreck, but he looked more angry than anything else.

"I betcha he's getting ready to tell us we're closing down shop," Jennifer said.

"I'm sure he is," I replied as we began to proceed across the street.

As soon as we were face to face with him, he said, "Let's go." Jennifer and I both looked at each other. We already knew what time it was. Before we started the walk back to the apartment, he demanded that all of us hand him all the money we'd made for the night. As instructed, we reached into our money stash and pulled out every dollar we made for the entire night. Luckily Jennifer and I had already made our dope purchases for the night, or we would have been knee deep in trouble, because my body would not have lasted that long for my next fix.

After we gave him all of our money, he made us march down the block like we were in a rush. "Y'all need to walk faster than that," he said.

During the walk back to the apartment Slim looked over his shoulder at least eight times to make sure we weren't being followed. But I knew what time it was. Police didn't follow someone unless they suspected that you sold drugs. Now if they believed you were selling sexual favors, then they would set up a sting and solicit sex from you like they did with Sabrina. So Slim was really wasting his time by looking over his fucking shoulder. No one was looking for him now that they had Sabrina.

The moment we entered the apartment he really showed his ass. He became really aggressive, so I tried to stay out of his way. I went with my first reaction and headed toward the bedroom. But he stopped me in my tracks and instructed me to take a seat on the couch beside Jennifer and Tacora. Tacora was on the verge of tears when I sat between her and Jennifer. I assumed she was upset about her hanging partner getting arrested. I thought Slim would have asked her what was wrong, but it was apparent that he wasn't the least bit concerned about her feelings. As he stood before us, we all gave him our undivided attention.

"I know y'all saw Sabrina get arrested by an undercover police officer for prostitution. Right now my mind is going around in fucking circles, and I can't figure out what I am going to do."

"I know you ain't gon' let her sit in jail!" Tacora blurted out as tears fell from her eyes.

"Did I tell you to open your motherfucking mouth?" he roared.

"No, but I—" she started to say, but he cut her off in mid sentence.

He was fuming and I could tell that he was about to get really physical. "Tacora, shut the fuck up! Now if you open your mouth again, I am gonna stuff my fist down your goddamn throat. Do you hear me?"

She nodded. After he realized that he'd gotten her attention, he continued. "Now I don't know what happened tonight because it happened so fast. But I do know that we are gonna have to lay low until I can figure out something. Right now the block is hot, so we can't go back to that spot. We might have to go over to the corner of Okeefe and Goff Streets and start with a clean slate. But y'all still gonna have to be careful and make sure y'all ain't talking to the police. Remember you gotta ask all your customers if he's the police, and he's gonna have to answer you whether he wants to or not. I'm thinking Sabrina forgot to ask that nigga in that BMW tonight, because if she had asked him, then she wouldn't be on her way downtown. As far as getting her out of jail, I'm gon' send somebody down there to get her, but it ain't gon' be tonight 'cause I know I ain't gon' be able to find a bondsman out this time of night. But I will make sure I get somebody to bail her out tomorrow. And until she comes back to the apartment, make sure you don't ask me anything about her, because I'm gonna smack the hell out of you if you do. Do y'all understand?"

All three of us said yes in unison. When he realized that we completely understood, he dismissed us and gave us the green light to carry our butts to our rooms. While Jennifer and I headed to our bedroom, Tacora headed to hers. The moment we closed our door, we heard Slim join Tacora in her room. Jennifer and I knew what time it was. He saw how vulnerable her dumb ass was, so he was using this opportunity to get his rocks off and ease her mind about her friend. I wished Sabrina could see her sugar daddy now, banging the hell out of her home girl while Sabrina was behind bars rotting.

It was somewhat quiet in the other room, but we knew what was going on. Jennifer started cracking up about the whole situation. We kept our voices down so neither one of them would be able to hear us. "She is so fucking stupid!" Jennifer said and chuckled softly.

"Yeah, she's a class A clown if you ask me."

"Yeah, she is, because I swear I couldn't let a man curse me out one minute and then try to slide in my pussy the next minute. She is fucking whack for that."

"She's young and gullible, Jennifer. What more can we expect from her?"

"I don't know, but she's getting on my fucking nerves with this kissing-ass shit! I wish she would've gotten locked up too."

"Do you think he's gonna go get Sabrina out?" I whispered.

"Can dogs fuck cats?" she asked and chuckled.

"Not the ones I've seen running around Huntersville."

"Well there's your answer."

"So why would he tell us that was his plan?"

"Come on now, Faith, do I have to spell it out? Slim doesn't give a fuck about no one but himself. When Sabrina got arrested, she took his money with her, which was money he can't get back. So why would he go out and lose more money when he doesn't have to?"

"To keep her from giving the cops any information about Paris's murder."

Jennifer hesitated for a moment and looked at me very strangely. "Has it ever occurred to you that he might've set up Paris to get killed?" she asked.

Uncertain as to what to say, I thought for a second, and then I replayed that entire incident over in my head. When I remembered the exact words Paris said before she got in that man's truck, I looked back at Jennifer and said, "I know you hate Slim's guts, but I know for a fact that he didn't have anything to do with Paris's murder. That guy who shot her was a regular customer of hers. I heard her say that before she walked away from me."

"Well that might've been true, but I still don't trust that motherfucker in there. I ain't gonna put shit past him," Jennifer said, and then she fixed her blanket so she could get cozy in her bed.

We talked for a little while longer until I decided to pull out my personal stash of my get-high supply. I had even bummed a needle from one of the junkies out there on the streets, so I was well equipped to get that monkey out of my back.

I Brought This On Myself

The very next day Slim roamed in and out of the apartment all day long. I wanted to ask him what the fuck was wrong with him, but I decided against it for fear that I'd get on his bad side, and then he'd have a reason to go upside my head. I watched a little bit of TV in the living room and then I made myself a grilled cheese sandwich to put something in my stomach before I went back into the room to lie down. Jennifer was already in the room lying down. She told me she had a headache, so I decided to leave her alone and I headed back to the living room.

Tacora was in the other bedroom doing God knew what, but I guess she decided to join me in the living room, because she came prancing out not too long after I had sat on the sofa. I hoped she wasn't looking for conversation, because I was not in the mood to socialize with her, especially after all the shit I'd been through because of her. She strutted her stinking ass over to the sofa and took a seat beside me. I pretended to be engrossed in the show that was on cable, but that didn't matter to her, because she made sure I knew she was in the room.

"Whatcha watching?" she asked me with that squeaky voice of hers.

I started to ignore her simple-minded ass because she knew what I was watching. She saw that it was Martin Lawrence and Gina, so she knew it was an old episode of *Martin.* But I smiled and played her game. "It's *Martin,*" I told her.

"When did that come back on? I used to love that show before they canceled it a few years ago."

"Yeah, I used to love it too," I responded, but didn't turn my head once to look at her.

Before she could make more conversation, Slim walked into the apartment, but he didn't come in alone. He had this pretty young girl with him. I knew right off the bat that he had recruited another victim. Too bad she hadn't been warned that she was in over her head with that joker, because it was only a matter of time before he flipped the script on her. He was smiling now, but give him another hour or two, and he would be right back to his regular self.

"Come on in here," he instructed her as if he was the most gentle man on the face of the earth.

Listening to him sweet talk this young girl made me want to regurgitate my entire grilled cheese sandwich. He was pouring on his phony ass charm too thick for me, and I wanted to expose him for who he truly was. But Tacora beat me to the punch.

"Who the fuck is she?" she asked.

Ignoring Tacora, Slim closed the front door and pointed the young girl toward the bathroom. Immediately after she closed the door behind herself, Slim rushed toward Tacora and grabbed her around her neck. I could tell that he was squeezing the hell out of her windpipe because she was gasping for air like her life depended on it. Well, I guess her life did depend on it.

"Bitch, don't you ever question me about who the fuck I bring in this house!" Slim said. "Do you understand?"

Tacora wasn't able to respond verbally, but she was able to make some type of eye signal to him, I guess, because he ended up letting her go. Several minutes later the young girl came out of the bathroom and noticed that Tacora was massaging her neck. She gave Tacora a really goofy expression. I spoke to the young girl and she spoke back to me, but Tacora wouldn't open her mouth. She focused her attention on the TV, ignoring the new chick.

Slim finally introduced the new girl. "This is Stacy," he said. "She will be staying with us until she can get back on her feet."

I nodded, because I didn't care one way or the other. I already knew that whatever he told her to get her to come here was a lie. And to say that she was going to be here until she could get on her feet was definitely some bullshit. I couldn't wait to see her face when he removed the blinders from her naïve eyes.

Like I said earlier, Stacy was a very pretty girl. I could tell that she wasn't over the age of twenty-one. Her body was nice and ripe for this line of work, so I knew Slim had major plans for her. She reminded me of the R&B singer Rihanna. She had that innocent girl look and she was petite like Rihanna as well. As I watched how Slim interacted with her, I knew that he had no intentions on springing Sabrina from jail. As far as he was concerned, she was a distant memory. She was just another young and gullible streetwalker that could be replaced at the drop of a hat. That was how he rolled.

"Where do you want me to put my stuff?" she asked him in her childlike voice.

"Come here and let me show you where you gon' be sleeping," he replied, and then he escorted her to Tacora's room. Right after he entered the bedroom, he called Tacora's name and told her to come into the room to help Stacy put away her things. I laughed softly, but Tacora heard me anyway. She sucked her teeth, jumped up from the couch, and stomped her way into the bedroom where Slim and Stacy were. Stacy's arrival had become so comical that I needed to share, so I got up from the sofa and snuck into my bedroom.

"Hey, Jennifer, wake up," I whispered as I nudged her on the arm.

She turned over and looked at me. "What's wrong?" she asked.

"Shhhh! Don't talk so loud," I told her.

"Why? What's the matter?" she asked, and then she turned her body around to face me.

"You were right," I said.

"About what?"

"Slim doesn't have any plans to bail Sabrina out of jail."

"How do you know that?"

"Because he just brought this new girl in the house and told Tacora she was going to be sharing the room with her."

Jennifer's eyes bulged. "You lying?" she whispered.

"No, I'm not. He got the girl and Tacora in the other room now."

"You fucking kidding me? " Jennifer asked and then chuckled.

"No, I'm not. Go in there and check for yourself," I said. So she got out of bed and walked toward the door. "Don't be so obvious. Act like you're going to the bathroom," I told her.

Jennifer fixed her shirt and shorts and then she opened the door. I followed her and acted like I was heading to the kitchen, just to see the reaction on her face. After she got an eyeful she marched back into the bedroom and I joined her about five seconds later.

"Oh my God! You weren't lying," she whispered as she took a seat on the edge of her bed. "She's cute too."

"Yeah, she is, and Tacora hates her already."

Jennifer chuckled. "Boy, I would have given up my last dime to see her expression when that girl first came in the house."

"Trust me, you would've died from laughter."

"I believe it," she replied, and then she asked, "Did he say what her name was?"

"Yeah, her name is Stacy."

"How old is she?"

"He didn't tell us that. But she's probably around twenty or twenty-one."

"You're probably right, because she looks young."

"I wonder what they're in there talking about now," I said.

"Probably not much of anything. But I betcha Tacora is kicking herself in the ass now."

"Girl, you know she is. You should've been in the living room earlier when Slim first walked into the house with her."

"What happened?"

"Tacora got really bold and asked him who the fuck she was."

"And what did he say?"

"He ignored her at first, but as soon as he showed his new moneymaker where the bathroom was, he ran up on Tacora and damn neared choked the life out of her."

"Oh, so she got the same treatment that I got, huh?"

"You better bet it. And she didn't like it either."

"That's good for the bitch! Now I bet she feels really fucking stupid."

"I'm sure she does, especially now that she knows he isn't springing Sabrina from jail."

"Wow! Unfucking believable!" Jennifer commented, and then we both shook our heads.

We stayed in the room for about another hour and chitchatted. We got quiet a few times when we heard Slim making conversation with Stacy. She giggled the entire time they were talking. I made a bet with Jennifer that Slim was going to fuck her by nightfall. Jennifer's bet was that he was going to get her before nightfall. So we sat back and waited to see who would win the bet. The loser had to spend ten dollars on the drug of the winner's choice.

Nightfall finally seeped through the mini blinds of the living room windows. And since Slim had not yet christened Sabrina's bed with Stacy, I was the winner of the bet. Jennifer assured me that she would happily pay her debt as soon as we got on the block.

"Y'all need to get ready because we gon' be heading over to Goff Street in the next thirty minutes," Slim announced.

"I'm ready now," Tacora replied as she sat on the living room sofa.

"Well, I'm not, so just chill out until I tell you we're leaving," he replied sarcastically.

Jennifer and I were in the bedroom with the bedroom door cracked, so we heard everything.

"She better step back before he fucks around and hurts her really bad," I said.

"I don't think she believes that he'll hurt her," Jennifer said.

"I don't see why not, especially after the way he choked her earlier."

"Well all I'm gonna say is that she's either stupid or she's a glutton for punishment."

"At this point it doesn't matter to me. Because

whatever she gets from him is what she deserves," I said and then I grabbed my purse and headed to the living room.

Jennifer followed me a few minutes later. She had already introduced herself to Stacy earlier, but they hadn't had a chance to really talk. As a matter of fact, Stacy and I had not had a chance to get acquainted either since she had been trying to get her living area situated. Once she had taken care of that, she accompanied us into the living room. The sight of her made Slim smile from ear to ear. He lit up like a fucking Christmas tree. And she had a glow as well. I saw them looking at each other through my peripheral vision. I was sure that Jennifer and Tacora saw the way they were acting too, but no one dared to make mention of it. I had a feeling we wouldn't be able to ignore Stacy for too long, though.

Let the Games Begin

When it was time to head outside Slim made the announcement that he was splitting up me and Jennifer. Then he went into the spiel about why he was doing it. Apparently he wanted someone who had been with him the longest to show Stacy the ropes, and since Jennifer was that person, she was appointed that job. Now I was left with Tacora's silly ass, and I was not at all happy about it. Jennifer looked at me and shook her head to indicate that she was disgusted too. I responded by nodding so she knew I shared her sentiment.

As Slim had planned, we all headed over to the corner of Goff Street and Okeefe. As soon as we arrived at our spot, which was in front of the Huntersville Recreation Center, Slim pointed out where he wanted me and Tacora to stand. He told Jennifer and Stacy he wanted them to stay close to him. Our post was right at the corner where the playground was located. When I saw the playground I couldn't help but think about my baby girl Kimora. I imagined how it would be if I had a chance to see her. I knew I would never bring her out here, but being able to spend time with her was something I wanted more than anything. But since Eric was doing everything within his power to keep her away from me, all I had left was the ability to dream. I just hoped that one day she'd grow up and come look for me. That would make me the happiest mother in the world.

"Get ready! Here comes a car!" Slim yelled, which of course brought me back to reality.

The car approached the side of the street where Jennifer and Stacy were located, so Tacora and I just stood around and waited for our turn. As we waited Tacora sparked up a conversation with me. At first I had no intentions of entertaining her. But she started saying some very interesting shit. And while she was talking, she gawked at Slim the entire time.

"I swear, I hate him," she said. "That punk ass nigga left my best friend in jail so he could go out and find another bitch to take her place."

"Yep, that's what it looks like," I said.

"And look at that bitch! She thinks she's pretty, but she ain't all that to me, especially with that big ass nose she's got."

"Well I think she's pretty," I said in an effort to piss her off. And it worked.

"Please, she ain't pretty nowhere. I look better than her."

"If you say so," I replied as I laughed to myself.

Tacora was being really pathetic. She was all broken up because Slim had used her dumb ass like he'd done to everyone else. She finally saw that he was the dirt bag that everyone had pegged him out to be.

"The first chance I get, I'm leaving," she blurted out.

"You're gonna do what?" I asked her. I knew what she'd said, but I just wanted to hear it again. I had to make sure I'd heard what I believed I'd heard.

"I said I'm leaving," she repeated.

Stunned by her boldness, I looked at her with a newfound respect. I sensed that this young girl wasn't so dumb after all.

"And how do you think you're gonna do that?" I asked her. It was important for me to know what her plans were, because Jennifer and I had been trying to figure out an escape plan of our own. Unfortunately we hadn't been able to devise one. But hopefully Tacora could help us out. I figured she must know something we didn't, and I was ready to hear what she had to say. I stood there and waited for her to divulge her plan.

"I haven't figured it out yet, but it's coming," she assured me, and then she fell silent.

Well that just dashed all my hopes. She had me thinking that I could use her to get away from Slim. But then something inside me ignited the possibility that she could have been lying to me. I mean why would she tell me how she planned to escape Slim? She and I weren't on the best of terms. She knew she was on my shit list. And she knew that I did not care for her, so why would she tell me?

Looking at it from her perspective, she would have been really stupid to do that. I could very easily have dropped the ball and told Slim her intentions. Now that was not something I would do, because that wasn't how I did things, but she wasn't aware of that. So if I were in her shoes, I would be leery too.

After about five minutes of complete silence between Tacora and me, a car pulled up. She insisted that I take the first customer, so I didn't argue with her and accepted the offer. Her generosity took me aback for a minute, but I bounced back quickly.

After I hopped into the car with my customer, I did my regular routine of giving out the prices of my services and waited for him to tell me what he wanted. I knew I was supposed to ask the customer whether he was a police officer, because Slim had drilled it into our heads all last night and the entire walk over here, but I didn't care. I wanted to run into a cop so he could take me away from this mess. And if it meant I had to get a prostitution charge to be free of that maniac, then so be it.

"I think I'd just like to get my dick sucked," my customer said. So I took his money and assumed the position. It took me no time to make him cum. He was definitely what one would call a minute-man. I was in his car and done with serving him in less than seven minutes flat. I was literally fifty dollars richer for doing a seven-minute job. Shit, if I could perform six blow jobs an hour and keep going for eight hours straight, I would make more money than I did as an assistant principal, and I didn't need a fucking six-year degree to do it.

Immediately after I finished my job with my first customer, I used one of the tissues I had stuffed in my purse to wipe my mouth, and then I grabbed the door handle to open the passenger door. The moment I put one foot outside the car, I saw another car pull up behind the car I was in. Tacora didn't hesitate to approach the next customer. By the time I removed myself from the car and closed the door, Tacora had already said a few words and was in the passenger seat ready to handle her business. I stepped away from the curb in order to give them some privacy. The last thing I wanted to do was watch them fuck, so I made sure I backed away enough to give them all the space they needed.

As I waited for another car to pull up, suddenly the car Tacora was in took off at full speed. I couldn't believe my fucking eyes. Slim couldn't believe it either. It definitely caught him off guard, because he had a delayed reaction. He didn't start running behind the car until the car was already halfway down the block. By then it was too late.

I just stood there and watched the whole thing unfold. Slim cursed out the driver of that car like he knew him personally. It was funny seeing him run down behind a car driving at forty miles per hour. When the car drove up to the traffic light, it made a sharp right turn onto Tidewater Drive and kept going. After Slim saw that happen, I guess that was when it registered for Slim that he wouldn't be able to stop the car, and Tacora was gone.

Jennifer rushed across the street to where I was standing. Her mouth was wide open. "Oh my God! What the fuck just happened?" she asked and then burst into laughter.

I was still in shock and didn't know how to answer her question. I stood there and watched Slim as he made his way back down to where we stood.

"I can't believe that bitch had the balls to hop in a car and leave just like that," Jennifer said.

"Me either. I mean she had just told me that she was going to dip on him, but I didn't know she was going to do it so soon."

"Get the fuck out of here! She told you that?" Jennifer whispered.

"Yeah. She and I were just standing here and she told me that she was tired of Slim's shit and that she wasn't taking it no more, especially since he let Sabrina stay in jail."

"Girl, Slim is going to hit the motherfucking ceiling when he finds out this shit!" she said, and then when she noticed how close he was to us, she said, "Oh, shit! Look at his face. He looks mad as hell! And it looks like he's coming over to you, so let me carry my ass back to the other side of the street." And then Jennifer left me standing there alone.

I didn't have the slightest idea what Slim was going to say to me. But I was prepared to listen, because I knew he was very angry. He'd lost two chicks in the last two days. And last week he'd lost another one to murder. I couldn't tell you what was going on in his mind, but I was sure that whatever it was, it wasn't pretty.

As soon as he got within arm's reach of me, he lunged forward and punched the shit out of my face. I never saw that one coming. He didn't give me any warning that he was going to hit me.

"Why the fuck did you let that bitch get away from me like that?" he screamed. Spit flew out of his mouth with every word he uttered.

I hadn't done a thing wrong, yet I was still getting shit on. It wasn't my fault that the bitch ran off. And I made sure I let him know it. "I didn't know she was gonna get in that man's car and get him to pull off," I finally said as I pressed my left hand against the left side of my face.

"I don't give a fuck if you didn't know. When you saw him drive off, you were supposed to stop them." He continued yelling as he got closer to my face. Spit continued to fly out of his mouth with every word.

"Stop them how? You saw how fast that car sped off," I pointed out.

I guess that was the wrong thing to say, because Slim lunged forward and hit me two more times. I saw stars when the first blow hit me. And all I could hear was him telling me that it was my fault and that I wanted her to run off, and that was why I didn't try to stop her. By the time the second blow hit me, the impact of it caught me off guard and I fell to the ground. Before I could gather my thoughts, he started kicking me. I knew all this aggression he was taking out on me wasn't all about Tacora leaving. He had to be mad about Sabrina's departure as well, and he just found an outlet in me on which to exert all of his frustrations.

Thank God a car started rolling our way, because if it hadn't, Slim would still be kicking me while I was down on the ground. As the car drove by, the driver slowed down, I guess to see if I was all right. Slim noticed and demanded that I get up from the ground. While I tried to gain the strength to get back on my feet, something told me to look up, and when I did my heart dropped.

Riding by in a gray Nissan Altima was Denise. She was the driver of this car. I couldn't believe it. She was approximately six to seven feet away from me, and when our eyes connected, she chuckled as if she was laughing at me. I knew it made her feel good to see me down and out like this, especially after I betrayed her by stealing her money. When she turned her head and kept going, my assumptions were confirmed immediately. It was fate that brought her through here at the exact time I needed her.

By the time I picked myself up from the ground and brushed myself off, Denise was long gone. She got her chance to see me reap what I had sown, so I figured she was satisfied.

Easy Come Easy Go

Whoever said that life was what you made it, lied. I knew that I had made a lot of wrong choices in my life, but I had also made some good ones and still came out on the losing end. Standing out here on this corner, making money for a nigga who beat me, cursed me out on a daily basis, and called me a dope fiend ho bag wasn't what I deemed an even trade. I literally sucked dick and allowed men to either fuck me in my pussy or my ass for money that I didn't get to spend. Not only that, I had a fucking dope habit and Slim refused to give me part of the money I made to support my addiction. Was he fucking nuts or what?

Back at the apartment I thought about how Denise had seen me at my worst point. I was relieved that she had not said anything to me, but the fact that she smiled at me spoke volumes. She saw me getting exactly what I deserved, and that was all she needed to see to get justice.

While I lay there in my bed and replayed the

whole scene in my mind, Stacy knocked on my slightly opened bedroom door and asked me if she could come in.

"Yeah, come on," I replied. It totally shocked me that she wanted to come into my bedroom, so I was curious to know what she had on her mind. Jennifer was in the shower at the time, and I heard Slim go outside right before Stacy knocked on my door, so she and I were alone.

"Can I sit down?" she asked.

I was lying on my side in the fetal position, so I slid backward so she could sit on the edge of my bed.

"Thank you," she said, and then she sat down.

"What's up?" I asked.

"I just came in here to see if you were all right," she replied with the sincerest expression she could muster.

"My knees are pretty scraped up, but I'm cool," I assured her. "And thanks for asking."

"Oh, you're welcome." She smiled and I smiled back. "You know what?" she asked. "After I saw Slim hit you all those times, I got really scared. I mean, I didn't think that he was the type of guy who'd hit a woman."

"What made you think that?" I asked.

"When I met him yesterday he was so nice."

"Where did you meet him?"

"He was standing outside talking to two other guys and saw me walking by and stopped me."

"You from Huntersville?"

"No, I'm from Portsmouth. But I got a friend who lives on Bower Street. I was staying there with her and her mama, but her mama got tired of me living there and told her to tell me I had to go. So I packed up my stuff and left."

"Do you have any children?"

"Nope. I don't want any rug rats." She smiled. "Do you?"

"Yes, I have a daughter."

"How old?"

"She just started grade school."

"Oh, wow! That's cool."

Before I could throw another question at her, Jennifer walked into the room wrapped up in a bath towel. I could tell she was shocked to see me talking with Stacy.

"Excuse me," she said, and then she slid by us and stepped into the closet.

"Oh, you're fine," Stacy assured her.

"Oh, yeah, we weren't talking about much," I added.

While in the closet, Jennifer peeped her head around the door and said, "Don't let Slim see y'all talking. You know he's paranoid and will probably think that you're trying to corrupt her."

"She ain't got to worry about it. If it got to that point, I'd straighten it out," Stacy responded.

Jennifer burst into laughter. "Faith, she sounds like she has it all under control, huh?"

I chuckled. "Yeah, she does."

"Can I ask y'all something?" Stacy asked.

"Yeah, go ahead." I encouraged her.

"Why did that other girl get in that man's car and leave?"

Jennifer and I looked at each other to see who

would answer the question. And since Jennifer acted a little hesitant, I asked, "What would you do if you didn't want to stay around any longer?"

"I'd leave," she answered.

"Well there's your answer."

"Well, if she didn't want to be around anymore, then why did Slim beat you up for it?"

Jennifer stood there by the closet, facing Stacy and me, and waited for me to answer. Now I wanted to tell her how much of a women-beating asshole he was, but I couldn't chance her repeating what I said to him. So to play it safe, I was vague with my answer.

"I'm not sure, Stacy," I said. "But when I figure it out, you'll be the first to know."

While we were talking Slim came back to the apartment. I thought he would come in the back to check up on us, but it sounded like he went into the kitchen for something, and then he went right back outside.

Stacy chilled in the room with Jennifer and me for another twenty minutes or so and then she expressed how tired she was and retired to the other room. After she left, Jennifer and I got into our little huddle to express a few things of our own.

"What do you think about her?" Jennifer whispered.

"She seems like she's cool, but I still don't trust her."

"Yeah, me either. There's just something about her that doesn't sit right with me."

"I sensed that too," I agreed.

"Well you know what that means?" Jennifer asked.

"Yep. That means we gotta keep our eyes on her."

Jennifer nodded. We wanted to give Stacy the benefit of the doubt, but we lived with a crazed maniac, so we couldn't take any chances.

A Couple Days Later

Things around the apartment calmed down after Tacora's unexpected departure. Jennifer and I thought that Slim would recruit another young girl to add to his harem, but he hadn't as of yet. Jennifer, Stacy, and I had been getting him his money, so he had no reason to complain about anything. But then I remembered whom I was talking about. Slim was a very miserable guy. His happy episodes were only temporary. We had all learned very quickly how to take the bitter with the sweet, and we also knew that it was smart to always walk on eggshells around him.

Just as I suspected, very little time passed before Slim returned to his psycho ways. One morning, Jennifer and I were awakened to noises from the other bedroom.

What's that sound?" Jennifer asked, her voice still groggy from sleep.

"That's Slim in there banging the hell out of Stacy," I told her.

"Do they have to be so loud?" Jennifer asked, and then she turned over on her stomach and buried her face underneath her pillow.

I didn't respond to her question because I didn't have an answer for her. But she was right. Did they have to be so loud? Well let me correct that, did he have to fuck her on that loud ass squeaking bed? It was obvious that they were on an old mattress. But I was sure that didn't bother him. He was getting what he wanted, so why would there be a need to change anything?

Slim banged Stacy's brains out for at least thirty minutes straight. I had no idea he had that much stamina. When I first came to the apartment, he didn't have any desire to fuck me, so I didn't have the slightest idea about how much of a champion he was in bed. Sabrina and Tacora knew what he was made of, though. And now that I thought about it, I was sure Paris and Jennifer knew as well.

After their little rendezvous, Slim and Stacy went into the bathroom and took a shower together. They acted like they were newlyweds. Stacy giggled like Slim was tickling her the entire time. I wanted to throw up because that bastard always seemed to know how to woo a young girl. I mean I was sure it wasn't hard to pull the wool over the eyes of gullible young girls. But how was it that he was able to keep them underneath his wings so long? I'd only been here for two weeks, and I was ready to go after the first night. I couldn't say how much longer I was going to be in this rat hole, but I knew that if I wasn't walking out of there by the end of this week, the paramedics would be dragging me out in a body bag.

I got up and went into the kitchen to get a bowl of cereal. I needed something in my stomach before I got my early morning fix. While I was minding my business, someone knocked on the front door. Usually no one was allowed to open the front door, but Slim was in the shower with Stacy, probably going for round two, so I didn't want to disturb him. He'd probably bite off my fucking head if I interrupted him while he was trying to bust another nut.

Whoever was knocking on the door had to be one of Slim's lookout buddies, because they were the only ones who ever knocked on the door. I took the liberty to make sure that was who it was by looking through the peephole. When I saw that it was indeed one of his flunkies, I yelled through the door and asked him what he wanted.

"Where's Slim?" he yelled back.

"He's in the shower," I said.

"Tell 'im Big Rob needs to holler at him when he gets out."

"OK," I replied and backed away from the door.

I went back to the kitchen to eat my bowl of cereal. Right around the time I was done, Slim brought his dusty ass out of the bathroom and walked in the kitchen with his fucking boxer shorts on like he was the king around here.

"Was somebody knocking on the front door?" he asked.

I swallowed the cereal I had in my mouth, and

then I said, "Yeah, it was a guy named Big Rob. He told me to tell you to come holler at him."

"Did you open my front door?"

"No, I didn't."

"You better not have," he warned me, and then he walked back into the living room. It didn't take him long to change into a pair of shorts and one of his regular white T-shirts. After he slipped on a pair of sneakers, he left the apartment. If he had not had his house key on him, I would have locked that loser outside. I mean what kind of question was that? He was more concerned about whether I had opened his door than who had come to visit him.

If Slim knew that his fucking time with me was coming to an end, he'd enjoy pimping me while he had me. As soon as I got the prime opportunity, I was dipping on him faster than Tacora had. But I was gonna be smart about it and take some of the money I made out there in those streets with my blood, sweat, and tears.

Before Stacy had a chance to come out of the bedroom, I had already gone back into my room and closed the door. I got in my bed and prayed that she wouldn't want to come in the room to talk, because I wasn't in the mood to chitchat.

I heard her roaming around in the kitchen, so I assumed she was getting herself a bite to eat. I also heard Slim reenter the apartment. His voice was more upbeat than it was before he left. I thought it was because of Stacy's presence, but then I found out it had something to do with him stacking a few more coins.

"We ain't going on the street tonight," I heard him say.

"What's wrong?" Stacy asked.

"Ain't nothing wrong. I just decided to have a strip party here at the house," he told her.

"You want me to dance?"

"Yeah. But cha got to get naked."

"OK," she said as if she had no problem with this arrangement.

I, on the other hand, was furious. I wasn't in the fucking mood to dance my old ass off in front of a room filled with a bunch of niggas. Not to mention I'd never done anything like that before. I did not know the first thing about stripping to a fucking song. That wasn't my forte. And not only that, I figured what man would want to pay to see me strip? I used to look good, but now my body was all bruised up from track marks, so I knew I would be making a spectacle of myself.

"Did Faith go back to her room?" Slim asked Stacy.

"I haven't seen her. She wasn't in here when I came out," she told him.

Hearing my name made me realize that Slim was coming into the room to look for me. I knew it had something to do with that stupid ass strip party, so I braced myself. The moment he entered the room, our eyes connected. He looked at me for a brief second, and then he turned his focus toward Jennifer, who was still asleep. Her back was facing both of us. It didn't matter to him that she was asleep, because he was the man, so whatever he needed to do to make us aware of that fact, he'd do it.

"Jennifer, wake up. I got something to tell y'all," he yelled.

Jennifer turned over in the bed and tried to adjust her eyes so she'd be able to see what was going on. She looked directly at Slim and then she looked at me. But once he started talking, she put her focus right back on him.

"I came in here to let both of y'all know that we ain't working the streets tonight, because we gon' have a strip party for a couple niggas I know," he said.

"We having it here?" Jennifer asked.

"Yeah. And it's gon' start about nine o'clock, so find something sexy to wear, 'cause you gon' be dancing with Stacy."

"I ain't no stripper," Jennifer said, trying to protest. But Slim made her turn down her volume.

"Look, I don't give a fuck if you're a stripper or not. You gon' get your ass in that living room and you gon' take off your motherfucking clothes. So please don't give me no more lip about this, because it's gon' really make me angry."

Jennifer sucked her teeth and threw her blanket back over her face. I thought she was going to give him more drama about the decision he made, but she didn't open her mouth. When he was done talking to her, he looked directly at me and said, "I ain't gon' have you dancing because your body don't look all that hot. You got too many of them nasty ass track marks and shit, so I'ma have you back here doing jobs if one of them niggas wanna fuck or get their dick sucked."

"OK. I'm fine with that," I told him.

As soon as I responded to him, he walked out of the room. He must've thought I was going to be offended by his comments. I didn't care how he looked at me. Yes, I had track marks all over my body! So what! My track marks represented what I was about. And if that meant that he didn't want me to shake my ass in front of his loser ass friends, then I was happy. He just didn't know that he'd made my fucking day.

Now as far as Jennifer was concerned, that was a whole different story. She was livid that she had to prance around these idiots for a few dollars. But she didn't make that known until after she heard Slim exit the apartment.

"Girl, you know I really wanted to say something slick out of my mouth," she whispered after she removed the blanket from her face.

"I know. I saw your facial expression," I told her.

"What made him wanna have a fucking strip party in the first place? We ain't strippers!" she snapped, but kept her voice down so Stacy wouldn't hear her.

"Well, you may not be one, but when I heard him tell Stacy about it, she acted like she was all excited and shit!"

"That's because she's stupid!"

I chuckled. "So what are you going to put on?" I asked.

"Nothing sexy!" She gritted her teeth. "I mean who the fuck he thinks he is inviting some local ass niggas over here so we can take off our clothes and dance around them? I ain't into that type of shit. It's bad enough I gotta fuck them niggas on the streets and then give all my money away."

"Don't worry about it! It could be worse."

"I know, Faith. But I'm just tired of all this shit that goes on around here. I'm tired of fucking for these pennies and getting treated like shit in the process. And not only that, I miss Paris so much. At least when she was here, me and her made the best of this fucked up situation."

"Yes, I've got to admit that she was definitely cool."

"You damn right. That chick always had my back. And you know what, it bothers me that Slim didn't give a fuck about her and just left her lying dead on them streets," Jennifer said as her eyes filled with tears.

"Don't get yourself all worked up. Something is going to happen for us and we're gonna be all right," I tried to assure her, but in all honesty, I didn't believe what I was saying myself. I knew she was still hurting behind what had happened to Paris. And I also knew that she wanted the guy who shot Paris to pay for what he did, but our hands were tied, and there was nothing that we could do about it at this point. We just had to bite our tongues and deal with whatever Slim threw our way.

Jennifer lay there in her bed as if she was in deep thought. She was silent for at least five minutes as she looked up at the ceiling. I grew concerned and had to say something.

"You all right?" I asked.

"I gotta get out of here before I kill him," she said, and when she said it, I could see the chilling look in her eyes. Looking into her eyes made the hair on my arms stand up. I knew she wasn't just talking. She was deadly serious.

"Look, Jennifer, you ain't even gonna have to put your hands on him. He ain't even worth going to jail behind. Trust me, God is going to look out for both of us. He is going to make a way for us to get out of here. We just got to believe it."

"No disrespect, but I ain't gonna be able to wait on God. I'm gonna have to do this myself," she said, and then she got out of bed.

She scared me when she hopped out of bed. I had no idea what she was about to do. I got out of my bed and followed her to the bedroom door until I saw her go into the bathroom. I honestly thought she was going to pick up something and try to attack Slim. But after I witnessed her close the bathroom door, I calmed my nervousness and got back into the bed. I left the bedroom door open to see straight down the hallway. As a matter of fact, I could see the front door from my bed, so I was in a good position to stop Jennifer from doing anything that she and I would both regret.

Dropping It Like It's Hot

The strip party was about to start and Slim had the men lining up to come inside the apartment. He was charging twenty dollars at the door, plus he was charging for drinks. He had this whole thing figured out. Jennifer and I were in our bedroom when Stacy joined us. She was dressed and ready to flaunt her stuff. I looked at her see-through black lace top and hot pink booty shorts with her ass cheeks bursting out underneath. It looked disgusting to me, but I knew the men would love it.

"Jennifer, you ready?" Stacy asked. "Because I was thinking about a dance move me and you could do together while we're stripping." She smiled as if she was excited.

Jennifer gave Stacy a nonchalant look and asked, "Do I look ready? And, anyway, what made you think I would do a stupid ass dance move?"

"Jennifer, what's wrong?" Stacy asked.

Jennifer ignored her and continued to buckle

her stilettos. I knew she didn't want to talk about anything dealing with Slim for fear that Stacy would go back and tell him, so I jumped in for Jennifer and answered Stacy's question.

"She's not feeling that dancing stuff," I said.

"Why? It's gonna be fun!" Stacy insisted. But Jennifer wasn't trying to hear her.

"Look, Stacy, don't come in here with all that giddy shit, because I am not in the mood!" Jennifer snapped.

Stacy was shocked at Jennifer's outburst. I could tell that she did not know how to respond, because she just stood there with an odd expression on her face. Again I had to step in and save the day. I stood and embraced Stacy. She was stiff as a board, so I tried to warm her up a bit.

"Look, Stacy, don't mind Jennifer right now," I said. "She's just not feeling this strip party stuff, so she's upset with the world. Don't take what she said personally."

"OK. That's cool," she replied, and then she stepped away from me and headed toward the door.

"Why you leaving?" I asked. "You don't have to go back out there with all the guys."

"I'm a'ight. I'm gonna go into my room until Slim tells me he's ready," Stacy said.

"OK. Suit yourself."

Stacy backed out of the room and closed the door behind her. When I heard her step away from the door, I turned to Jennifer and asked, "Why you had to bite off her head?"

"Fuck her! I don't care about her feelings. She's

his little flunky, so let her carry her dumb ass right back in there with him."

I chuckled at Jennifer because I understood her frustration. She was tired of walking on eggshells around here, and so was I. But until we were out of this apartment and out of Slim's life for good, then we had to tolerate all this bullshit.

Jennifer and I weren't able to dwell on the Stacy situation, because five minutes after she left the room, Slim came in.

"Jennifer, you ready?" he asked her.

Jennifer looked up at him with the most disgusted expression she could muster and replied by asking, "Do I have a choice?"

Slim laughed. "Bitch, getcha ass up and be out there in that living room in the next two minutes or suffer the consequences!" he threatened, and then he stepped out of the room and slammed the door.

"Come on now, Jennifer, let's be on our best behavior," I said. "Let's not give that monster any reason to put his hands on us tonight."

"Fuck him!" she whispered bitterly. "I wanna see if he'll put his hands on me in front of all them niggas in there."

"Jennifer, don't test him. You know he's not dealing with a full deck of cards. Let's just let it go and move on." Not only was I tired of seeing Slim beating on me, I was tired of him beating Jennifer. And at the rate she was going, I figured it wouldn't be long before she unleashed all of the anger she had built up over the time she'd been in the company of Slim. I could tell that she was preparing herself to go to battle with him, so I knew I had to be on guard at all times.

Finally Jennifer left the room and joined the men in the living room. They cheered on her and Stacy as they entered the room. I stood behind the wall of the entryway to the living room and watched the expressions on all the men's faces. They looked like pussy hungry derelicts with their tongues hanging out of their mouths. Slim stood in the kitchen so he could monitor everything. He also controlled the music.

Right after he put on the first song, the men started getting amped up. Stacy shook her ass and bent over to make her booty clap. I saw Jennifer being very cold and evasive while she was on the floor. Her facial expression was also cold. She refused to crack a smile at anyone. A couple of the guys asked her to smile, but she frowned at them instead, so they took their attention off of her and started rooting for Stacy. And Stacy was eating it up for what it was worth. I also noticed a few of the men whispering to Slim and then looking in my direction.

While all the entertaining was going on, Slim left his post by the CD player and walked in my direction. When he approached me he said, "That big nigga over there with the dreads wanted you to get butt naked, but I told him I wasn't gon' waste his time because you weren't young and fresh like them. But I did tell 'im you'd suck his dick for fifty dollars, so go in the room and get ready, 'cause he gon' come in there in a few minutes."

I was appalled at the way Slim talked to me. He

basically handled me like I was a fucking dirt bag bitch. How dare that bastard tell that guy that I wasn't young and fresh? Shit! I wasn't that much older than those girls, so what the fuck was his problem? But instead of expressing how I felt about what he'd said, I kept my mouth closed. Why should I set myself up to be cursed out? Slim was an immature little boy with dreams of becoming someone he would never be, and I was his means of getting there.

Shortly after I walked away from the party and headed into the bedroom, I was joined by the big guy who wanted to get his dick sucked. He was too big to sit on the edge of my twin-sized bed, so I sat on the bed and convinced him to stand in front of me. Immediately he unzipped his pants and pulled out his shriveled up dick through the opening of his zipper. I looked at that itty-bitty thing and almost laughed. I could not believe how small his penis was. He had to be over three hundred pounds, so to be that big and only have a dick that was the size of a five-year-old's had to be humiliating.

I stared at it and wondered how I would hold it in my hand and suck it at the same time. It looked impossible. While I contemplated another way to do it, he became frustrated.

"Why the fuck you staring at my dick?" he yelled. "Just put it in your motherfucking mouth and suck it, bitch!"

It took everything within me not to curse out this fat motherfucker. I mean, who the fuck did he think he was talking to like that? I was the chick whose mouth he wanted to slide his dick in. So I wasn't his bitch for real, and I wanted to express that to him. But I figured if I gave him a hard time, he'd run in the other room and tell Slim, so I kept my mouth closed and worked with what I had. Dreading servicing this disrespectful ass nigga, I grabbed the tip of his penis with my thumb and my pointer finger and began to lick the head.

I tried to block out the musty smell that was coming from his ball sack, but it was becoming unbearable, causing me to gag a couple of times. He looked down at me twice and asked me what the fuck was wrong. The second time he asked me, I had to be honest with him and tell him his mess stunk. He was utterly offended by my comment.

"Bitch, did you just say my ball sack stinks?" he snapped.

"Look, I don't know what it is, but whatever it is, it's sweaty," I replied.

"Well deal with it, 'cause I done already gave that nigga Slim my dough. So shut up and make my dick cum before I make that nigga come in here and straighten out your ass!" he barked, and then he shoved his penis right back into my mouth. He grabbed the back of my head and forced my head back and forth. He was literally forcing his dick in and out of my mouth.

I gagged at least five more times, but he ignored me and continued to gyrate against my face. I held my breath to eliminate the smell and went with the motion until he ejaculated into my mouth. The moment he pulled his nasty ass dick out of my mouth was the moment I spit all of his semen onto the floor. He picked up a shirt from Jennifer's bed and wiped off his dick with it, and then he threw the shirt in my face. "Thanks for nothing, bitch!" he said, and then he waddled his fat ass out of the room.

Feelings of humiliation grew inside me rapidly and I wondered how much longer I would be able to take this treatment. I wasn't a bad person. And even though I'd done some fucked up things, I'd never treated a human being the way I'd been treated. I was at my wits' end.

After fat boy walked his ass out of the room, Slim escorted another guy in. This time I had to let this one fuck me in my ass. So I assumed the position and let him go for what he knew. And for the first time since I'd been on the streets, I wanted to put a gun up to my head and pull the trigger. I simply wanted to end my life. I was nothing but a dope fiend. No one respected me. Not even my own ex-husband respected me. He threw my ass away and re-married the next best thing that came along. So why continue to live?

As I wallowed in my grief, I heard a loud scream from Jennifer followed by a thud. My first intention was to break free of this moron who was banging the hell out of my rear end, but I knew he wouldn't let me go, so I stayed where I was and wondered what had happened. After several minutes of continuous pounding, the guy ejaculated on the back of my ass and then left the room.

After I wiped off the back of my ass, I quickly pulled up my panties and rushed to the door to see what had happened. I heard the music still playing, so I figured everything was all right, but when I opened the door, my eyes told me a different story. Slim was holding Jennifer off the floor with his arm around her neck. He had her in a fucking chokehold and her face had turned at least three different shades of red while I was looking at them. I couldn't believe how all the men were just standing around watching. She was naked, so I assumed that she had undressed herself completely to dance, but clearly something else happened in the process.

I rushed down the hallway toward them and yelled for one of the guys to help her. "Can y'all please help her before he kills her?" I begged. But every last one of those men in there kept their distance and either threw their hands in the air or left the apartment altogether.

Before long the apartment became empty, and the only person left standing there with me was Stacy. Her eyes were glassy and she looked scared as she stood there butt naked. By this time Slim had dragged Jennifer into the kitchen and he was trying to choke her until she had no breath left in her body. I couldn't stand there and watch this go on any longer, so I jumped in to save her.

"Get off her!" I screamed and locked my arm around Slim's neck. I immediately applied enough pressure around his neck, hoping he would realize that he had to let her go so he could save himself. When he let her go, I knew he was going to focus his anger on me. Slim was a much bigger man than I was able to handle, so I knew it would only be a short matter of time before he was able to maneuver out of the hold I had around his neck. I heard Stacy in the background crying, asking me to stop, but I tuned her out. My life was at stake, and I didn't care about that bitch.

Finally Slim released Jennifer, but I maintained my hold on his neck. I hadn't noticed at first, but Jennifer had gotten off the floor. Once she had gained enough strength to help herself, she came to my defense to keep Slim down on his knees. It was an uphill battle, but we were gaining some leeway.

While we kept Slim pinned to the floor, Jennifer and I tried to figure out a way to knock him out so we could escape. But as soon as Stacy saw Jennifer reach for the pot on the stove, she ran over and snatched it from her. The next thing we knew, Stacy had jumped on Jennifer's back.

I couldn't help but wonder why all these stupid ass bitches kept coming to this guy's rescue? Did they not see that he was dangerous and that he would kill us if he had to? For the life of me I couldn't figure out why Stacy prevented me and Jennifer from knocking out Slim. All we wanted to do was knock him out long enough to get away. But it looked like that wasn't going to happen tonight.

Once Stacy intercepted our plan, Slim was able to regain his control of me. As soon as he removed my arm from around his neck, he turned to face me and I saw nothing but rage in his eyes. Before I could blink, he hit me so hard on my head that he knocked me unconscious.

Rat Poisoning

When I regained consciousness, my head hurt like crazy. The lights from the kitchen and the living room blinded me the moment I opened my eyes. I tried to block out the light with my hand, but it didn't work, so I dealt with it and looked around the room. I saw Jennifer lying beside me on the floor, but she wasn't moving. Fear crept into my heart. She looked like she was dead as she lay there naked, but I had to check to make sure.

I reached over to check her pulse and realized that she was indeed breathing, so that relieved my heart. And all I could do was lay my head against her arm because I felt her pain.

"Y'all thought y'all could take me down, huh?" I heard Slim ask, startling me. I couldn't see him, although I now knew he was in the room with us.

He spoke again, so I was able to follow his voice. And when I looked around the entire room, I noticed he was sitting on the living room couch with his gun in his right hand. I also saw Stacy sitting next to him fully dressed. There was no doubt in my mind that he was going to pull the trigger and kill both me and Jennifer.

"Getcha ass up!" he roared as he pointed the gun directly at me. I turned over on my stomach and pushed all the weight of my body onto my hands and feet to lift myself from the floor. After I stood, Slim instructed me to pull up Jennifer as well. I turned toward Jennifer, got down in a squat, and grabbed both of her arms. When I tried to lift her, it seemed impossible. Jennifer's body was too heavy for me to lift, so I did the next best thing, and that was to wake her.

At first trying to get her to regain consciousness was also impossible, so I dragged her across the kitchen floor and onto the living room rug. Halfway across the rug she began to wake up. She broke away from my grasp and became a little hostile. She started kicking and swinging her arms. I looked at her until I noticed that her eyes were fully focused.

"Jennifer, stop, it's me," I told her. Once she realized that I was the one who had her arms, she calmed down.

Sitting on the sideline looking at us, Slim burst into laughter. I guessed Jennifer and I looked somewhat comical to him. I stood over Jennifer and assisted her off the floor. After I helped her stand to her feet, Slim made yet another one of his announcements as he waved his gun around at us. Jennifer was still somewhat dazed, but she caught the gist of his statement.

"Both of y'all bitches made me lose a lot of money tonight. And then on top of that, y'all hoes tried to hurt me. Now I oughta kill you standing right there. But since I'm a good nigga at heart, I'ma give y'all a chance to make it up to me by taking you back to the corner so you can get the money you owe me. But I'm warning you this time that if y'all ever try to jump on me again, I'm gon' blow your motherfucking brains out! Now get out my face and go get dressed. We leaving in ten minutes."

After Slim dismissed us, I grabbed Jennifer by her arm and helped her walk back into the bedroom. I was appalled that he wanted us to go out on the corner, especially after all the dick I'd sucked tonight. Jennifer was the one who'd prevented him from making money, so why make me pay for something she did? I knew I wasn't in a position to protest considering that she and I were both on his shit list, so I did what I was told, and got ready to head back to the corner to turn more tricks.

While Jennifer and I were in the bedroom, I helped her get dressed. She was slowly coming around. She and I didn't say much to each other because we feared that either Stacy or Slim would be standing outside the door eavesdropping. But when we got outside, Jennifer definitely had a few choice words. She kept her voice down to a minimum during the walk to the corner.

"You know we almost had him, right?" she whispered as we walked ahead of Slim and Stacy.

"Yeah, I know. And we would've had him if that bitch wouldn't have jumped in it."

"I know. But I'm not giving up. I'm gonna get away from him the next time around, even if it's meant for me to die while I'm doing it."

I couldn't comment after Jennifer made that statement. When I looked in her eyes, I knew that she meant what she said, so I knew there was no need for me to try to sway her thinking. I just looked straight ahead and decided to go with the flow.

While we were on the corner, I noticed how Jennifer wasn't her usual self. Normally she'd leave all the bullshit we went through back at the apartment and turn over a new leaf while we were out here. But tonight she was just dragging herself from one car to the next. Slim had to talk to her a few times, but whatever he said went right over her head. She was really testing him to see how far she could go. I was beginning to get scared for her. As soon as she finished with her next customer, I rushed over to her and grabbed her to the side. Slim stood a couple feet away and watched us, so I knew I had to be fast.

"I don't know what you're trying to do, but you need to chill," I said.

"Whatcha talking about?" she asked, giving me a funny look.

"Look, Jen, all I'm saying is for you to chill out for me, please. I saw Slim pull you to the side a couple times to talk to you. And you know he's kind of fed up with us right now, so please, let's behave. Can you do it for me?" I begged.

"I'm cool. We gon' be a'ight!" she said, and then she walked over to the curb. Two cars pulled up. Stacy took the first one and Jennifer hopped in the second car. I waited patiently for the next car, and finally one pulled up and I got inside. Slim instructed him to turn off his car. He wasn't allowing that drive-off stunt to happen to him again. He had become quite hip to our games.

After I sat down on the passenger seat, I did my routine spiel about what kind of services I performed and how much they had to pay. I never bothered to ask my customers if they were the police, because I always hoped they were. Unfortunately this one wasn't. I was disappointed to say the least. After he gave me his money for a standard blowjob, I instructed him to pull out his dick and then I went to work.

"I wanna see if you can deep throat my dick," he said.

I looked up at him, and then I looked back down at his penis. Now I had to admit that he was working with a monster. His dick had to be at least nine inches and it wasn't fully erect. And the head of it was huge. I couldn't see how I could push the entire thing in my mouth if I wanted to. So I continued to do what I knew how to do and occasionally I pressed my luck by pushing a third of it to the back of my throat.

Suddenly while I was servicing my customer I heard Stacy scream. "Oh, shit!" she yelled. "I think she's having a seizure or something!"

I immediately stopped what I was doing. The guy whose dick I had in my mouth was not pleased with me at all. He was already erect and was at the peak of ejaculating, but I stopped stimulating him without any warning.

"What the fuck you doing?" he snapped.

"Shhh!" I hushed him.

"Shhh, my ass! Bitch, you better keep sucking my dick or give back my money," he told me.

"Slim, what are we going to do?" I heard Stacy ask. "What's happening to her?"

She sounded distressed. I sat up in my seat and looked out of the passenger window of the car. From where I was sitting, I really couldn't see what was happening, but I did see Stacy and Slim hovering over Jennifer. And then I saw her feet kicking, and my mouth dropped open.

"What the fuck!" I said as my heart dropped. And without saying another word, I jumped out of the guy's car. He grabbed my arm before I could close the door.

"Where the fuck you think you going?" he yelled. "Bitch, you better give back my motherfucking money before I kick your ass out here."

Without even thinking about it, I reached down in my bra, grabbed the fifty dollars he'd already given me, and flung it back at him. After I slammed his car door, he sped off down the street and I ran over to see why Jennifer was lying on the ground kicking.

As soon as I got within two feet of her, Slim grabbed me by the arm and demanded that we leave. "Let's go! We gotta get out of here," he yelled.

By this time Stacy was screaming hysterically, so

I looked over her shoulder and saw Jennifer lying on her back kicking frantically. Her eyes were in the back of her head, and she was foaming at the mouth. My heart was already in the pit of my stomach, but it felt even worse now.

"She's ODing!" I screamed, and pushed Stacy to the side. But before I could get by her, Slim grabbed me with his other hand and locked me into a bear hug. I started kicking and screaming uncontrollably. "Let me go, Slim. I gotta stop her from dying!" I sobbed.

Slim ignored my cries and threw me over his shoulder, but he couldn't manage my weight, so he dropped me to the ground. And as soon as I hit the concrete, I felt a massive pain shoot through my knee. I screamed at the top of my voice. Instead of picking me back up from the ground, Slim pulled out his pistol and pressed it against my head.

"Bitch, shut up right now!" he roared and pressed the gun against my temple as hard as he could. I closed my mouth immediately. Tears were still falling from my eyes, but I wouldn't utter a sound. When he figured that he'd calmed me down, he helped me back up to my feet and instructed me to leave with him immediately. I had no other choice in the matter, so I allowed him to escort me back to the apartment without any protests.

The walk back to the apartment seemed very long. I cried the entire time. Stacy was a complete wreck herself. Slim had to tell her over a dozen times to walk faster. But when we finally got back to the apartment building, he didn't have to open his mouth again, because she ran straight for the front door and didn't look back.

Two of his outside watchmen walked up to him with expressions of concern. They saw how upset Stacy was, so they wanted to know what had happened. Slim told them to help him carry me upstairs and he'd tell them what happened on the way. By the time we all made it to the second floor, Slim had given them the 411. After they got the gist of everything, they acted like they didn't want to be around. But before they bailed on Slim, they wanted to know if he was going to leave Jennifer's body out there.

"You damn right I'm gon' leave that shit out there! What the fuck you think I'm stupid enough to bring her dead ass back here? Hell, I told her about snorting that shit while she was out there on the block anyway. But she didn't want to listen. So I ain't taking the blame for that shit! Hell nah!" he replied, and then he unlocked the front door so Stacy and I could get into the apartment.

After Slim watched me and Stacy go inside, he pulled the door closed, leaving him outside to chat with his two friends. I never knew what their names were, but I knew they worked for Slim by making sure we couldn't leave without Slim knowing.

While Slim stayed outside, Stacy retired to her room and closed the door, so I found myself standing alone in the living room. I sat down on the sofa and reflected on Jennifer's death. The thought of it ate me alive on the inside. And to know that she'd died the exact same way my old friend Teresa died made me feel even worse.

I remembered Teresa's death like it was just yesterday when I walked into that shooting gallery and saw her lying dead against the wall. Her body grew colder with each passing minute. I had shown up two minutes too late to save her, and now here I was again coming two minutes too late. It seemed that everyone around me kept dying. First it was Teresa, then Jennifer, and even though we weren't friends very long, I couldn't forget about Paris. All those women meant something to me one way or another, and now they were gone. I hoped I wasn't going to be next.

Stacy's cries from the bedroom became louder and louder. The fact that she was crying made me sick to my stomach. I mean how in the hell could she shed a fucking tear when she helped Slim knock out Jennifer not even two hours ago? What the fuck was her problem? To me it was just a classic way to get some attention from Slim. She just wanted to show that asshole that she had a heart. But I couldn't stand it anymore.

I knew I couldn't be here another night with these two sickos. Paris was dead. Jennifer was dead. Sabrina was in jail, and Tacora bailed out on us. I refused to be the last one to stick around so he could torture, use, and abuse me. I felt just like Jennifer did. She wanted to die if that meant it was the only way she'd be able to get out of here, and now I was willing to do the same. I had no reason to live anymore. I'd done everything underneath the sun. I'd lost my family, my car, and my career, I couldn't complete a twelve-step substance abuse program, I stole money, I stole drugs, I had sex with a woman, and I'd fucked over two hundred different men, so what else could I possibly do? Absolutely nothing.

I got up from the sofa and raced to the back where the bedrooms were located. My intention was to lock Stacy inside her room, but first I wanted to ask her if she heard Jennifer say anything before she died. I knocked on her door softly.

"Come in," she said.

When I opened the door, she was lying on her stomach with her face buried in the pillow. She turned over after I entered the room. I stood by the door because what I had to ask her wasn't going to take very long.

"I just wanted to know if Jennifer said anything to you before she overdosed?" I asked.

Stacy wiped the tears from her puffy eyes and said, "No, she didn't say anything. One minute she had her back turned to me and Slim, and then the next minute she was wiping her nose with the back of her hands. Slim must've known she was getting high because she started acting strange, and he fussed at her and told her to put that shit away. And then a couple minutes later she started trembling and collapsed on the ground. I didn't know what was happening to her at first. Slim was the one who told me she was ODing."

"All right," I said to her, and then I backed out

of the room to leave. While I was leaving she turned to lie back on her stomach.

I closed the door very softly and locked it at the same time. Slim had the bedroom doors fixed so we couldn't lock them from the inside. It was for his benefit only to be able to lock them from the outside. But today I was going to put that shoe on my foot and benefit from his psycho ways.

After I locked the door I eased away and raced toward the kitchen. With Stacy out of the way, I had a better chance to escape. Tonight I wasn't going to have any interruptions when Slim got back to this apartment. I was going to fight my way out of here even if it killed me.

The Last Straw

I was very nervous. I didn't have the slightest idea of how I was going to get out of this apartment, but I knew that whatever I decided to do, it better be a very clever idea. When I reached the kitchen, I looked through all the drawers and cabinets, trying to find something sharp. Slim kept the sharp knives hidden so we wouldn't use them to stab him in his sleep. I needed to find something that would invoke the same pain as a knife. I searched everywhere, but I couldn't find one sharp object. But then a light went off in my head when I saw a corkscrew on the countertop. Slim had brought it in the apartment earlier tonight for the liquor he served at the strip party. It would be my best choice for a weapon, so I grabbed it and stuffed it in my pocket.

As soon as I placed the corkscrew in my pocket, I started shaking really badly. I guessed it was the mere fact that I was about to put my life on the line, and in the process take away someone else's life. I figured all I had to do was get him when he wasn't looking and stab him in his neck. I knew I only had one chance to make it count. If I screwed it up, I knew my ass would be blown to smithereens.

I paced the kitchen floor. My nerves were completely haywire, and my armpits started perspiring like crazy, all because I knew I was about to tread on some very dangerous waters. As I was deep in thought about a plan to take out Slim, I heard Slim grab the doorknob and turn it. Immediately my heart rate took off at the speed of lightning. Something on the inside of me told me to back out of my plans to escape, but then the courageous side of me told me to go for what I knew. I didn't have a thing left to lose. I took a deep breath and waited for my opportunity to strike.

When Slim saw me standing in the kitchen, he looked at me strangely and asked what I was doing. I played it off and acted like I was deep in thought about what had just happened to Jennifer. I guessed I must've said the wrong thing, because he blew up. He walked away from the front door without locking it and headed straight toward me. I didn't know where his gun was because I couldn't see it from where I was standing, so I braced myself.

"Why the fuck are you bringing up her name in my house?" he roared. "Don't ever let me hear you talk about that fucking junkie again. Do you hear me?" he asked as he buried his mouth in my ear. His words echoed in my eardrums.

I reached inside my pocket and grabbed the corkscrew. I wanted to bring it out at just the right time. I knew I couldn't be one second off from sticking him in the right spot. I had to paralyze him long enough to get his gun away from him and perhaps take away his cell phone so I could use it to call the cops. Unfortunately something unexpected happened just as I was ready to strike. Stacy started banging on the bedroom door.

"Who looked the door?" she yelled. "Somebody let me out."

My heart stopped beating and then it sunk deep into the pit of my stomach. Shocked by Stacy's sudden outburst, Slim looked away from me. It seemed like his head turned in show motion. In the next few seconds I knew he would realize that what Stacy was yelling was entirely true, so I needed to act quickly. The entire left side of his neck was exposed for me to plunge the sharp end of the corkscrew deep inside the veins he had popping through his skin. I pulled the corkscrew from my pocket, closed my eyes, raised my weapon as high as I could, and plunged it directly at Slim's neck, hoping it landed in the right spot. I needed it to land in a vital place to cripple him long enough for me to grab his gun and his cell phone, and then make my escape.

"Owwwwwwwww!" Slim screamed in agony.

When I heard Slim cry out, I opened my eyes and noticed that I'd definitely stuck him, but I didn't punctured his neck at all. The corkscrew was sticking straight out of his shoulder blade. He must've moved when I closed my eyes.

Angry by what I had just done, Slim's eyes became bloodshot. I knew that whatever he was about to do to me, it would end my life. I had nothing else in my grasp to defend myself with, so I pushed him out of my way and tried to make a run for the door. But before I got the opportunity to make it out of the kitchen, he pulled the corkscrew out of his shoulder and grabbed me by the back of my shirt.

"Come here, you bitch!" he roared and yanked me back in his direction.

I lost my balance and fell backward onto the floor. Meanwhile Stacy was still banging on the bedroom door yelling for someone to let her out of the room. But she was the least of our concerns. My focus was on getting away from Slim, and his focus was to prevent that from happening.

Right after I hit the floor, Slim reached behind him and grabbed his gun out of his waistband. When I saw that semi-automatic weapon flash before me, I nearly had a heart attack. As I closed my eyes, believing I was about to take my last breath, I heard him pull back on the chamber, and then the gun went off. *CLICK.*

By some miracle, I was still alive. I opened my eyes and realized that his gun had jammed.

"What the fuck!" he yelled. Frustration covered his face. In that moment I knew without a doubt that this guy was trying to kill me, so I kicked his dick, and luckily my kick was dead on target. Caught off guard, he dropped his pistol to grab his genitals. When the gun hit the floor, it fired a shot. *BOOM!*

I screamed because the shit sounded like a fucking cannon was being fired. I got up from the floor and tried to make it to the door, but when I got there I saw Slim from the corner of my eye going for the gun. I quickly turned the doorknob and snatched open the door. What I saw outside made my heart drop to the pit of my stomach.

"He's trying to kill me!" I screamed. And at that moment one of the three police officers standing outside grabbed me and snatched me away from the apartment. Slim had no idea the police had grabbed me, so he came out behind me with his pistol in hand, ready to fire.

Unfortunately for Slim, all three police officers stood in the doorway and let off every round their magazines had. I watched as Slim's body took one bullet after another. His body jumped after every single piece of lead entered it. The officers didn't stop shooting until his body finally fell to the ground.

Once the smoke cleared from all the ammo being fired, the officers rushed inside the apartment. I was escorted downstairs to a nearby paramedic so they could nurse my battle wounds. While I watched them treat my wounds, a black female police officer walked up to the back of the ambulance and said, "I was told that you had some information that could help apprehend the suspect who murdered a woman by the name of Paris Dozier."

I looked at her like she was crazy. How would she know I had information about Paris's murder? But before I could ask her that question, Jennifer stepped around the door of the ambulance. My heart was overjoyed when I saw her face. I was on the verge of tears and I couldn't hold my composure. I literally jumped off the chair where I was being examined.

"Oh my God! Jen, you're alive!" I screamed.

Tears fell from her eyes as she embraced me. "I had to fake my death, or we wouldn't have gotten out of there."

"But how did you do it?" I asked as tears started falling from my eyes.

"Right before I got out of my last customer's car, I found a pack of Alka-Seltzer on the floor and picked it up. I quickly realized that this was the perfect opportunity to escape. Slim already thought that I was out there getting high, so what better way to escape than by faking an overdose by foaming off at the mouth, making my eyes go to the back of my head, and causing my body to tremble?"

"Well why couldn't you tell me that was what you were going to do?" I asked.

"Because I didn't have time," Jennifer said, and then she hugged me again.

It felt good to know that she was alive after all this time. I wasn't where I wanted to be, but I knew that I'd get there one day.

A Sucker 4 Candy

Amaleka McCall

Prologue

Brooklyn, New York
June 2010

"Nigga, you are a broke muthafucka and you ain't got shit to offer nobody!" Celeste Early screamed at the top of her voice. "I'm 'round here struggling to feed my kids and all you wanna do is come up in here and lay up!" she continued as she went toe to toe with her baby daddy.

"Shut the fuck up!" Drake screamed back at her. "Why don't you get your lazy ass up off the system and stop waiting for a man to give you money and get a job, bitch!"

"If you got a fucking job like any responsible man would do and bring some money in this house, instead of hanging out and chasing every piece of ass you see running around town, then I wouldn't have to be on the system!"

This was their normal routine whenever Drake decided to show up at Celeste's house. Ben sat at the edge of his bed listening to yet another argument between his mother and her no good baby father. He rolled his eyes. "Fucking losers, both of them. They both need to get a job," Ben said to himself. He often spoke to himself. "Ain't neither one of 'em got no money. That's why my ass hustling now. Fuck 'em. I'ma keep money in my pocket."

Ben pulled out a wad of cash and flipped through the bills. He sniffed the money and then exhaled. He smiled. He was making paper hand over fist now. He had moved up. "Fuck delivering newspapers," Ben said with the smile still on his face.

Just sixteen, Benjamin "Ben" Early had been hustling since he was thirteen. He knew his mother would probably flip if she knew, but in his household it was survival of the fittest. His mother was broke as shit and that was the bottom line. Celeste had him when she was young and she wasn't much for working. Everything Ben got, he got on his own. He realized his mother couldn't possibly miss that he had new clothes, sneakers, fitted hats and always had money in his pocket. Since she didn't say anything, Ben didn't say anything either, primarily because he always bought his baby brother a new pair of kicks when he got himself some. Both Ben and the baby stayed in the latest Jordans and LeBron James sneakers.

Ben was the de facto man of the house. He bought groceries for the house when his mother had prematurely used up all of the food stamp credits on her EBT card. Celeste was horrible about that. She would sell half her food stamps, which meant she only could afford to buy half the amount of food it took to feed a growing boy like Ben and his baby brother.

Ben had found his own way to get food. He learned to make his own paper and buy his own food at an early age.

"Two stacks!" Ben whispered excitedly as he put the rubber band back around the wad of money he had pulled out. Excited about counting his money, he had filtered out the noise coming from his mother's bedroom for a while. "Gotta get this dope bagged up and hit the block," Ben said to himself. He wasn't trying to stay in the house much longer.

"Stupid bitch!" Ben heard Drake yell, once again interrupting his thoughts.

Ben shook his head, trying to ignore Celeste and Drake as long as he could. He wondered whatever attracted them to each other. He pulled out a medium sized Baggie of dope. Ben had just picked up the bag from Deezo, the dude he sold for and who had told him to go home and bag it up. Deezo had told him to make nicks and dime size bags out of the package.

Ben was excited. He had finally graduated to having his own package and not just doing hand-to-hand for other dudes. He had also moved up from straight cheap ass crack to heroin, which was making a strong comeback in the hood.

"You're a trifling ass bitch anyway, Celeste!" Drake screamed.

"Yeah, and you're a broke ass nigga with a little ass dick!" Celeste screamed back.

Ben shook his head. He was getting angrier by the minute with all the commotion. "I gotta get outta this house," he mumbled, getting ready to start bagging his shit so he could bounce. BAM! Ben's concentration on his task at hand was interrupted. He jumped when he heard something slam.

"Ahhh!" his mother screamed. BAM! The sound of thumping and banging came again.

"I know this nigga ain't up in here hitting on my moms," Ben said to himself.

"Bitch!" Drake hollered. WHAP! Ben knew he heard a slap.

"Oh, hell naw!" Ben huffed.

"Get off of me!" Celeste screamed at the top of her lungs.

Ben jumped up. Just then his baby brother, Keon, came waddling into his room. Keon had a look of terror on his face and he threw his arms up for Ben to pick him up.

WHAP! Ben heard another slap. He threw his drugs into an open nightstand drawer and scrambled out of his bedroom, headed for his mother's room. He ran past his baby brother, leaving the baby standing in his bedroom whining.

"I'm coming right back, Keon!" Ben said as he ran to help his mother.

"Get off me! Agghh!" his mother screamed.

Ben kicked Celeste's locked bedroom door, but the door didn't bulge. "Open this door!" Ben screamed from the other side.

"You wanna talk about me, bitch!" Drake growled.

Ben could hear his mother gasping for breath. *This nigga is choking her!* Ben's mind raced. He kicked the door again, this time with all his might. The door flew open with a bang and the doorknob hit the wall.

"Get the fuck off my moms, you punk ass nigga!" Ben screamed, grabbing Drake's shirt. Standing five eleven, Ben was almost as tall as Drake.

"What? Mind your business, this between me and your moms," Drake barked, shaking himself free of Ben's grasp as he finally let Celeste go. She was rolling on the bed, holding her neck, trying to catch her breath.

"Get the fuck outta my crib!" Ben gritted, stepping close to Drake and getting up in his face. "You don't help out in this place, you ain't shit. Get the fuck out!"

Drake poked his chest out, equaling Ben's status. Celeste finally caught her breath and got up to step between them. She didn't want her son and her baby daddy to fight.

"Wait—" She started to say something, but her words were interrupted. Before she could say another word screams cut through the air. They all froze. Celeste's eyes stretched wide.

"That's Keon!" she screamed. They all whirled around. "Keon?" she called out, kicking off her slippers and running towards her boys' bedroom. Ben was right behind his mother and Drake was on his heels.

"Ahhhhh!" Celeste belted out when she crossed the kids' bedroom door. The baby was flopping on the floor and foaming at the mouth. His eyeballs were completely rolled up into his head and his body jerked horribly.

"Keon! Oh my God!" Celeste let out a blood-curdling scream.

"What the fuck!" Drake screamed as well, running over to Celeste and Keon on the floor.

With her hands trembling fiercely, Celeste hoisted the baby's limp body off the floor. Baby Keon had stopped moving and his eyes were still rolling. White foam continued dribbling out of his lips.

Celeste rose from the floor and started running with Keon still in her arms. There was no phone in the house. "Somebody call 911!" she hollered as she tried rocking the baby back to consciousness. "Keon, wake up, baby!" she repeated as she ran towards the front door. "Help me! Oh God! Keon!"

Drake fumbled with his cell phone, dialing 911 as fast as he could. His car had just gotten repossessed so they had to wait on 911 to send an ambulance. Celeste was going crazy outside their apartment, with Keon still in her arms.

"Keon!! Wake up, baby!" she continued to plead with her baby as she tried shaking him back to life.

Ben was paralyzed with fear.

"What the fuck is goin' on?" Drake huffed, grabbing Ben by the shoulders, trying to find out what happened. "What happened to him?" Drake screamed at Ben.

"I . . . I don't know," Ben lied, his eyes opened as wide as they could go.

Drake raced back outside when he heard the ambulance sirens. Ben went back into his bedroom and stood there staring down at the nightstand drawer he had left open. He tightened his fists. Like a robot, Ben reached into the drawer and picked up his Baggie of dope. It was more than half empty. In fact, there was just a dusting of the drugs left. It looked as if Baby Keon had spilled the dope, gotten it on his hands and put his hands into his mouth. It was high grade uncut heroin. A small amount of the drug could've put a grown ass man six feet under.

Ben was supposed to get fifteen stacks for the bundle he had once he broke it down, cut it and bagged it into nicks and dimes like Deezo had told him to do. Now he had to get rid of what wasn't spilled out all over the floor. He couldn't let his mother find out that he had dope in the house and left it around for the baby to get. She would break his neck if she ever knew about it. He started wiping up the rest of the powder with his hands. His heart was racing like crazy and he was sweating now.

"What the fuck I'ma tell Deezo," Ben whispered to himself. His stomach cramped up. He was thinking about the consequences that might come from Deezo for this one. But he was also very worried about the condition of his baby brother. Ben could hear his mother outside screaming as the ambulance sirens pierced his ears. Ben continued to frantically clean up the powder. He had to get the drugs out of the house right away.

"Ben! What the fuck you doing? Let's go, the ambulance just left!" Drake boomed from the doorway.

"I'm not going. I . . . I can't see him like that," Ben said nervously.

"Fuck you, lil nigga!" Drake cursed. He didn't have time to even see what Ben was doing. Drake left and Ben felt like somebody had just kicked him in the heart. He was scared and nervous. He didn't believe in God, but he started to pray that Keon didn't die. That occupied one part of his brain. The other part was worried about how he was going to make the money back for the package. Deezo was expecting some loot off the package as well.

When Ben had gotten all of the drugs cleaned up, he left the house. With the money he had counted prior to the incident in his pocket, he hailed a cab and went to the hospital. Ben ran into the emergency room entrance and looked around for his mother and Drake. He spotted Celeste sitting in a chair rocking back and forth and Drake was standing up with a seriously angry look on his face.

"What did they say?" Ben asked his mother nervously. She looked up at him with swollen eyes.

"They are working on him, Ben. . . . He can't die, Ben. What happened in there?" Celeste cried, looking at her oldest son pitifully.

"I don't know," Ben lied. "I came out there to get this no good nigga off you and I left Keon in the room. I thought he was gonna follow me out the room. I was only gone for a minute, Keon was only in there for a minute." Ben knew the half-truth had to do, he couldn't tell his mother the whole story.

Drake was too distraught to even respond to Ben's smart-ass comment about him being a no good ass nigga. Celeste continued to rock, trying to calm herself down. Then she looked up and saw the doctor walking towards them. She stood up, her knees practically knocking against each other.

"Ms. Early?" the doctor asked.

"Yes," Celeste answered, her voice hoarse from screaming.

"I'm very sorry," the doctor began. "We couldn't save your baby—"

Celeste exploded into ear shattering screams. "Noooo! Please! God! No!" She doubled over like she had been gut punched. She was in great pain. Ben had tears welling up in his eyes too but he tried to play tough. He wanted to be strong for his mother.

Drake punched the wall, and then kicked a waiting room chair. Keon was not Drake's only baby, but it didn't matter. He was still feeling hurt over the death of his son.

"Why?" Celeste screamed.

The doctor held his head down. "Ms. Early, we have to do an autopsy since whatever caused the baby's death happened outside of the hospital. It seemed like the baby's pupils were severely dilated, indicating that he may have ingested something into his system," the doctor tried explaining through Celeste's screams.

"Whatcha mean, like he ate some shit that killed him or something?" Drake asked in a gruff tone.

That was how he dealt with his grief, he got angry and violent.

"Yes. Like he took in something that poisoned his system or caused him some kind of toxicological shock." The doctor continued using big words none of them could understand.

Ben was silent. His heart was beating out of control.

"You can see him before we take him down," the doctor said.

Celeste was so weak she could hardly walk as they all followed the doctor to the room where Keon lay on a small bed. When they walked into the room there were nurses cleaning up all the papers and tubes and mess from where they had tried to work on the baby to save him.

Celeste opened her swollen eyes. "Agghh!" she hollered when she saw her baby lying there. His little eyes were closed and his cherubic face looked like he was just sleeping. Drake and Ben helped Celeste over to the bed. Her knees buckled. "God! Why! Why my baby?" she continued to cry. She reached out and touched him. His skin was still a little warm.

"You can hold him," one of the nurses said softly.

She picked up Keon's limp body and handed him to Celeste. Celeste cradled the chubby, lifeless toddler against her chest. "Mmmmm," she moaned as she rocked her baby back and forth.

Ben stood close, watching, his mind racing with thoughts. It was his fault. *If I had just put the drugs away before I left the room, none of this would've hap-*

pened, he thought to himself. Now his brother was dead.

Celeste had to almost be peeled away from her baby. Drake had forgotten all about their fight and Ben just stayed quiet. In his head, he kept blaming himself repeatedly. There was no way he could tell his mother what happened. He knew he had to keep his secret to himself—hopefully forever.

The next day, Celeste was asleep. The doctor had prescribed her a sedative so she could sleep without the memories of Keon keeping her up. The loud knocks on the apartment door stirred Ben from his sleep. Drake had left. He was in and out. He didn't really live with Celeste and the kids.

Ben jumped up and looked around as the knocking continued. His heart started racing, thinking it might be Deczo looking for him. Ben listened and heard the knocks again. He got completely up and pulled on a pair of basketball shorts. He rubbed sleep from his eyes and made his way to the door. He looked through the peep hole, and felt a sigh of relief when it wasn't Deezo.

"Who is it?" he screamed.

"It's the police! We're looking for Celeste Early," a voice filtered through the door.

Ben's heart started hammering in his chest. "She's asleep!" he yelled back.

"Wake her up. This is about her baby, Keon. We need to speak to her immediately."

"Shit," Ben said under his breath. He walked to his mother's bedroom, wishing he could undue all of this. *Maybe they want to tell her something else,* Ben rationalized in his mind. He shook Celeste's shoulder, but she didn't budge.

"Ma!" Ben called her and shook her some more.

"Mmm," Celeste moaned. The sedatives had her in a deep sleep. There was no way with her baby being dead that she would've been able to fall asleep.

"Ma, the cops are at the door. They wanna speak to you," Ben told her.

Celeste fought against how drowsy the sedatives made her feel and opened her eyes. "What?" she asked, still dazed.

"There are cops at the door," Ben repeated himself. "They said they need to talk to you about Keon."

Celeste sat up. "Open the door," she grumbled.

Celeste forced herself to get out of bed. Feeling tired and depressed, she put on her bathrobe and went into the bathroom. She splashed water on her face and looked at herself in the mirror. Her eyes were puffy and looked as if somebody had used her as a punching bag. Celeste didn't care. She could hear the police talking in her tiny living room. She dragged her feet out of the bathroom and went into the living room. Her hair was wild and unkempt on top of her head, and she still looked a little drowsy from the sedatives. "Can I help y'all?" Celeste said in a raspy, hoarse voice.

"Ma'am, we need to talk to you about your baby son, Keon Early," the plainclothes cop stated. "The hospital social worker contacted us today."

Celeste looked the cop up and down. Since he wasn't in uniform, she knew he was a detective. That was common knowledge in the 'hood.

"And," Celeste said, moving closer to them.

"Ms. Early, you're gonna have to get dressed and come with us," the detective retorted. "We need to ask you some questions down at the station."

"Questions . . . about what? My son is dead, that's all the answers you need," Celeste snapped, hugging herself tightly.

"Ms. Early, it's important that you cooperate. Your baby's autopsy and toxicology report show that he died of an overdose of heroin," the detective said flatly, showing no emotion or respect for a grieving mother.

Celeste couldn't react. The sedatives had her brain on slow motion. "What? No, you making a mistake here, officer . . . don't nobody in here take no heroin," Celeste said, her voice firm, yet slurred, with denial.

The other detective walked closer to her. "Well, you look pretty high right now," he said snidely.

"I don't get high!" Celeste growled at him.

"From the looks of things around here, it seems like you might be lying to us," detective number one interjected. They were looking around at the cramped and junky apartment. There were clothes piled up on the couch, dishes spilling out of the sink and the furniture was old, some of it broken down. Celeste wasn't the best at keeping a clean house, but she wasn't on drugs.

"Oh, now being poor means I'm on heroin! I

may not have much but I ain't no dope fiend. I know y'all think all us mothers in the 'hood get high, but I got news for you . . . this one don't. Ain't no way my baby got no heroin in his system . . . I don't even allow drugs in my damn house!" Celeste spat.

Ben felt like he was going to faint. *Shit! Now they know Keon got to the drugs!* Ben screamed in his mind. Now he not only had to worry about what he was going to tell Deezo about the missing package, but the cops were investigating. He felt as if he would throw up.

"Miss, you can get dressed or we can take you down like this," the detective said, his tone nasty and demanding.

Celeste began to cry. "What about my baby? He gotta have a funeral! Y'all arresting me? I can't believe this shit! I can't even grieve for my dead child!" she screamed, shaking her head left to right.

"We want to take you down for questioning. You may also have to submit to a drug test and we'll be back with a search warrant for the house," the detective explained. It was as if they didn't even care about her feelings. Celeste knew that shit meant she was not coming back home. Shaking all over, she dragged her feet towards her bedroom. One of the detectives followed her.

"Can I get dressed in peace?" she growled. He stepped back and stood outside her bedroom door while she pulled on some clothes. Celeste stepped back into the hallway with tears in her eyes. This was like her worst nightmare coming to life.

She looked at Ben with sadness and tears in her eyes. "Ben, how did this all happen?" Celeste asked.

The detectives started escorting her out of the apartment. "You got somebody to take care of him?" the detective asked Celeste, nodding at Ben.

"No, it's just me," she said sadly.

"C'mon boy, you gon' have to come with us too, until we figure out whether or not your mother is coming home," one of the detectives told Ben. Ben just stood there dumbfounded. He knew leaving his apartment with the cops wasn't a good look. Deezo always had people watching.

"Ben, how did all of this happen?" Celeste asked again, looking at him, desperate for an answer or any words that could help her figure it all out.

Ben had a simple look on his face. His mind was going a mile a minute. He was thinking about how this all happened—how it all got started.

Chapter 1

Three years earlier

"Oh daddy, yeah, you fuck me so good! Yeah, beat this pussy up! Ohhh, I'm cumming, daddy!" Celeste screamed in ecstasy as yet another one of her boyfriends laid the pipe.

Ben lay in his bed with his arm over his eyes, listening to his mother fuck once again. This was nothing new to him. His mother's door had been like a revolving door since he was very young and she was still broke as hell. Ben pulled his knees up to his chest when he felt the hunger pains ripping through his belly again. That made him angry. His mother had all of these dudes in and out, but there was never anything to eat in the house. He turned over onto his stomach thinking that maybe laying on it would help the hunger pains subside. It didn't help one bit. He put his pillow over his head to drown out more sounds of his mother getting her back blown out. "Fucking ho!" Ben cursed, jumping up out of the bed. He could see the sun rising out of his window. It was almost time for him to run his paper route and make some money. That was the only way he would eat. It was far from the first or the fifteenth of the month, which meant Celeste couldn't afford any food.

Ben walked into the small kitchen in the project apartment he shared with his mother. He opened the refrigerator, there was nothing inside but an open can of Budweiser beer. It was the same story in the cabinets, minus the beer. When Ben opened the shabby cabinet doors, inside was bare except for the one or two hungry roaches that ran. He knew this beforehand but it was force of habit to open the refrigerator and cabinet doors with the hope food suddenly appeared.

"Shit, y'all niggas at the wrong house looking for crumbs," Ben said to the roaches. He slammed the cabinets, hoping the noise would disturb his mother's groove. It didn't work. She just kept right on doing her thing.

Ben went back in his room and slid on the one pair of sneakers he owned—a beat down pair of Nike Uptowns that used to be white but now looked more like dark brown. Celeste had finally broken down and bought Ben a pair of sneakers about eight months prior. The shits were run down in the back, dirty and starting to rip on top. Ben was embarrassed to wear them to school. At thirteen, while other kids were rocking fly gear, Ben had two pairs of jeans that he played switch-a-round with, two hoodies, and a few dingy white T-shirts. That was all his wardrobe consisted of. He had stopped going to school because of the way the kids teased him about his clothes.

As soon as he had turned thirteen, fed up with being hungry, Ben had walked his Brownsville neighborhood trying to find a job. Then he happened upon a new store that had just opened up near Pitkin Avenue. The owner told Ben if he delivered flyers to houses and other stores he would get paid for each one that he got rid of. That worked for a while, but the owner caught on that Ben was just dumping the flyers and coming back to get paid. Finally, Ben graduated to a full-time paperboy route. He would ride his pieced-together bike to the Daily News newspaper depot, pick up his papers for the day and make deliveries in nice neighborhoods. Ben was making $100 a week and he thought it was so much money. It was to him. At least he could buy some food. Celeste always had her hands out for a little bit of the money too.

Ben hurried up and got dressed. He was too damn hungry to play around. He needed to do his paper route, get his chips up and get something to eat quickly. He walked to his mother's bedroom door and kicked the bottom of it. "I'm going to work!" Ben yelled to his mother. "Shouldn't tell your ass shit," he said softly to himself.

"A'ight, go make that paper, boy," Celeste replied, giggling at the man she was locked up in the room with.

Ben shook his head in disgust and prepared to leave the house. He picked up his raggedy bike and wheeled it out of his small apartment. Outside, he climbed onto the bike and rode down his block. He passed the usual neighborhood corner boys with their flashy chains and fresh gear. They were out there playing CeeLo and talking shit, their usual daily routine.

Ben knew they were doing their thing and making money. He slowed his pace when he noticed a candy apple red Cadillac Escalade pulling up to the group of boys. Ben's heartbeat quickened. He felt a pang of excitement come over him. Everybody knew who drove that boss ass Escalade.

It was Deezo, a big time hustler whose reputation preceded him. Deezo was known to be notorious and he didn't play with his workers or his paper. He was also like the hood's Robin Hood. He would hand out turkeys at Thanksgiving and give kids sneakers and toys at Christmas. Ben had been the recipient of a few of Deezo's generous gifts. Deezo was both feared and revered in Brooklyn. In Ben's assessment, Deezo was the man.

Ben stopped for a minute when he noticed Deezo's ride. He wanted to catch a glimpse of the man he admired so much. He had been looking up to Deezo since he was a little boy. In Ben's eyes, Deezo was more than the man around his way. Deezo had everything, a bunch of fly ass cars, more than one diamond encrusted chain with chunky platinum pieces hanging from them, huge diamond earrings in each ear and every type of designer clothes you could think of. Ben had made a mental note to check out Deezo for a month. Every time he turned around, Deezo had on a different color pair of Prada sneakers to match all of his Yankee fitted caps. Ben used to daydream about being just like Deezo when he got older. The hood's Robin Hood was Ben's role model.

Deezo pulled the Escalade up to the corner and all of the boys stopped what they were doing. Dice stopped flying, the talking stopped and so did the drug sales. It was like the corner boys were in the army when Deezo came through. They all stood up straight and at attention, looking at the Escalade.

"Ayo' Quan, wassup?" Deezo called out from the window of his ride.

Ben had also noted that Quan was the dude in charge of that corner. He was the one who collected on Deezo's loot from the corner boys whom Deezo allowed to slang there. Quan walked over to the Escalade and gave Deezo a pound. With the slap of the hands, Ben saw them pass the money.

Smart, Ben thought to himself. He was making notes. Ben wanted to be just like them. Getting mad paper and fly as hell.

"Yo, lil nigga, whatcha looking at?" one of the corner boys said to Ben after noticing him watching Deezo so closely. Ben averted his eyes and rode off to do his paper route. Ben turned back one more time before he left the block and he noticed Deezo looking at him. Ben almost crashed his bike when he saw Deezo's eyes on him.

Chapter 2

That evening after Ben had finished his paper route, he slung the empty cloth newspaper bag on his bike handlebars and headed home. He was tired and hungry but he was happy to have gotten paid, which meant he had money for food. Ben got to his block and as usual the same corner boys were still out there doing the same thing—slanging them thangs. He pulled his rickety bike up to the side of the store, leaned it against the wall and passed the boys to get into the store. Ben unfolded the five crumpled twenty-dollar bills he had just earned. He was proud of his payday. He went around the store picking up stuff he wanted to eat—a box of Apple Jacks, half a gallon of milk, a pack of Lorna Doone cookies and three bags of barbeque potato chips.

"She better not ask for none of my stuff either," Ben mumbled about his mother. He went to the counter and put his stuff down. "Yo A-rab . . . let me get a hero," Ben called out to the man behind the counter. "I want ham and American cheese, lettuce, tomatoes, mayonnaise, mustard and oil and vinegar." His mouth watered as the man set about making his hero, which would be his dinner. He was sure his mother probably hadn't cooked shit.

As Ben waited for his sandwich to be ready, he glanced out of the store window at the corner boys. He daydreamed for a minute, thinking about all the things he would buy if he were in their positions. The first thing Ben thought of was new clothes. Clothes were a big status statement in Brooklyn. Most people in his neighborhood judged you on what you wore and how often you changed to something new.

The storeowner startled Ben when he told him his stuff was ready. He pulled out his bills and paid for his meager groceries. Ben stepped out of the door of the store and just as he did he noticed all of the corner boys starting to scatter.

"Five-o niggas, five-o en route!" one of the boys called out with his hands cupped around his mouth.

Ben looked around in confusion. Then he noticed the cop cars speeding down the streets, flashing lights but without any sirens blaring. The cops were trying to sneak up on the boys, but all corner boys had lookouts. The word had already gotten out and the scrambling had begun. Ben grabbed up his bike and threw his grocery bag into the newspaper delivery bag that hung from his handlebars.

"Yo Shorty, take this and put it in your bag,"

Quan, the lead corner boy who Ben had seen talking to Deezo, shouted at Ben. Ben's eyes widened as Quan stuffed something into Ben's newspaper bag. "Get the fuck outta here now, Shorty! I'll see you later on about that! I know where you live at!" Quan barked frantically.

Ben nodded at Quan and did as he was told. With his heart hammering wildly in his chest, Ben climbed onto his bike and rode off doing top speed. He turned to look back once and noticed that the jump out boys had all of the corner boys lined up against the wall near the store, including Quan. Ben inhaled deeply and peddled his bike even faster. When he got to his building, he snatched the cloth newspaper bag off his bike and raced into his apartment. He was so nervous his hands shook. He raced past his mother, who was in the living room with a new boyfriend that Ben was seeing more often now.

"Damn, you don't say wassup?" Celeste called after him.

Ben ignored her. He went into his room and closed the door. He set the newspaper bag down on the floor and flopped on his bed. He was scared to look inside the bag at first but curiosity was killing him. He took out his grocery bag first, and then slowly he peered down into the cloth bag. His eyes lit up and he swore he could feel his blood pressure rising. Ben swallowed hard as he stared at the contents of the bag. In the bottom of the bag lay three bundles tightly wrapped in plastic. Ben slowly and reluctantly picked each of the bundles up. One bundle was a bunch of red-capped containers with white rocks in them. The second bundle was a bunch of brown and green grass-looking stuff in small Baggies, and the third bundle was a bunch of tiny Baggies with white powder in them. Ben knew all three bundles were drugs—crack, weed, and either powdered cocaine or heroin. Although he was thirteen, growing up in the hood afforded Ben a vast street knowledge about drugs.

"Ben! Open this door!" Celeste hollered from the other side.

Ben jumped. He snatched the bundles of drugs and lifted his thin mattress and slid all three bundles under it. Inhaling and exhaling to get his nerves together, he walked over and opened his door. His mother eyed him up and down suspiciously.

"Did you get paid today?" Celeste said, letting her eyes scan his room. Ben sucked his teeth and rolled his eyes. He could not stand his pain in the ass mother when she acted so money hungry.

"Whatcha was doing up in here with the door locked? Trying to hide ya little bit a money?" Celeste snapped as Ben pushed past her to go into the kitchen.

"Nah, I ain't hiding nothing from you!" Ben snapped back. He started unloading his little bit of groceries.

"Well, give me what's mine, nigga. Ain't no free stays up in here . . . shit your ass getting grown," Celeste told him, sticking her hand out.

Ben did as he was told. He handed Celeste $40 out of the money he had left. That left him with about $30 after he had already spent about $30 on groceries. He acted angry but he wasn't really mad. He didn't mind helping his mother out, she was a single mother with no help from whoever his no good ass father was. However, Ben didn't appreciate it when men came over and he and his mother were hungry and those niggas didn't even help out by buying as much as a loaf of bread. Ben thought his mother was real stupid for giving up her ass to no good niggas for free.

Ben sat down to eat his hero, but when he lifted the greasy sandwich to his mouth he found that he didn't have an appetite. He was thinking hard about the packages under his mattress. He thought he could go out there and sell every bit of those drugs and make good money. He also knew if he did that, Quan and Deezo would surely be looking for him. Ben decided to just wait and see if they ever came to claim what was theirs. After thinking about the drugs, the money and Quan and Deezo repeatedly, Ben finally forced himself to eat his sandwich. He went to bed full and worried. All he could do was hope that things were going to start looking up.

Chapter 3

Ben didn't hear from Quan for the entire night. He tossed and turned all night knowing that the package was under his mattress. The next day, he woke up to knocks on his door. Ben scrambled out of his bed and raced to the door before his mother could answer it. When Ben pulled back the door, Quan and Deezo were standing there. Ben almost shit his pants.

"Whaddup Shorty? I came to pick up my shit," Quan said. Deezo stood silently with a serious glare on his face. He didn't look happy.

Ben shook his head up and down absentmindedly, too star struck to even speak. Quan and Deezo stepped inside of the apartment without Ben inviting them in. Ben knew Celeste slept late so he wanted to hurry up and get what they came for before she got up and saw the two biggest neighborhood hustlers in her living room. He rushed to his room, retrieved the three bundles and proudly handed them over to Quan. Deezo kept his eyes on Ben while Quan surveyed the bundles. Ben could feel sweat dripping down his back.

"It's all here Shorty. Good looking out. You did a'ight," Quan said, smiling at Ben.

Ben's shoulders slumped in relief. Although he knew he hadn't taken anything out of the bundles, he was still scared as hell.

"That's wassup, Shorty. Here, this is for ya troubles. Look like a nigga could use the help and shit," Deezo said, handing Ben two crisp one hundred dollar bills.

Ben's eyes lit up. "Thank you," he smiled up at Deezo.

"Buy ya self something, Shorty. Ya moms be trippin' the way she got this crib looking. This ain't no way for a lil' nigga to live," Deezo commented, turning around to head for the door. Ben shook his head, agreeing with anything Deezo had to say. "And Shorty, since you did so good with this little job, I got something you can do to make some money if you want to. I'ma see you out there. I might can help you get ya chips up, feel me?" Deezo stopped walking and told Ben.

Ben couldn't stop smiling. He couldn't believe Deezo was offering him a job. He had dreamed about being down with Deezo. When Deezo and Quan left, Ben raced over to the window and watched them get into Deezo's Escalade. He could see all of their bling sparkling against the sun. The whole scene excited Ben. "I'ma have that car when I get older," he said to himself, gripping the money Deezo gave him.

* * *

Ben was too excited to eat his Apple Jacks that morning. He rushed and got dressed. He didn't take his newspaper bag or anything else. He left the house, grabbed his bike and headed for downtown Brooklyn. Ben went straight to Footlocker first. He copped a fresh, crisp new pair of white Nike Uptowns. Then he went to several other stores and copped a traditional navy blue Yankees fitted cap, a brand-new pair of Sean Jean jeans and a five pack of crisp white tees. He felt good about himself now. He wore his new sneakers right out the store, the same for his jeans and one of the T-shirts. Ben even had enough money to eat a super-sized meal from McDonald's. He felt like a man. No, he felt like *the* man. He felt independent. It was a feeling Ben wanted to have all the time. He was definitely going to take Deezo up on his offer.

When Ben returned to his hood that evening he rode his bike past the corner store. He was secretly hoping he would run into Deezo or Quan.

"Shorty!" Quan called after Ben. Ben smiled to himself and stopped his bike.

"Yeah," he answered. His prayers had been answered.

"Deezo told me to hook you up, son. All you gotta do is go getcha newspaper bag, come get a package, and deliver it to an address across the way. . . . Two stacks is what Deezo paying for the one trip," Quan told Ben.

Ben felt like he would piss his pants. Two hundred more dollars just like that! Ben thought excitedly. "A'ight. I'll be right back," Ben said, excitement lacing his words. He took flight on his bike, and ran into the house in a huff. He scrambled to his room to get his bag. But his activity was interrupted.

"Where you been at?" Celeste said dryly, stepping into Ben's bedroom with her arms folded. Ben stopped like a deer caught in headlights.

"I went to work and then shopping," Ben lied.

"Where you get money to shop?" Celeste asked suspiciously. She always wanted to know every dollar he had.

"I saved it up from the newspaper route," Ben told her impatiently. He didn't know why his mother was sweating him. It was annoying. Ben screwed up his face at Celeste.

She looked at him up and down. "I got something to tell you," she said. Ben gave her a blank stare. He wanted to tell her to get the hell out of his room so he could get his bag and be out. He was preoccupied and full of anticipation for the job he had coming up.

"I'm pregnant. You gon' have a brother or sister," Celeste said dryly.

"And," Ben answered, being a smart ass.

"You too grown for your own good, Ben. I'm just telling you. I ain't have to tell you shit," Celeste snapped.

"So you shouldn'ta told me then," Ben said with an attitude. He grabbed his bag and brushed past his mother, bumping her slightly. "Another mouth to feed and she don't even feed me," he mumbled on his way out. He knew whoever his mother was pregnant by was probably not going to be around or help out in the house. This annoyed him even more. Ben snatched his bike and started out the apartment door. He didn't have time for his mother and her bullshit right now.

"Where the hell you goin' at this time with that bag?" Celeste asked.

Ben didn't answer his mother. He felt like she wasn't in any position to question him. Thirteen or not, Ben was the breadwinner in their household.

"Benjamin Early!" Celeste called after him.

Ben let the door slam behind him. He had to get back outside. Quan was waiting on him. "A'ight, I'm back," Ben huffed, putting his feet on the ground to stop his bike.

Quan dropped a package into Ben's newspaper bag. "Take this across the way to Howard Houses; there's a kid named Spider waiting on you. Don't fuck this up, lil' nigga," Quan warned.

Ben pulled himself up on his bike and was out. He had a new job and it paid more than he could ever dream of making as a newspaper delivery boy.

Two weeks had passed and Ben had made eight deliveries for Deezo. He had more money than he could have ever dreamed of. Each time he earned another two hundred dollars, he would buy another full outfit, complete with fitted cap. Ben started giving Celeste $100 instead of the $40 she was accustomed to getting from his paper route. Celeste was happy as hell. She had only questioned Ben once about where he got the extra money. He told her he had picked up a new route that paid more money, which was not a complete lie. Celeste was satisfied with the answer . . . at least, that is what she told herself.

Chapter 4

It had been a year since Ben had first got down with Deezo. He had graduated from delivery boy to an actual hand-to-hand corner boy. It had happened one day after Ben had made all of his drop-offs with his newspaper bag. He had come back to the block to let Quan know that everything had been delivered as planned and to collect his money. That day when Ben rode up on his bike, Deezo was talking to Quan. They both noticed Ben at the same time.

"Yo, Shorty, come here and let me holla at cha'," Deezo called out to Ben.

Ben looked at Quan and then back at Deezo. *He wanna holla at me!* Ben thought to himself. He nervously wheeled his bike over to Deezo's ride.

"Nigga, you can't get up in my shit with that piece of shit bike," Deezo said, chuckling. Ben smiled and put his bike down on the sidewalk. He could not believe Deezo was letting him get into his car. "Get in, lil' nigga, I ain't got all day," Deezo demanded.

Ben climbed the high step of Deezo's luxury SUV and got into the passenger seat. Deezo rolled up all of his smoke-out black-tinted windows. Ben swallowed a lump of fear that sat at the back of his throat and stared straight ahead. He wouldn't dare grill Deezo straight on; that was a violation he had seen another little corner boy get slapped for in the past.

"Yo, you been real good with them deliveries and real smart about how you handle yours, Shorty," Deezo complimented. Ben was smiling inside but he didn't dare part his lips into a smile. "I like that you stay hungry and humble, feel me? I can tell you want this real bad and shit. Some of these niggas I got working the block is cocky. They make a lil' bit a money and they think that make they dick grown and shit. Feel me?"

Ben shook his head eagerly. "But you . . . I been watching you, Shorty," Deezo continued. "You keep your humble attitude all the time. That's the right way to be. . . . When you get cocky is when you get caught. A kid like you can make it far in this game, Shorty. How old is you?"

"F . . . F . . . Fourteen," Ben stammered, his nerves on edge.

"Shiiit, I remember when I was fourteen. I was in the same boat as you. Mother was single, a bunch of fucked up niggas in and out the house and shit. No food up in the crib. House dirty. She having a baby every year and shit . . . I was just like you, I worked hard and made my way in the game.

I stood up and made my own money and ain't never ask my moms for shit again. I was the man in my crib after a while, feel me?"

Ben was hanging onto Deezo's every word. He couldn't believe Deezo had compared himself to him. He felt really good inside. He was ready to do anything Deezo asked of him.

"Now, I wanna move you up from deliveries. You know . . . give you your own lil' candy shop and shit. If you thought two stacks was good, how you feel about making a stack every two to three days . . . that's the type of money I'm talking," Deezo said seriously.

"Yeah, yeah . . . I'm down . . . I can do it," Ben said excitedly. He had goose bumps just thinking about that kind of money. He could see himself buying a chain down on Canal Street as soon as he made his first stack.

Deezo laughed. "Damn Shorty, I love that hungry attitude," Deezo said. "You gon' be a'ight in this game. I'ma tell Quan to start you out light . . . let me see how you handle yourself and then we'll talk." He extended his fist towards Ben for a pound. Ben responded in kind and bumped his fist against Deezo's. Ben went to get out of the car.

"Shorty, just don't ever try to cross me or fuck with my paper. Don't become a sucka fo' candy like some of these lil' niggas I gotta deal with," Deezo warned.

"Nah, I won't," Ben said sincerely.

"Good, cuz niggas don't survive crossing me," Deezo said seriously.

With that, Ben climbed out of the SUV with a

wide smile on his face. He would never dream of crossing Deezo. He knew he could be loyal since Deezo was good enough to give him a chance. *My own spot!* Ben thought excitedly.

"Damn, lil' nigga, you look like Deezo just gave you a million fucking dollars," Quan said, laughing when Ben walked back over to him. That was exactly how Ben felt. The only obstacle he had was hiding his new job from Celeste. Although she was money hungry, she was totally against hustling. She had warned Ben repeatedly that he better not ever try to sell drugs or bring them into her home. Ben was determined to make money so he would just have to find a way around his mother's rules.

Quan started Ben off with his first package of weed to sell. It was a couple of ounces with a real good street value. Ben was responsible for getting rid of three bundles of weed a day. The weed had a street value of three thousand dollars. He would get $300 off each thousand. Ben had already started planning what he would do with his money.

Quan assigned Ben to a spot in front of an abandoned building ten blocks from his house. That worked for Ben because he didn't want his mother to see him on the corner of his own block by the store. Ben's business immediately started booming on that block. Quan had told him to keep his stash in a paper bag behind a rotting piece of wood that was nailed to the building's missing windows. Ben was only supposed to grab something from the stash when he had the money in hand from the customer. He followed his directions to the letter. Quan would come by and check on Ben every so often. Quan had given Ben a disposable track phone. When Ben had burned through his package, he would call Quan for instructions. Most of the time it was still before dark so Ben would wait for Quan to pick up the money, give him his cut and then Ben either got a new package or rode his bike back to the block. Word on the street was that Deezo was supplying the best weed in Brooklyn so Ben's product really sold itself. Ben had to admit that this was the easiest money he had ever come by.

After working for Deezo for a while, Ben had become more distant with his mother. Celeste was into her new man, Drake, and she was just about to give birth. Ben had been buying clothes and sneaking them into the house. He could count on Celeste being asleep when he left every day with his new gear on, and if she ever caught him in something he would just lie and say he had, yet again, moved up at the newspaper. In actuality, Ben had long since gotten fired from the newspaper route after he just stopped showing up. With his weed spot booming sales, he started giving his mother even more money and he noticed she had started picking up stuff for the baby that was coming. She still didn't buy food, but that was fine with Ben because he never ate at home anymore. He considered life to be good.

Chapter 5

Summer came and went and before Ben knew it winter had reared its ugly head. One night, he was standing up against the wall near his spot. He was wrapped tightly in his brand new North Face snorkel and his toes were toasty in a brand spanking new pair of Timbs. Quan had just left. He had given Ben three more bundles of weed to get rid of. He had stepped up his game and his first three bundles had disappeared within four hours. Peering from under his fur trimmed hood, Ben noticed that one of his regular customers, a dude named Rambo, was walking his way. Ben turned and went into the stash real quick. He took out three bags of weed and held them tightly in his hands. He was so used to seeing Rambo he knew just how much weed Rambo was going to cop and Ben wasn't worried about Rambo not paying. He felt it was all gravy.

"Wassup," Ben said. It was his customary greeting to his customers.

"Let me get five dime bags," Rambo replied. Ben was thrown off. Rambo was buying way more than he usually did.

"Shit," Ben mumbled. He had already taken out three nickel bags, now he would have to show this nigga his stash spot. Ben decided to play smart. "All I got left is three nicks, son," Ben lied. He would just take an L on the sale because something about Rambo's new request didn't sit right with him. Rambo just gave off the aura that he had larceny in his heart and Ben's gut didn't take to Rambo.

"C'mon, nigga, I'm having a get together at my crib," Rambo complained. "I done collected everybody money and told them I was coming to get that bomb bomb zee shit and now you fronting on a nigga."

"Yo, I'm dry," Ben lied again. He was starting to get nervous. Something told him to take out his track phone and call Quan, but Ben wanted to be a man and handle it.

"Nigga, why don't you stop fronting! I just saw that nigga, Quan, leave from over here. That nigga replenished your shit . . . why the fuck is you fronting on me?" Rambo barked, his words making frosty puffs of smoke into the night air.

Ben's heart started racing. Something was telling him to run, but he kept thinking about Deezo's package that was behind the wood planks. He was also recalling Deezo's words in his head: "just don't ever try to cross me or fuck with my paper." Although it was about thirty degrees outside, Ben was sweating now.

"Yo, do you want the fucking three nicks or what, nigga!" Ben growled, he decided to play tough.

"Nah . . . I want all your shit!" Rambo barked, rushing into Ben and sticking a black handgun in Ben's face. Ben's heart felt like it would pound through his chest. He clenched his ass cheeks to keep from shitting on himself. "Now muthafucka, I want you to give me all the fucking weed from behind that fucking wood plank in the window!" Rambo growled, pushing the gun further into Ben's forehead.

"A'ight, but I gotta get it," Ben said, his words coming out shaky.

"Nah nigga, we gotta go get it. Now I'ma walk with you over to that window and you gon' hand all the fucking weed over to me or else your little young brains gon' be laying on this fucking ground," Rambo hissed menacingly.

He roughly turned Ben towards where the stash was hidden. Ben walked over slowly, the gun up to the side of his temple now. Ben gulped deeply. With trembling hands he reached out to the third piece of wood, hit it twice and when the wood gave a little Ben slid his hand behind it and picked up the stash. Quan had given Ben a small .22 caliber handgun, but it was all the way down in the side of his boot. Ben was too scared to reach for it.

"Here," Ben whispered.

"You got something else for me too nigga . . . don't try to play me," Rambo growled.

"Nah, I ain't got nothing else," Ben said, his voice quivering.

"Nigga, you pro'bly got a pocket full of loot!" Rambo spat.

"I'm telling you Quan just collected all the loot," Ben lied. Quan had taken the first part of the day's take, but Ben was still holding a couple of stacks for Deezo.

"See . . . see, you think I'm playing," Rambo muttered. He lifted the gun, slammed it hard against Ben's head.

"Agghh!" Ben screamed. Blood immediately began leaking down the side of his face. "Yo man . . . I ain't got no money on me," Ben cried.

"Next time it's gon' be a bullet in ya fucking head! Now gimme the fucking money," Rambo barked.

"It's . . . it's in my . . . my inside po . . . cket," Ben stuttered. His head was throbbing and he was feeling dizzy. Rambo leveled the gun at Ben's chest and began digging in his pockets. When he found the wad of crumpled up bills, Rambo grabbed them by the handful. Some dropped on the ground, but he couldn't worry about those. Now he had the weed and the money. "Turn towards the wall and get down on your knees, little nigga," Rambo demanded.

"Please don't kill me, man." Ben was crying hysterically now. It was times like this that brought the little boy out of him. He turned around slowly and put his knees on the freezing cold concrete. He could feel the icy ground through his jeans. When he was completely down, Rambo took off running.

Ben was so scared he waited a few minutes before he turned around. Rambo had taken his track phone so he couldn't even call Quan. When he thought Rambo was finally gone, he got up off his knees. His head was killing him, but Ben felt even worse now that he had to tell Quan and Deezo that he had lost all of the weed and the money. Ben was freezing as he walked the ten blocks to Quan's corner as slowly as he could. Ben was thinking of all kinds of things to say, when he finally decided that telling Quan and Deezo the truth was his only option.

When Ben rounded the corner by the store, Quan was sitting in his new car. He had risen so high in Deezo's camp that he was now the proud driver of a brand new Infiniti QX56. When Quan spotted Ben, he rolled down his window slightly. "Yo lil' nigga, whatcha doing around here now? Did I fucking say you could leave the spot?" Quan barked.

Ben felt like his heart would jump out of his chest. "I . . . I . . . n . . . n . . . need to talk to you," Ben stuttered. His bladder all of a sudden felt filled to the brim.

"Get the fuck in here, nigga!" Quan commanded. The other corner boys were all bundled up in their snorkels looking at Ben like he was walking into doomsday. Ben used his frozen hands to open the car door. He flopped into the seat and timidly took his hood off his head. "What the fuck happened to you?!" Quan said, alarmed by the bloody cut on Ben's head. Ben couldn't even speak. He just busted out crying. "Yo, what's going on, nigga? You better start talking fast," Quan told him.

"I got robbed. . . . He took all the weed and all the money," Ben blurted out. "He hit me in the head with his gun. He made me give him everything or he said he was gonna kill me. I couldn't get to the gun you gave me cuz it was in my boot and it was too cold and I am sorry—" His words were running together one after the other like a string of pearls.

"Slow down!" Quan said, trying to get a grasp on just what Ben was telling him. "Now . . . you got robbed?" He wanted to make sure he had heard Ben correctly.

Ben shook his head yes.

"Who was it?!" Quan asked through clenched teeth.

Ben swallowed hard. "It was Rambo but he told me if I told y'all he was gonna come and shoot me." Ben cried some more. He felt like he was in double jeopardy.

"Fuck that weed head nigga! He gon' be dead so how he gon' shoot you!" Quan said, hitting Ben upside his head.

"Ssss," Ben winced. "What I'ma tell Deezo?" He cried harder as he thought about what Deezo might do to him.

"You gonna fucking tell Deezo the truth. I'ma call that nigga right now," Quan said, picking up one of his track phones. Ben slumped farther down into the car's seat. He could just imagine how Deezo was going to react.

Ben listened to Quan recount the story to Deezo over the phone. Ben kept his eyes closed. Quan hung up the phone. "Yo, Deezo said to take your lil' ass home and he gon' deal wit' you tomorrow. That nigga laying up with a bitch so you lucky tonight, Shorty," Quan told Ben. Ben made a long sigh of relief. "Don't go nowhere until you hear from me. You gon' have to face Deezo tomorrow," Quan instructed.

Ben shook his head. He got out of Quan's car and walked up the block to his house.

Ben turned the key in his apartment door and before he could push inside someone else was pulling on the door. Ben jumped. He was suddenly face to face with Drake, his mother's boyfriend and soon-to-be baby father.

"Wassup? Yo, we about to head out . . . ya moms in labor," Drake said, sounding a little shaken up. Ben just looked at him. Celeste came waddling out of her bedroom.

"Ben, I'm going to the hospital. Stay here and Drake will let you know when the baby comes," Celeste said. Ben could tell she was in pain. She was too distracted by her labor pains to even notice the big cut on his head or to ask him why he looked like his life was about to come to an end.

Drake and Celeste left for the hospital. Ben was kind of happy they were gone. He didn't want to answer any questions about his ordeal anyway. All he wanted to do was lie down in peace and quiet so he could think about what Deezo was going to do to his ass the next day.

* * *

Ben didn't get even a full hour of sleep. He had tossed and turned all night. Every time he closed his eyes he would see Rambo with the gun to his head and then he would see Deezo's face. Ben was lying in his bed wide awake when the knocks on the door finally came. The sound had made his stomach instantly cramp up. He got up, pulled on the jeans he'd had on the night before, and answered the door. Of course, it was Quan.

"Get dressed, nigga. Deezo wanna see you," Quan instructed, stepping into the apartment without an invitation. Ben hung his head, dragged his feet back to his bedroom, and threw on some clothes. He headed towards the bathroom to brush his teeth.

"Yo! Where you goin'?" Quan barked.

"I'm going to brush my teeth," Ben replied in a shaky voice.

"Hurry the fuck up son, Deezo don't like to wait. Especially when it's about his paper." Ben rushed into the bathroom and brushed his teeth and washed his face. When he came out he knew it was time to go face the music.

When Quan pulled his car up to a desolate area in East New York, Ben's heart felt like it would explode. He could just imagine what they would do to him inside the warehouse-looking building that sat in the middle of nowhere. He knew that nobody would be able to hear him scream all the way out here.

"Get the fuck out. Whatcha staring like a dummy for?" Quan snapped. Ben did as he was told. The cold air against his face didn't even bother him. His entire body felt overly hot with fear. Inside the building, they walked all the way to the back of a large room. There were a couple of chairs scattered around. Deezo was standing up and so were five other mean looking dudes. There were a few lights dangling from the ceiling, but the place was still drab and dim. Ben stopped walking when Quan stopped to give all the dudes a pound. Ben was blinking rapidly he was so scared.

"Shorty . . . get the fuck over here," Deezo demanded. Ben walked over, his head hung low. "Now . . . tell me what the fuck happened out there and you better tell the fucking truth. I know I told you not to fuck with my paper!" Deezo barked.

Ben's eyes were as wide as marbles and he shook his head up and down. He began recounting the robbery. Ben told Deezo how Rambo had hit him in the head with the gun, took all the drugs and how he'd made him kneel down like he would shoot him. Deezo was rubbing his chin.

"A nigga named Rambo, huh?" Deezo asked. Ben shook his head. Deezo looked like he was in deep thought. "Did you tell this nigga that the weed and the fucking money belonged to me?" Deezo asked seriously. Ben shook his head yes. "A'ight, Shorty, this what I'ma do. I ain't gonna fuck you up like I planned on doing since it seems like a nigga really robbed you. I'ma cut you some slack, but you gon' have to work off that debt. I'ma give you a new spot, a new product and you gon' work sun up and sun down until you fucking repay that debt. You ain't getting no paper until my money is back in my pocket. You understand?" Deezo told and asked Ben at the same time.

Ben shook his head eagerly. He was just happy and relieved that he wasn't going to get his ass beat or killed. "And you gon' go out with Quan and these niggas and help them find this Rambo dude. I wanna meet the muthafucka bold enough to take something they know belongs to me," Deezo continued. Ben shook his head some more. "Yo Quan, show this nigga what happens to niggas that cross me. Because if this little nigga lying about what happened I want him to see what I'ma do to him." He was looking at Ben but speaking to Quan.

Quan forced Ben down into a chair. Ben emitted a small whimper because he didn't know what to expect. Then he watched as Quan pulled out a manila envelope. Quan slid several pictures out of the envelope and held them up to Ben's face. Ben shrunk back in the chair at the sight. The first picture was of a dude with his face busted up beyond recognition. There was so much blood Ben couldn't even tell where his eyes really were. His mouth hung open and his own dick had been shoved inside it. Ben felt waves of nausea flash through his stomach as he was forced to look at picture after picture of Deezo's torture victims.

"Now since you know what the fuck is gon' happen if I ever find out you crossed me, I want you to get the fuck out there and work hard," Deezo said, his breath hot on the side of Ben's face. "Don't make me have to send you home to your trifling ass mama in a body bag."

Ben had already made it up in his mind that he would never, ever let anything happen to one of Deezo's packages again. He told himself he would be extra careful and he would work extra hard.

Ben drove around with Quan and three other dudes for hours before they finally found Rambo. Ironically, Rambo was copping weed from another kid not too far from where Ben had his spot and where Rambo had robbed Ben.

"That's him!" Ben screamed.

Quan skidded his tires trying to stop so fast. When the car lurched to an abrupt stop, Quan threw it in park and they all hopped out. When Rambo noticed Ben and company, he tried to take off running. He wasn't fast enough. Quan had grabbed a hold of him, and the other dudes immediately started pummeling Rambo. They punched him, kicked him, and when he was flat on the ground, unable to really move, Quan lifted his Timberland boot and stomped Rambo in the head.

"We ain't finished, nigga. . . . Deezo wanna see you," Quan snarled. He had one of his posse call somebody and a black van pulled up shortly thereafter. Rambo was thrown into the van, never to be seen again.

Ben worked every day from sun up to sun down, tirelessly, to pay Deezo back. He wasn't making any money and Celeste was starting to take notice. She had been waiting to see just how long it was going to take Ben to bring her the usual $100 a week she had grown accustomed to. She waited and waited, but nothing.

Ben's baby brother, Keon, had just turned a month old and Celeste was back to arguing and fighting with her baby father, Drake, over money. Frustrated that she couldn't get shit out of Drake, Celeste turned her attention back to Ben.

It was an early morning and Ben was getting ready to hit the block. Deezo had told him the night before that he was more than halfway paid up, so Ben wanted to get outside early to get it in. The faster he paid Deezo back, the faster he could make more money. He shuffled around his room, layering on clothes to combat against the brick cold winter morning air he knew he would have to contend with standing outside doing hand-to-hand sales. But before he could get finished dressing, Ben's plans to get out of the house before his mother got up were broken up.

"Where the fuck are you going so early in the morning?" Celeste asked, standing in his doorway. Ben jumped; she had startled him. He furrowed his eyebrows as he stared at his mother. She had been up all night with Keon, who in Ben's assessment did nothing but cry day and night. Celeste looked as if she had been to war. Her eyes had bags under them and her hair resembled a wild bird's nest on top of her head.

"I'm going to work," Ben mumbled, thinking to himself that his mother looked like shit. He sighed when he saw that she wasn't going to leave his room. His mother stressing him was the last thing he needed right now on top of the shit he was going through with Deezo.

"Well, I ain't seen no fucking money from you in a minute so how you mean you going to work!" Celeste snapped. Ben didn't want to hear her mouth. He rolled his eyes in typical teenager defiance. But Celeste kept on talking. "You think this a free ride up in here, nigga? I noticed you been eating shit I put up in here lately too! I ain't seen a dime from you since before I left to go to the hospital to have Keon. You got all these sneakers and shit though," Celeste hollered, walking over to Ben's stack of sneaker boxes and slapping them down from where they were stacked neatly.

"Eating shit you put up in here? The last time I checked you was the mother and I was the son . . . so ain't that how it's supposed to go?" Ben snapped. He was really blown by his mother's audacity. She was acting like she was talking to her man and not her son. "I gotta go!" he snapped at his mother like she was a lunatic.

"You ain't goin' no fucking place 'til I get my money, Benjamin Early!" Celeste screamed. Just then, at the sound of Celeste's high-pitched, screechy voice, baby Keon started to scream from Celeste's bedroom. She rolled her eyes in disgust.

"I don't have no money for you. I will soon," Ben tried to reason with her. Between the baby crying and her stressing over not having any money, Celeste seemed to snap. Her eyes were wild and she turned her face into a scowl.

"What? I said I want some fucking money now!" she screamed. Then she stretched her arm out and slapped Ben across his face. He was shocked. He rocked on the balls of his feet. He wanted to punch his mother in her face so badly.

"What the fuck you doing!" he screamed, holding the side of his face. He had drops of blood on his hands. Celeste's nails had scratched him on the cheek and drawn blood. She seemed to have caught herself. She had never really hit Ben before. He knew she was stressed over money, the baby crying all the time and her no good baby father who was in and out the apartment and fucking with every Thelma and Louise in the hood. Celeste's eyes went low and she wore a sorrowful look.

"Ben . . . wait . . . I'm just—" she started. Ben didn't allow her to complete her apology, he didn't wanna hear what she had to say. He stormed past her, grabbed his coat and headed out the door. Baby Keon was still screaming his head off. "Ben! Wait . . . I'm sorry!" Celeste cried out to no one. It was too late. Ben was already gone. She just didn't know how far gone he was.

Chapter 6

Ben had worked hard and paid off his debt to Deezo. He was back in Deezo's good graces and he had graduated from his old weed spot to one of Deezo's main crack spots. Ben was fifteen now and he had shot up at least six inches in height. His voice had gotten deeper and he considered himself a man now. When Ben first got started at his new hand-to-hand crack spot, he immediately noticed the difference between the customers that he used to sell weed to and the customers who bought crack. Ben's weed customers had been mostly young dudes and girls, some college students and even some white kids that drove to Brooklyn from Long Island to get the best weed. All of the weed customers, with the exception of a few, still appeared to be "normal" in Ben's eyes. But he noticed that his crack customers were a lot of women, some he knew from his neighborhood that were mothers. He also noticed that all of the crack customers, men and women, looked horrible and would always try to beg for a freebee. Ben often wondered how crack had made them so skinny and fucked up their teeth so bad.

Ben was starting to learn from his environment. He had grown to have a hardened heart towards fiends and people in general. He had learned from Deezo that it was either kill or be killed out on the streets. Being as young as he was, Ben had gotten his first blowjob from one of his customers. It was a hot summer night and Ben was standing on his corner. He was partnered up with three other dudes that worked for Deezo. Quan had told Ben the partnership was for their own protection. They were all standing around talking shit as usual, waiting on their regular customers to come back for the fifth or sixth time that night.

A female fiend came rushing over to Ben and his crew. She was moving back and forth like her ass couldn't stand still. "Whatcha want tonight, Trisha?" Ben asked, knowing the woman by her first name now. He knew she was notorious for begging. Trisha would always try to sell them some shit they didn't need, like used batteries and other junk. Ben had a scowl on his face as he waited for her to say some dumb shit.

"I need to borrow something," the woman said nervously. The monkey was on her back big time and she couldn't keep still.

"Yo bitch, you can't borrow shit!" Ben snapped at her. "If I loan you a rock you gon' give it back? No! Then it ain't borrowing, bitch. Now get the fuck on." Ben had been in the game long enough now to pick up on just how the corner boys spoke to the fiends. He had gotten his bark down pact.

"C'mon . . . please!" Trisha begged, still moving like she was being eaten alive by ants.

"Trisha, whatcha gon' do for my man if he give you a free cap?" one of the boys that was with Ben called out to the skinny, drawn up, poorly dressed woman. It was a joke, but they wanted to see how far she was going to stoop to get that crack.

"I'll do anything he wants," Trisha said, sounding real desperate. Her voice cracked and her lips were white with ash.

"A'ight . . . let me see you drop down and suck his dick right here," the boy said. Ben's eyes grew wide. Getting his dick sucked was a dream of his. He had heard so many of the dudes he hung around talking about girls sucking their dicks and how good it felt. Ben was dying to receive that first blow job.

"I'll do it. I'll do anything right now for a cap," Trisha pleaded, rubbing herself. They all started laughing cruelly.

"Go 'head Ben, take that bitch behind the building and let her suck you off," one of the boys demanded. The other boys started chiming in.

"That's part of the game, son . . . let a bitch suck ya dick for that good good," they all joked. Ben didn't know if they were serious or not. He was young and although he had been slanging for two years now, he wasn't as worldly as some of his older counterparts.

"C'mon baby, I'll suck you off good," Trisha

said, making a failed attempt at trying to be sexy. Although Trisha was dirty, her skin was ashen and she looked like a bag of bones, the possibility and thought of having a mouth on his dick made Ben get hard. Trisha's missing teeth gave Ben more hope that it would feel real good too.

"Nigga, you better go before I do," another boy said.

"Yeah, I'll let that bitch suck my dick if you don't," another one of the boys called out. They all started laughing.

"Let me find out you're scared to let a bitch suck on ya little dick," they teased. They were ramping up the peer pressure. Ben was hesitant, but the taunts and jeers from his boys started getting to him.

"Nah, why the fuck I'ma be scared for? Ain't like I never had my dick sucked," Ben said, fronting hard. The boys started laughing again. Now they were jeering him even more.

"You ain't never had that baby dick of yours sucked yet," they taunted.

"Fuck this! C'mon bitch," Ben grumbled at Trisha. He was so mad at his boys now he was shaking. Trisha was excited about the possibility of getting a freebee. She needed it badly. She obediently followed Ben around the back of the building. His heart was beating fast and his palms were sweaty. Trisha noticed Ben's reluctance and decided she was going to try to run game on him.

"Give me the cap first," Trisha begged, she was pressing her luck. Trisha thought she was going to outsmart this young boy. Ben looked at her and took notice that she really looked horrible. He couldn't help but wonder where her kids were right now while their mother was at the back of a building begging to suck the dick of a fifteen-year-old boy for crack. Ben had to put the thought out of his mind. There was no way he was going to let the other dudes on the corner clown him if he gave Trisha some free crack and didn't let her suck him off.

"Nah, you gon' have to do it first," Ben told her, finally calming his nerves enough to speak.

Trisha smacked her lips and twisted her face up. Ben nervously fumbled with his zipper and got his dick out of his pants. The air hit it and it started to get hard. He didn't want to look down at Trisha's ugly, pock-marked faced and her thinning, unkempt hair. He was afraid his dick would wilt, so he closed his eyes. Trisha got on her knees and put her dirty hands around his dick. Ben jumped a little, but when she put his now rock-hard dick into her warm mouth he felt a tingling sensation all over his body. Trisha slid her rotten mouth up and down his dick hard and fast. Her slob was falling onto her hands and the ground.

Ben swallowed hard and imagined that she was a beautiful, sexy girl giving him head. He leaned back on the abandoned building and let her go to town on his dick. He could feel the cum welling up inside of him. Trisha started sucking on it harder.

"Take that shit like it's candy," Ben moaned. He was breathing hard and pumping into Trisha's mouth now. Ben opened his eyes and put his hand on the back of her head. He couldn't control himself. This was his first time ever feeling something so good. He started fucking her in the mouth as if it was a straight up pussy. Trisha moaned and gagged. Ben was now banging her face fast and furious.

"Arrghhh!" Ben sang out while he came. He wouldn't let Trisha's head go. She gagged more because he was shooting his cum forcefully into the back of her throat. His body shuddered. He had never felt anything like that in his life. He opened his eyes in disbelief. Trisha was trying to spit out his cum. She was wiping her mouth fiercely. What she hadn't swallowed had dripped onto her lips and chin.

"Give me the cap now," she pleaded. She was disgusted and pissed with Ben. Trisha had been giving head for years and never had she been manhandled like that. Ben dug into his pocket and took out two dimes. He dropped them into her waiting hand and she scurried away. He wiped off his dick and folded it back into his pants. He was trying to get his legs straight before he went back to the spot with the rest of the dudes. When he was satisfied he didn't look too whipped, he started walking back.

When Ben emerged from the back of the building all of the dudes were waiting on him. They rushed at him. "Yo, how was it?" one asked. Ben just nodded. He didn't want them to think he was feeling a crackhead bitch like Trisha.

"I hope you told that bitch to fucking kick rocks after she sucked you off," another dude said. Ben looked at him confused. "Yo! I think this nigga really gave that bitch a cap after she sucked his shit," the same dude announced. Ben stood in silence. Now they were making him feel like a fool all over again. He didn't speak to them. He just wore a dumb looking expression on his face.

"Yup! You did, didn't you?" another boy said and they all busted out laughing.

"You ain't supposed to ever give none of these fiends no free caps. I don't care if a bitch suck the skin off your dick!" one of the boys lectured Ben. "Shit, you better not let Deezo find out you gave that bitch a free cap," the same boy told Ben.

Ben was shaking now. The possibility of pissing Deezo off again weighed heavy on his mind for the remainder of the night. He replaced the money for the missing caps into what Quan was going to collect for Deezo. He wasn't going to ever give Deezo a reason to think he was trying to cross him again. Ben didn't plan on ever fucking up none of Deezo's money or drugs. There was one thing that Ben was learning, and that was that there were hard-learned rules to the drug game.

That same night Ben was put to yet another test. Before he left the block to go home, Deezo had asked him to stash drugs in his house. He had been reluctant at first, but Deezo had convinced him that it was the only way he could gain enough trust to move up to the next level.

The money lured Ben in.

He was making enough money now that he was able to stash some and buy clothes with the rest.

He had continued to hit Celeste off with a few dollars too, but he couldn't give her too much, because then she would figure out that it wasn't coming from a newspaper route.

"Yo Ben, I'm trying to move you up in this here game. But you gotta pass a couple of tests," Deezo told Ben as Deezo sat behind the wheel of his brand new Porsche Cayenne. Deezo had been changing cars more often now.

"Yeah wassup, Deezo?" Ben had asked eagerly.

"I need you to stash some bundles in ya crib for me," Deezo told him.

Ben's heartbeat immediately dropped when the words had finished leaving Deezo's mouth. That was the one thing he was afraid to do. Celeste had always warned him that if she ever found out that he was using or selling drugs she would beat his ass and then call the police on him herself. She had implicitly warned him against bringing any drugs anywhere near her house. But Ben wanted to be down so badly he'd do just about anything for Deezo. He also wanted to keep making money to feed and clothe himself.

"A'ight Deezo, I'm down. You know I'ma do what it takes to be a soldier . . . I'ma rider," Ben had replied enthusiastically.

Deezo starting laughing. He was clearly pleased. "You muthafuckin' right. Nigga, you been riding since I put your little ass on," Deezo replied. Then he reached his fist out and gave Ben a pound. Ben returned the gesture.

He felt good getting a compliment from Deezo, but Ben's mind was racing with how he was going to pull off stashing the drugs. The apartment he shared with his mother wasn't but so big and when Celeste got ready to search Ben's shit for money she would go through all his belongings with a fine-toothed comb. When Ben agreed to stash the drugs for Deezo he had stepped over an invisible boundary that his mother had put up. Still, Ben didn't go back on his word with Deezo.

That night, Ben slid into the house as quietly as he could. He was hoping his mother would be asleep or fucking—her favorite pastimes. As he tiptoed into the darkened apartment, he held onto his fat pockets, which were loaded down with five bundles of crack.

"Fuck you, Drake, you piece of shit!" Celeste's voice boomed.

Ben was startled. His mother's screams stopped him dead in his tracks. His heart starting racing like crazy.

"You ain't never got shit. No money, no time. Barely giving me any dick! What the fuck I need you for," Celeste continued her tirade.

Ben listened for a few minutes and was relieved that his mother was preoccupied with her usual argument with Drake. He knew that would give him a few minutes of free time to get the bundles hidden. He was breathing hard but he was concentrating. When he rushed through his bedroom door, he was caught a little off guard when he noticed that baby Keon was in his bed.

"What the fuck she put the baby in here for?"

Ben said under his breath. He looked over at his baby brother, who was surrounded by pillows on the bed just in case he rolled over. Ben shook his head. He kind of felt sorry for baby Keon because he had to be stuck inside the house with their crazy mother all day long.

Ben eased down onto his knees. He stopped and listened again. Celeste and Drake were still at it. "Good. These assholes just don't know how stupid they sound," Ben mumbled to himself. He pulled his nightstand drawer out of the base of the nightstand and set the heavy drawer down. He slipped the drugs in the slot where the drawer was supposed to be, and then he spread the packages out so that the drawer could fit back in the slot. He carefully fit the nightstand drawer back into its place. The drawer wouldn't close all the way, but it was good enough.

Ben figured at least if Celeste came searching while he was sleeping, he would be able to hear her since the nightstand was right next to his bed. Ben took his clothes off and moved some of the pillows. He sucked his teeth when he looked at his baby brother taking up most of the bed. He was scared to move Keon. He didn't want to risk waking him up and having to deal with him while Celeste dealt with Drake. Ben folded his body around his brother's and when he did, the baby nuzzled in closer to him. He hugged his baby brother back. As thugged out as Ben thought he was, this was the most affection he had had in a very long time. He started to think he could get close to baby Keon and maybe even love him.

Chapter 7

It was Ben's sixteenth birthday and he was surrounded by his new family—his street crew. Deezo raised a glass in preparation to make a toast.

"Y'all niggas pipe the fuck down! I got something to say!" Deezo screamed over his underlings' chatter. Everybody lowered their voice in response to the boss's command. He had that kind of power over his younger posse. They all turned to look at Deezo. "Let's make a toast to this little nigga, Big Ben, right here. This nigga graduated from delivery boy to weed spot to crack spot, now this nigga slanging that girl to those rich white muthafuckas," Deezo sang out, lifting his glass high over his head.

Ben was smiling from ear to ear. Deezo had summarized his story perfectly. Quan and a bunch of other dudes all made cheering sounds and took their drinks to the head. Ben couldn't wipe the smile from his face. He took a swig of the Hennessey Deezo had given him. Ben was feeling good. Deezo and his dudes had treated Ben better than his own mother, Celeste, had. He was feeling like shit was all gravy. He was sitting on top of the world. He was back making good money and since he had been stashing drugs in his crib on a regular for Deezo, he had made his way to the top of Deezo's "good guy" list.

When Deezo had first told Ben he wanted him to stash and bag heroin for him, Ben was a bit reluctant. Ben had become comfortable doing hand-to-hand on his corner. But Deezo had convinced him that standing out on the street for years wasn't the way to get to the top. It didn't take much convincing. Ben had been taking home Baggies filled with heroin for a month now. He would put the high-grade heroin into smaller Baggies, which Deezo referred to as nicks and dimes, and Ben would distribute packages to other dealers that got their weight from Deezo. It was a much better arrangement for Ben, because he was able to be home and spend more time with Keon.

Ben had grown closer to his baby brother, especially since Ben had started buying all of Keon's clothes, sneakers, and necessities. Ben regarded his mother and her baby father as a waste of sperm. He had stopped giving Celeste any money. He was tired of supporting her lazy ass. She just didn't want to get out there and find a job, and Ben wasn't a little kid anymore. The first time he had refused to give her any money out of his so-called "pay check," Celeste had gone nuts, screaming and trying to hit him. Ben had grabbed her wrists and pushed her back. It didn't take long for Celeste to realize her son was growing up and he wasn't about to let her take all or any of his money anymore. Celeste was on her own. Of course, she turned her sights to Drake for money, which was a lost cause. Ben was the man now and he was making more money than he could've ever dreamed of when he first started hustling for Deezo.

"Yo Ben, tell us about the first piece of pussy you got last year from that bitch down on Halsey," Deezo said, laughing. Deezo had noticed that Ben had zoned out. He didn't want the party to end just yet. He knew how to keep his little soldiers loyal to him. The little birthday party he was throwing Ben was just a part of Deezo's plan. "C'mon Big Ben, tell us about that tight ass pussy you got from that ho," Deezo said again, his words slurring.

Ben smiled, just thinking about it now. He had been a virgin before Deezo made an older woman give him some pussy. Ben was blushing as Deezo started telling the story. Everybody started laughing. They partied all night in celebration of Ben. He hadn't gone into the house until after five o'clock in the morning. Celeste didn't care. She had been too wrapped up in her own life chasing after Drake to even remember that it was Ben's birthday. He took note of his mother's blatant disregard for his birthday.

* * *

Two weeks after the party, Ben was doing his usual—stashing, bagging and selling weight for Deezo. Ben was in a routine. He had walked into the dark, quiet apartment. He listened closely when he first went into the apartment, but he didn't hear anybody screaming and cursing. He was relieved. He wasn't in the mood to hear Celeste and that bum ass nigga, Drake, argue. He went into his room and unloaded some of the new stuff he had purchased. He pulled out three different colored fitted caps, three pairs of high-end jeans, and then he walked over and added two new shoeboxes to his collection. His sneaker collection was off the chain now. He had three stacks of boxes that towered almost to the ceiling.

When he was done situating his new clothes and shoes, he took out the clothes and sneakers he had purchased for Keon. Ben smiled at how cute some of the miniature high-end items were. He took Keon's stuff out of the shopping bags and folded them up. The baby was asleep in Ben's bed, which told Ben that Drake was in his mother's bed. He had gotten kind of used to sleeping with the baby in his bed now.

Ben finished putting the stuff away. Then it was down to business for him. He pulled out the half-gallon–size Baggie that Deezo had given him that night. He examined the heroin inside. He couldn't really understand how something that looked like an off-white version of cooking flour could be so powerful and so expensive.

"Shit, I ain't complaining—that shit keeping my

pockets laced," Ben said to himself, giving the Baggie a squeeze. He pulled his nightstand drawer out and then laid everything he needed to bag up on top of the nightstand. He pulled the drawer out to keep from having any accidents on the floor. If he spilled any bit of the drugs it would fall into the drawer, which he would be able to clean up later. Ben spent his entire night bagging up. He was exhausted afterwards and all he wanted to do was go to sleep.

Ben pulled the rubber gloves that Deezo had given him off and dropped them into the emptied big Baggie that had previously contained the heroin. He balled the plastic items up and put them into his old newspaper bag. He would discard the empty plastic and gloves later, he told himself. He usually took the newspaper bag out with him whenever he left the apartment and threw the drug paraphernalia down into the sewer grates a block up from his house. Ben had a system and he followed it to the letter. He couldn't take a chance with Celeste finding any Baggies with residue sitting in them.

"Ben . . . Ben!" Celeste called out, shaking Ben's shoulder. He moaned and shrugged her off. "Ben! Get the fuck up!" Celeste hollered.

"Mmm," Ben moaned and waved her off.

"Look, getcha ass up! I gotta go down to welfare and you gotta stay here with Keon," Celeste told Ben.

Ben perked up when she said that. "Nah! I gotta

go to work," Ben grumbled, rubbing sleep out of his eyes.

"Well, too fucking bad. That job don't benefit me no more. I don't see a dime of ya money, so I gotta go to the welfare office and let them lecture my ass on getting a job," Celeste spat indignantly with her arms folded across her chest.

"C'mon man! I gotta go to work," Ben complained.

"Like I said . . . you gotta watch the baby while I go get humiliated by these fucking uppity ass white people. So here he go," Celeste growled, pushing baby Keon down onto Ben's chest.

"Dayum!" Ben belted out.

"Oh yeah, he just took a shit so change him," Celeste said with an evil chuckle. She sashayed out of Ben's room and out of the apartment. Ben put Keon down on the bed and sat up. "What the fuck I'm supposed to tell Deezo now?" he said to himself.

Baby Keon was laughing; he thought Ben was talking to him. "Don't laugh, lil nigga! I gotta sell these fucking packages or else Deezo gon' kill my ass and you gon' be left here with ya trifling ass mother and father." Ben spoke to the baby like Keon could understand him. Keon just smiled.

"Yo, to be a poor ass lil nigga you a happy baby," Ben said, slumping down on his bed, putting his head in his hand. He thought for a minute, then lifted up his head like a lightbulb had gone off inside. There was no way he was going to let Deezo down again, not after all Deezo had been doing for him lately. He snatched baby Keon off the bed.

"Your hater ass mother can't stop me from making my paper. I'ma just have to take you with me," he said to Keon.

Ben changed and dressed the baby as quickly as he could. Then he dressed himself. He grabbed his packages and threw them into Keon's baby bag, which worked out perfectly for Ben. When he got to his first sale, he got strange looks from some of the hustling dudes.

"What the fuck is this, daddy daycare and shit," a dude they called Beast joked with Ben.

"Yo, my moms be wilding out. She left my brother and just bounced on a nigga," Ben explained.

"It's all good . . . as long as daddy daycare keep supplying that straight white girl, I wouldn't give a fuck if the baby brought it here by himself," Beast said. Ben got a good laugh out of that one. He got the same type of comments at every one of his spots. Word traveled fast and before long, Ben saw Deezo waiting for him at the corner of his block.

"A' yo, Ben, let me holla at you," Deezo called out. Ben had a smile on his face as he bopped over to Deezo's ride.

"Wassup boss," Ben said all cheery.

"What the fuck is up?" Deezo barked, his facial expression serious.

Ben immediately wiped the smile off his face. "I . . . I . . . I had to babysit so I couldn't leave him so I just took him with me to drop off the weight," Ben stammered. He knew Deezo wasn't happy.

"Muthafucka, you must be smoking that shit you dropping off! You gon' take a fucking baby around with you? Don't you know that shit would bring attention to your dumb ass!" Deezo screamed at Ben.

Damn, I fucked up again. Ben hung his head in shame.

"Gimme my fucking money and get the fuck away from my fucking car!" Deezo belted out.

Baby Keon started crying from his stroller at the sound of Deezo's deep, booming baritone. Ben dug down into the baby bag and handed Deezo all the money. He waited by the car window a few minutes, waiting for Deezo to give him his cut of the money.

Deezo flipped through the stacks of bills. Then he gave Ben an evil look. "What the fuck is you waiting for? You ain't getting shit off this run. You better be lucky I don't fuck ya ass up for having that fucking baby out here," Deezo said.

Ben stood up straight, gathered himself and began pushing baby Keon towards home. As soon as he and Keon were almost at their building, Ben spotted Celeste. She had her arms folded and her face was curled into a monstrous snarl.

"Where the hell did you have my baby at?" Celeste erupted, her voice high-pitched and shrill. Ben ignored her, he was too angry to deal with this shit right now. "I asked you a fucking question, Benjamin," Celeste continued, calling Ben by his government name, which told him that she was really upset.

"I was fucking at work!" Ben screamed back.

Celeste hadn't expected his defiance so she was quiet for a second. "You didn't take my baby to no newspaper route!" she continued to scream. By now, some of their ghetto ass neighbors were watching their altercation. "You think I didn't see you talking to Deezo!" Celeste belted out, dropping a bomb on Ben.

His eyes widened and he started to feel hot with embarrassment. "So what?" he spat, getting on the defensive.

"So he is a fucking drug dealer and I told you ain't no child of mine selling no drugs . . . not living up in my house!" Celeste screamed.

"Just because I was talking to him now I'm a drug dealer . . . whatever," Ben replied. He pushed the stroller towards Celeste and turned his back on her.

"Don't you fucking walk away from me when I'm speaking to you!" Celeste screamed at Ben's back.

He ignored her ranting and headed in the opposite direction. He needed to get his thoughts together. He didn't know what he was going to do if Deezo completely cut him off.

Celeste stormed into the building. When she got into the apartment she couldn't help herself. She was very angry with Ben, but she was more worried that her sixteen-year-old son might be into hustling drugs. She went into Ben's room and began tearing it up. "You wanna play with me? I am not to be played with," she said to herself as she pulled out Ben's dresser drawers. She sifted through all of his stuff that fell onto the floor. She didn't find anything except a few sealed condoms.

Celeste continued her whirlwind destruction of

Ben's room. She emptied every last one of his sneaker boxes. She shook the sneakers out and tossed them onto the floor if they were empty. "This boy thinks his mother is a joke," she continued talking to herself.

She went to Ben's tiny closet and started pulling stuff off the hangers and top shelf. She still didn't find anything that suggested that Ben was selling drugs. "I know where to look!" she beamed, having an ah-ha moment. She rushed over to the bed and struggled with the heavy mattress as she turned it over.

"This bastard thinks I'm stupid! His ass probably ain't been to no fucking newspaper job," Celeste stated as she strained to get the mattress off the bed. When it finally fell over, Celeste was disappointed that she didn't find anything under it. She was on a mission. She continued to destroy Ben's room. She walked over to his nightstand and picked up his newspaper bag. She examined it. She peeked inside, but there was nothing inside the bag except an empty, balled up plastic Baggie. She balled the bag up and put it under her arm.

"How he go to work and his newspaper bag laying right here. I'ma keep this shit and let me see how long it take him to look for it," Celeste said to herself out loud. She had seen Ben leave every day with his bag, but not today. "Just because he took the baby wouldn't mean he wouldn't need his bag . . . he think he slick," Celeste continued.

She had made herself exhausted going through Ben's room and belongings. She hadn't found anything of substance that pointed to Ben selling or using drugs. "He better be lucky I ain't find no bullshit up in here," she said.

She took Ben's bag and hid it in the closet in her room. She wanted to see how long it was going to take before Ben asked or looked for it. Although she expected to find drugs, Celeste was really secretly relieved deep down inside that Ben might've been telling her the truth. She reminded herself that the next time she saw her no-good ex-boyfriend, Deezo, she would be sure to tell him to stay the fuck away from her son. Celeste and Deezo had history and she hated the very ground he walked on.

Chapter 8

It had taken a few days but Deezo finally started speaking to Ben again. When he calmed down, Deezo realized that taking a baby with him to do drops wasn't the worst thing Ben could've done. At least Ben was focused and determined enough to still go after the loot.

"Yo son, I'ma give your little ass this last chance. That baby shit was your second chance . . . one more strike and your ass is out," Deezo said, his tone grave and serious. He couldn't let Ben know that it was all good. Deezo would never admit he reacted too fast and harsh and made a mistake.

Ben immediately felt better. When he had taken the baby out with him, all Ben was trying to do was make sure he met his commitment to Deezo. "I'm sorry Deezo, I was just trying to make sure your paper got collected and the shit got out there," Ben explained apologetically.

Deezo nodded in agreement. "We back on track and shit. Instead of every couple of days, I need you to stash and bag and get that shit out every day now. These niggas won't let me rest over that good good," Deezo told Ben.

Ben was happy as hell inside, but he tried to play it cool.

"You got the potential of making some real good paper off this lick right here. You better getcha mind right and stay focused," Deezo said, playfully slapping Ben upside his head. Ben gave Deezo a half-hearted smile. "Go get a new package from Quan. I'm sure you hungrier than a muthfucka since you ain't made no loot in a few days."

Ben shook his head. He didn't have much to say. When he got out of Deezo's car, he felt like he would vomit. *How the fuck am I going to handle stashing and bagging every single day?* Ben thought to himself. He knew his mother was already growing more and more suspicious of his "work" since he was doing a lot more shopping. He was going to have to be very, very careful. He was caught up now. He felt like he was in the middle. If he got caught with drugs in the house his mother was going to call the police on him herself, as she had threatened more than fifty times. If he didn't agree to stash, bag and drop the heroin for Deezo, he knew he'd be considered a sucker and Deezo would stop letting him get money.

Ben was at a crossroads in his life and unfortunately, he had nobody to turn to for advice on which road to take. He did what he knew best, he took the road he thought was going to keep him fed and clothed. He met up with Quan and picked up another large package of heroin. This time the gallon-sized Baggie was almost full.

"Deezo said to bag these small nicks and dimes with only a few twenties here and there. Deezo is upping the price on this shit," Quan told Ben. Ben nodded his agreement but didn't say much more. "Deezo said you can possibly make fifteen stacks off this one bag alone, so you better not fuck nothing up," Quan warned Ben.

Fifteen stacks! Ben screamed inside of his head. That was more money than he had ever dreamed of making in his short life. He grew excited. He was sure nothing would go wrong. He stuck the bag down into the front of his pants and gave Quan a pound.

"Tomorrow, have that shit bagged and ready to go," Quan continued. "Deezo ain't gon' care if you gotta sit up all night and bag that shit up. Just have it ready. Remember that is raw, uncut shit, straight from Asia, and it ain't no fucking joke."

Ben left and went straight home. It was time to start the stash and bag process all over again. He could only hope that things go smoothly. He wanted to please both his mother and Deezo, but they were polar opposites. Speed walking on his way home, Ben was kind of proud that Deezo didn't really trust any of his other younger workers to handle such a large amount of weight. He knew that Quan was Deezo's right hand man, but Quan had moved too far up to be stashing, bagging and dropping weight off. He smiled a little bit when he thought about his new role. He was officially Deezo's heroin boy.

Chapter 9

Present Day

"Let's go!" one of the detectives' voice boomed from behind Ben. The deep, base-filled sound snapped Ben out of his daydream. He had been reflecting on how this entire nightmare had gotten started. He shook his head left to right, trying to get the memories to go away.

"I need to put my clothes and shoes on," he complained to the detective.

Ben was trying to buy some time. He needed to get into his bedroom and grab all of the money he had stashed away. He had heard one of the cops say something about a search warrant and Ben knew if he didn't grab the money he'd been stashing away, those cops would get it and act like they had never seen it before.

"Hurry up and get your clothes on fast! We need to get out of here," the detective instructed.

"Why I gotta go with y'all anyway?" Ben nervously protested.

There was no way he could leave his building with detectives and let Quan and the rest of the corner boys see him. Ben knew the word in the hood traveled fast and that him being seen with cops would get out to Deezo faster than the speed of light.

"Look, don't ask any more questions. Get your clothes on before I make you go like that," the detective answered, irritated.

Ben rushed into his room. The detective stood by the door while Ben got dressed. Ben was able to secretly get all of his money before the detective noticed.

"We didn't do shit! How could y'all treat a grieving mother like this?" Celeste cried as they prepared to escort her out of her apartment.

"Look, if both of you wanna get froggy we can slap these cuffs on you for our own security. It doesn't have to be an arrest for us to do that, you know. Right now, we just wanna talk to you both down at the station . . . just questioning," one of the detectives said deceitfully.

Ben rushed back into the living room. He had put on a pair of jeans and a new pair of kicks; his money had been split between each shoe, and his jeans pocket.

"Hmm, those jeans look pretty expensive for a

boy whose mother is on welfare," the same lead detective commented.

Ben squinted his eyes. He didn't have any respect for cops. *Shut the fuck up, you hater*, he thought to himself. Like most boys in his neighborhood and all over Brooklyn, he had been taught to despise and never trust cops. It had been drilled in his head that all cops were crooked, even if they were members of your immediate family. Ben believed it too. He had witnessed many of his friends get stopped and frisked on the streets for absolutely nothing. Even if they were drug dealers, in his eyes, the cops had no reason to constantly harass his buddies. Now they were harassing him and his mother, which only made his feelings toward them worse.

"Like I said before, let's get the fuck out of here. You two can either go the nice way or the hard way," the other detective chimed in.

With tears soaking her face, Celeste followed the first detective out of the apartment. She didn't have any energy to fight them. She kept thinking about her dead baby, Keon, and she didn't have anything to hide.

Ben stood stoic, ice grilling the cop like he was a tough guy. The second detective pushed his trench coat aside and showed Ben his gun. The detective rested his hand on the top of the gun and looked at Ben with an evil glare.

"It don't matter . . . if you don't kill me, somebody else will anyway," Ben said gravely in response to seeing the gun.

"Just c'mon, Ben. I can't stand to lose another child, my only child left," Celeste pleaded, noticing Ben's defiance. His mother's words spurned Ben into action. He stepped out of his apartment and the detective was right behind him.

When they got outside, Celeste noticed that the word about Keon's death had already spread throughout the neighborhood. There was a makeshift shrine of balloons, teddy bears, and candles set up outside of her building with little signs saying *Rest In Peace.* That made Celeste break down even more.

"Oh God! My baby is gone!" Celeste cried out. She doubled over like she was in pain, the fresh cut of her grief rushing back. Her sedatives had fully worn off. The detectives helped her up, by placing their hands on her and helping her to the car.

Ben followed them with his head down. He didn't want to look up or look around. He was too scared that he would see some of Deezo's boys or worse, Deezo himself. There was a small crowd gathered outside. Once Celeste was in the car, one of the detectives grabbed Ben and put him in next. Although Celeste and Ben weren't in handcuffs, the way the detectives placed them in the police car, it looked to everybody in the neighborhood like Celeste and Ben had been arrested. Hushed murmurs of speculation wafted through the growing crowd. People started whispering things like, I think she killed her baby, and maybe the other son killed the baby and she allowed it. The entire incident was like a major tragedy in the eyes of their neighbors. First, her baby died, and now, Celeste and her older son were getting arrested. The rumors were flying for sure.

Ben could feel the eyes of his ghetto neighbors on him. He felt as if he was in a big fish bowl on display for everyone to see.

"Ben, what happened? Did you have something you wasn't supposed to have?" Celeste leaned over and whispered to him in the back of the police car. Ben shook his head in the negative, while he watched the backs of the detectives' heads. After he thought back on his start in the drug game and recounted all the warnings and close calls he'd had with Deezo, he realized this would be his third strike with Deezo. Something Deezo had already warned him about.

Ben had already made it up in his mind he wasn't confessing to having the drugs in the house. He figured if he just denied it and his mother denied it he would get away with it. He was sure the police wouldn't find any drugs inside the house. He was sure he'd been careful to get rid of all the drugs and everything associated with it every day when he was done bagging. He had cleaned tirelessly with all types of cleaning agents after Keon had spilled the heroin. There was no doubt in Ben's mind that all of the drugs were cleaned up and there was not even any residue on his floor or in his nightstand drawer. Ben was confident and he wasn't budging on his story. He was going to stick to his denial.

"I cannot believe this. I can't even grieve for my son," Celeste cried, putting her face into her hands as they started pulling down the block. It seemed as if the entire neighborhood was out watching now.

Ben looked out the window as the cop car drove slowly down his block. When the car got to the corner, Ben could see Quan and all of the corner boys glaring at him. Quan put on a screw face and did some hand signals that were meant to send Ben a serious message. It was ghetto sign language telling Ben that he better not fucking snitch on them. He swallowed hard and turned his eyes away.

Quan noticed that Ben didn't even want to have eye contact with him. Ben's apparent disregard immediately made Quan angry. Ben didn't realize that not acknowledging Quan with at least a head nod was the worst thing he could've done. Anytime corner boys or hustlers like Quan and Deezo saw one of their workers get bagged by the cops, they automatically erred on the side of caution that the person was going to snitch. That meant their block was going to be hot and shit was going to have to be shut down for a minute so they could gauge the fallout from the cops. To make matters worse, Ben didn't have Deezo's drugs or money and no way to explain to him what happened. That meant that all the people that bought weight from Deezo was going to be dry for a minute while Deezo got more from his connect.

For a hustler, something like that could spell disaster. The drug game was a heavy supply and demand type of business. If a dealer like Deezo couldn't supply for even one day, he could lose his demand to the next hustler. Deezo's money was going to be funny for a minute, all because Ben had been careless. All of these thoughts ran through Ben's mind, while his mother sat crying next to him in the back of the cop car and his baby brother lay dead in the morgue. He felt like disappearing. He wished he could disappear. At that moment, he felt like he would've probably been better off dead too.

At the precinct, the detectives separated Celeste and Ben into different rooms. They weren't going to question Ben initially, because he wasn't old enough to give consent and his mother couldn't sit in on his interview because she was also a suspect.

Celeste was in an interrogation room with her head on the table when the two detectives came back in. She lifted her head in response to them opening the door. Her head was booming with a massive headache, a testament to how much she had been crying.

"Ms. Early, we realize your baby is dead, but we need to find out how he got such a high concentration of heroin in his system," the lead detective said, acting as if he wanted to be nice to Celeste. She had heard about these types of tactics before. It wasn't going to work on her.

"I don't know! I don't use drugs! I don't allow my son to bring drugs or use drugs in my house and my baby's father is not on drugs," Celeste pleaded her case.

"Ms. Early, somebody in that house had heroin in the house. The baby didn't go outside and get drugs on his own. He ingested the heroin through his mouth according to the medical examiner's report," the other detective said, his tone cold and kind of cruel. His words made Celeste cry even harder.

"I'm telling you, I really do not know. I don't know what happened," Celeste cried out. She put her hands into her hair and began pulling it. She felt like she would go insane.

"OK. Well, if you don't want to tell us, I guess we're going to assume you're guilty," the second detective began. He was the mean detective or bad cop to the lead detective's good cop. "We are sending someone to the midnight magistrate for an emergency search warrant for your apartment. I guarantee you will be arrested within a few hours. We don't have mercy for baby killers, so I will work all night until I get what I want. You'll be attending your son's funeral in leg irons." The detective had a genuine disdain for Celeste. His face was curled into a frown to display his disgust for the grieving mom. A mom he thought was just faking grief.

Celeste continued to cry. The detective sucked his teeth at her, turned swiftly and stomped out of the room. "I didn't do anything!" Celeste screeched as he let the door slam.

The lead detective, the good cop, looked at Celeste with a little bit of sympathy. "Ms. Early, we want to speak to your son, Ben," the detective stated. "Maybe he can tell us something that he was too afraid to say in front of you. Will you give us consent to talk to him alone since he is a minor? It's worth a shot if he can tell us what happened without feeling the pressure of your presence." The detective was laying his game down thick.

Celeste shook her head yes and scribbled her signature on a consent form that the detective had slid in front of her. She didn't know that they weren't supposed to be speaking to Ben without the presence of a parent or an attorney because of his age. Her mind was too muddled to even realize anything. She just wanted to get out of there so she could go about making funeral plans for Keon. She pushed the paper back towards the detective.

The detective was happy he had been able to deceive Celeste.

"When can I go home?" Celeste asked. "I already told y'all everything I know. I will say it again. I was arguing with my baby father, he hit me, next thing the baby was screaming, I ran and found him having a seizure," she recounted the moment robotically.

"We've heard you, but some stuff just doesn't add up. We have to hold you here until we can figure out the one plus one of this whole thing," the detective replied. With that, he was gone. The door to the interrogation room slammed and Celeste was alone again. Once again, she put her head back down on the table, distraught. She was overcome with another wave of racking sobs and sadness. She was wondering what she did to deserve all of this.

Ben sat in an open room with a double-sided mirror. Because of the mirror and the missing door, the room couldn't be considered an official interrogation room. They weren't able to keep minors in totally sealed interrogation rooms. Due to his nervousness, Ben was battling a bad case of the bubble guts.

The detectives walked in the room and Ben jumped. They looked like they were ready to do the good cop, bad cop routine Ben had learned about from movies. They sat on either side of him. One detective sat on the edge of the table to Ben's right and the other detective pulled up a chair and sat very close to him on the left. He felt surrounded and he was, literally surrounded.

"Ben, we spoke to your mother," one of them started. Ben looked at him, expressionless. "And she seems to believe you might know how your baby brother got those drugs in his system," the detective lied, staring Ben dead in his eyes.

Ben just stared. Deezo had warned Ben against these types of tactics that cops used, when they lied and told one suspect the other had already told on him. Ben wasn't falling for that one.

"C'mon Ben, if you don't start talking you're going to juvie hall and your mother is going to Riker's Island," the detective continued.

Ben figured the detective that chose to threaten him with jail was playing the bad cop. The bad cop usually started the conversation and made the threats. Plus, he was usually the best of the two liars.

"Look Ben, we know people make mistakes all the time. This mistake cost your brother his life," the other cop, the supposedly good cop weighed in. "He was a baby, he didn't deserve to die like that. We know you didn't mean for it to happen. We can help you . . . all you gotta do is tell us if the drugs were yours or your mother's."

"There was no drugs in our house," Ben said robotically. He was too smart for their tricks. Both detectives bit down into their jaws. It would've been easier for them if either Ben or Celeste had confessed. Now the detectives would have to do a lot of work, which meant less time with their families. Something else they weren't happy about.

"Well, this is how your brother ended up!" the bad detective boomed. The detective placed a photograph of Keon's autopsy on the table in front of Ben. The detective was pissed off at Ben and he wasn't going to hold back any punches.

Ben almost threw up seeing Keon's chest cut wide open and blood everywhere. It looked like something out of a horror movie to Ben. He wanted to cry, but the tears wouldn't come. He was too angry. He was too much of a man. He kept holding out hope that this would all blow over after the cops realized there were no drugs in their house. At least, there was none now.

"You still don't want to tell us what happened in that house?" the mean detective grumbled.

"I don't fucking know!" Ben screamed, banging his fists on the table.

"Listen you little black bastard!" the bad detective snapped. "A fucking baby is dead . . . he is your fucking brother and you won't budge! I'm going to make sure you get locked up and your mother too. You ghetto fucks don't even care about a dead baby!" The detective gritted, grabbing Ben by the collar and putting his face close to his. Ben could smell the stale coffee and cigarettes on the detective's breath. He closed his eyes and he immediately saw Deezo's face. Even if he wanted to tell the detectives the truth, just thinking of his third strike with Deezo was enough to deter him from it.

Ben just kept his mouth shut until the two detectives became so disgusted they finally gave up. He thought his tactic was working. He put his head down on his folded arms. Ben was just waiting for the cavalry to come and release him and his mother.

The detectives were able to get enough probable cause for an emergency search warrant based on the fact that Ben, Celeste and Drake had been the only people in the house when baby Keon overdosed on heroin. The detectives gathered their squad and a few uniformed police and went in and executed the search warrant. They tore Celeste's apartment up. They went through both Ben's and Celeste's bedrooms with needle-in-a-haystack precision. They dumped out her dresser drawers, flipped her mattress, pulled things down in her closet, searched through her toiletries and even dumped out her powders and lotions. The detectives were determined to find something.

"Ay, I think I got something in here," one of the search team officers called out. About five other cops raced to Celeste's room. "It was down in the bottom of her closet," the cop who found the item told them. The lead detective on the case snatched the cloth newspaper bag from the cop who had found it. The detective used a gloved hand and reached down into the nearly empty bag. He pulled out a crumpled up, gallon sized plastic Baggie. He unfolded it and noticed a pair of latex gloves inside.

"What the fuck is this," he whispered to himself, noticing the Baggie had a white dusty residue inside. "Hey! Somebody get me a dye kit stat!" the detective hollered to the other cops, who were still ransacking the apartment for evidence.

One of the cops came with the dye kit that police departments used in the field to test substances that needed verification as to whether or not they were a narcotic. The detective carefully opened the Baggie and used a Q-tip to swab off a little bit of the white residue from the bag. He squeezed three drops of a substance from the dye kit onto the Q-tip. The end of the Q-tip lit up like a light bulb. The cotton tip immediately turned violet in color. The detective looked at the color chart for different drugs.

"Fucking bingo! We got her! We fucking got her!" the detective screamed out excitedly. Some of the other cops and detectives came rushing into

Celeste's bedroom to see what all the excitement was about. The detective was holding up the Baggie and the Q-tip like he had just won a gold medal at the Olympics.

"This bitch had a Baggie with heroin residue right in her closet inside of an old newspaper delivery bag!" the detective told the other cops and detectives who had rushed to the scene. "She let her baby ingest heroin and die. I have no sympathy for a piece of shit mother like her. She is going under the jail."

They all started mumbling and grumbling about Celeste. They were all seething mad. They all wanted to see Celeste go down for killing her baby.

Chapter 10

Celeste had been inside of the interrogation room at the precinct for hours. She had dozed in and out of sleep so many times she didn't even realize that an entire day had passed. Every time she closed her eyes for longer than a few minutes, she saw Keon's face and she could even hear him crying and trying to talk. She winced at the thought. Her back ached from sitting on the hard chair. She had walked around the room, sat down, laid on the table and stretched out on the floor all in attempts to get comfortable. A uniformed cop finally came into the room and Celeste stood up, her eyes stretched wide.

"Why are y'all holding me here? I should be free to go. I have to plan my son's funeral! I lost my baby and y'all treating me as if I'm a criminal. This is ridiculous," Celeste rambled, flailing her arms in protest.

Suddenly, Celeste noticed the two detectives that had taken her from her home step from behind the uniformed officer. Her eyes grew wide. She looked from the detectives to the uniformed cop and back again. "What is going on?" she asked, her voice edging on frantic.

"Ms. Early, you are under arrest for the death of your baby. You will be charged formally at your arraignment," the detective who played bad cop started. "Cuff her and take her for processing," the detective told the uniformed officer.

"Wait! What are y'all talking about? What are y'all trying to do to me?" Celeste screamed at the top of her lungs as the uniformed officer laid hands on her and started manhandling her to put the handcuffs on her. "Help me!" she cried. Celeste was moving around and making it hard for the cop to get the cuffs on her.

"You have the right to remain silent, anything you say can and will be used against you . . ." the detective continued, unfazed by Celeste's screams and cries.

"Where is my other son? I wanna see my son! I need a lawyer!" Celeste hollered as she continued to fight against the handcuffs. She was dragged kicking and screaming to a cell inside the precinct's detective squad room.

"When you get to central booking, you will see a judge for arraignment and then you will be given a public defender if you can't afford a lawyer," the uniformed cop told Celeste. Celeste couldn't stop screaming and crying. It was as if she was living in the nightmare from hell.

* * *

Ben was asleep on the hard table in the same room with the double-sided mirror. He was startled awake by the door opening.

"Let's go, boy," the bad detective demanded.

Ben rubbed the sleep from his eyes and stretched his arms out in front of him. "I can go home?" Ben asked.

"Nope. You're on your way to a group home. You are officially without a guardian," the smart mouth detective said snidely.

"What?" Ben asked, his voice low. He was afraid of what the answer was going to be.

"Well, you can't go back home alone. You're not old enough to be on your own. Your mother has been arrested and formally charged with the death of your baby brother," the detective informed Ben.

"She didn't kill nobody! She loved him!!" Ben cried out, jumping up like he wanted to fight the detective. His heart was beating unbelievably fast. He felt like he'd have a heart attack. A hot feeling of shame came over him. This is all my fault. I should've just told the truth. This is all my fault. The thoughts cried inside of his head.

"Sit the fuck down, boy!" the detective snapped back. "Your mother lied to you and everybody else. She had drugs in the house and we found them!" The detective thought he was dropping a bomb on Ben.

Ben tried to swallow the tennis-ball–sized lump of fear that had formed in the back of his throat. He started scanning his mind. He knew he had thrown out all of the evidence anytime he had stashed and bagged heroin in the house. He couldn't think. His mind was racing. He started sweating and his stomach began cramping again. Ben knew his mother was innocent, but if he confessed that the drugs were his, he knew the cops would be asking him who supplied him with the drugs. Ben couldn't afford to snitch on Deezo or Quan. He would surely be dead if he did.

Ben thought hard about confessing and then asking the cops to put him in the witness protection program he had seen on TV shows. He quickly dismissed that idea. He didn't trust the police at all. Messing with the cops, he knew Celeste would be losing another child.

"Where y'all taking me?" Ben asked one of the detectives.

"To the group home in East New York," the detective told him.

Ben felt slightly relieved he wasn't going to be in Brownsville in his own neighborhood. But the relief he felt was short-lived. He started thinking about some things Deezo had once told him during one of their conversations.

"I got peeps everywhere . . . all over Brooklyn. I know so many people, I'm like the mayor of the city, so if you ever think about crossing me and getting away with it, your ass better leave Brooklyn. Nah, better yet, you better leave New York all together," Deezo had said to Ben.

He felt he wouldn't be able to stay anywhere without somebody knowing Deezo. A fact that made Ben very uneasy.

He was dropped off and signed in at the Cleveland Street Home for Boys. Ben didn't plan on staying at the group home. He had cash on him and he planned on running far away from the group home as soon as the cops left.

He was signed in by a black female counselor who introduced herself as Ms. Tori. She was a nice looking lady with wide hips and a nice ass. Ben followed her on a short tour of the facility, but he wasn't really interested since he didn't plan on staying there.

"These are the dorms," Ms. Tori explained. "You will be in what we call the new entrant dorms. This is where you will stay until we can process you and see which other room would suit you best. If you behave well you will move out of this dorm quickly. If you don't you might stay a very long time and never have a semi-private room."

She led him inside of a large room with five sets of bunk beds and about eight other boys sitting around in various stages of recreation. Some were playing handheld game systems, some were listening to iPods and some were just sitting around looking miserable.

Ben put on his best mean mug on his face to send a message to the other boys that he was not to be fucked with. He sat down on the bed he had been assigned. He didn't have shit to unpack so Ben just sat down and looked around.

"Whatcha looking at, nigga?" a short, fat boy immediately barked at Ben.

Here we go. I knew somebody would start something, Ben thought to himself as he looked at the stupid boy. He didn't answer the boy or even acknowledge him. He wasn't there for that.

"Ohhh, he ignored your ass, Pudge," one of the other boys instigated.

The fat boy walked over to Ben and got in his face. "You new here and I don't like you," the boy they called Pudge gritted at Ben.

Ben stood up and faced Pudge nose-to-nose. He thought about what Ms. Tori had said about behavior and the possibility of getting a semi-private room, then he thought about the fact that he planned on running away from the home anyway. *This nigga don't know me*, Ben thought to himself.

"What pussy? Whatcha gon' do?" Pudge taunted some more.

Ben just hauled off and punched the so-called menace in the nose. Nobody saw it coming because Ben was quiet and calm.

"Ohhhh shit!" the crowd of boys sang out.

Pudge fell back, holding his nose. Nobody had been brave enough to stand up to the three-hundred-pound bully before Ben got there. The sounds coming from the new entrant room reverberated down the home's hallways. Three counselors, including Ms. Tori, rushed into the room and grabbed Ben.

"There is no fighting in this facility. I guess you won't be moving from this room anytime soon, Mr. Early!" Ms. Tori screamed at Ben.

"Get the fuck off me!" Ben growled at her. His adrenaline was pumping and he was ready for whoever was next.

Ben was given a citation on his first night in the home. That meant the next day he wasn't able to leave for any recreational activities when the other boys left. That suited Ben just fine. He just wanted to be left alone. He figured as soon as they stopped monitoring his every step, he would make his great escape.

Chapter 11

Celeste was arraigned and formally charged with possession of an illicit controlled substance with the intent to distribute, because of the pure concentration of the heroin residue in the Baggie. She was also charged with child endangerment and involuntary manslaughter for Keon's death. She was assigned a public defender that hardly even spoke to her. He looked young and inexperienced. One look at him, and Celeste lost all hope of getting out of jail.

Drake had to plan Keon's funeral by himself. He had not visited Celeste and whenever she used her collect calls to call him, he would not accept the charges. It was driving Celeste crazy that he wouldn't speak to her. In her mind, Drake was there the night Keon overdosed, so she couldn't understand why he would be blaming her for their baby's death.

Celeste wasn't even told about Keon's funeral arrangement. Her lawyer had to call almost all of the funeral homes in Brooklyn to find out when and where the funeral was going to be held. Her lawyer had petitioned the court to allow her to attend Keon s funeral. The judge reluctantly agreed.

Celeste was led into the funeral parlor in leg shackles and she had three armed escorts. When she walked in and saw her baby's tiny body in the casket, she broke down all over again. The reality of the situation had really settled in now and Celeste let it all hang out. She screamed and hollered for her baby.

Ben was also escorted to the funeral. He was allowed to sit next to his mother in the front row, directly in front of Keon's tiny white and gold casket. He was burdened down with guilt when he saw his mother surrounded by three armed officers like she was a mass murderer. It was especially hurtful for Ben because he knew Celeste was locked up for a crime she didn't commit.

His eyes had black bags under them because he had not slept well. Celeste gave a small smile when she looked up and saw Ben. He hugged his mother around her shoulders tightly and rocked a bit while he held on like he never wanted to let go. He had tried to keep his eyes on Celeste's face or on Keon, because it was breaking his heart to see his mother all shackled up like that.

"Ben . . . I don't know what is going on," she cried as he held onto her so tight he threatened to choke off her air passage. Her armed escorts moved in to break up their moment of affection. Celeste would only be allowed a few seconds of physical contact. Ben sat down next to her. He couldn't even say anything to his mother.

"I go back to court in three weeks. The lawyer is trying to get me to plead guilty for a shorter sentence," Celeste managed to say between racking sobs. "Ben, I didn't have any drugs in the house . . . you gotta believe me. I don't even know what they're talking about that they found a bag with drug residue in it."

Ben hadn't heard about the bag with residue in it. A cold chill shot down his back when his mother spoke the words. His heart started hammering against his chest bone. He remembered now that the very last time he had used his newspaper delivery bag to hide his Baggie after bagging up, he hadn't thrown it away. He had left the house with the baby instead. It was so long ago, Ben had forgotten all about it. Ben didn't even realize his mother had his newspaper bag, because he had started using Keon's baby bag to transport the heroin to his drops. With this new bombshell dropped on him, he had a hard decision to make. It was either confess and send the cops Deezo's way or let his innocent mother sit in jail for something he knew damn well she didn't do.

* * *

Baby Keon's funeral had gotten packed with people from the neighborhood. Some of Celeste's family came, but there was way more of Drake's family there. Drake's family members shot daggers at Celeste with their eyes. They had all read the newspapers and the pieced together story that the media was putting out about how Keon had gotten the drugs.

Ben had sat on the front pew with his mother the entire time, so he had not seen when Quan, Deezo and some of the other boys he had hustled with walked into the funeral parlor. But they all saw him.

The services for babies are always much sadder and more somber than for adults. The funeral director kept referring to Keon as "God's angel," which made Celeste feel even worse. She screamed and cried through practically the entire service. When it was over, she was escorted out of the funeral home.

Ben walked slowly next to his mother. There were so many people he couldn't look at every face. Instead, he just kept scanning the crowd. As he let his eyes roam, he almost fainted. He had noticed a few of the corner boys he knew and then he had locked eyes with Quan and Deezo. He felt like running out of the place. His palms became sweaty and he felt like he would take a shit in his pants. He could hardly walk once he saw them.

Deezo gave Ben the serious ice grill. Ben

averted his eyes away from Deezo's gaze. He knew that with the armed guards there and with the police and media outside, Deezo probably wouldn't call attention to himself and go after Ben. Not there anyway. If Ben had previously had any doubts about whether or not Deezo was looking for him, those doubts were put to rest. Deezo was definitely after him.

Ben walked slowly by Deezo, feeling the heat of Deezo's gaze on him.

"I'm gonna see you, Shorty," Deezo called out to Ben as he passed the row of seats Deezo and the crew sat in. Celeste whipped her head around, but she couldn't tell where the words had come from. There were just too many people.

Ben held his head down and didn't respond. He didn't know why he was acting so guilty. He told himself that he should have just told Deezo the truth about his mistake and dealt with the consequences. It's not like Ben had stolen the drugs or sold them for his own personal gain. Now Deezo was under the impression that Ben had crossed him with the drugs and to make matters worse, Deezo thought Ben had been talking to the cops to get around dealing with Deezo's consequences. Ben was in a lose/lose situation right now.

Outside, Ben gave his mother a final hug. He didn't know when or if he would see her again.

"Ben, you gotta help me find out what happened in the house. I gotta get out of here," Celeste pleaded, looking her son directly in the eyes. Ben could swear that his mother could read the guilt in his eyes. He lowered his eyes to the ground and walked away with Ms. Tori, who had accompanied him to the funeral.

Celeste wasn't allowed to go to the cemetery for Keon's burial after the funeral ended. She cried for the entire ride back to Riker's Island. Ben had told Ms. Tori he didn't feel up to going to the cemetery as well. He was driven back to the group home. A few times during the ride, he peered out of the back window of the car while they drove back. He was paranoid, but he also knew without even looking out the window that he was being followed.

Quan and Deezo had paid five of the group homeboys and gave them specific instructions on how they wanted things handled. The boys were so happy to get some money that the home counselors didn't know about; they probably would've done anything for it.

When Ben returned from the funeral, he just wanted to get in his bunk and go to sleep. He was mentally and physically exhausted. He signed in and went to his dorm. He sat down on his bed and pulled out the program from baby Keon's funeral service. He shook his head as he looked at the tiny bit of information about his brother. Ben stared at the picture of his chubby faced baby brother that was on the front of the program. He felt a stabbing pain in his heart. He put his head in his hands and for the first time since everything happened, he let himself cry for his brother's lost life. Ben realized that Keon was dead because he had been so selfish and desperate for material things. He had been a sucker for candy like Deezo had warned him against. And like so many suckers for candy before him, he had lost his entire family chasing behind the hood's deadly candy.

Ben held his head down for a while and let the silent tears run into his hands. He could hear the sound of footsteps moving towards him. But he didn't bother to look up. He just figured it was some of his bunkmates coming back from their daily activities. He didn't want to see any of them or deal with their bullshit. As he kept his head in his hands, he noticed that the sound seemed like it was a lot of footsteps, not just one set like he initially thought. He removed his hands from his face and went to lift his head up. Just as he did, BANG!

He felt a sudden explosion inside his head. He had been punched in the top of his head. Dazed, he went to put his hands up in defense, but he didn't have time to react before another closed fisted blow landed in the center of his face. He was seeing stars now. He tried to blink away the pain and confusion, but it was to no avail. Ben tried to lift his arms up to cover himself at least. He couldn't even do that. His arms were being held down on either side of him and so were his legs. He was rendered powerless. There were too many attackers for him to fight off. BANG! More closed fisted blows attacked his body.

Ben felt a sharp pain permeate his stomach, then his chest. He was dragged onto the hard tile floor now and his head landed with a thud.

"Kick him." Ben heard somebody whisper faintly. Then he felt a severe pain in his rib cage. His mouth popped open to scream, but nothing came out. He couldn't scream, somebody had stuffed a balled up pair of socks into his mouth. Ben bit down into the fuzzy cotton of the socks.

He was trying to move, to fight. His efforts were futile against all of the hands holding him down. He opened his battered eyes, just in time to see the front of a construction Timberland boot coming straight for his head. BAM! The boot came crashing down on Ben's skull. His head banged into the tile on the floor. He felt as if his brain would explode.

They punched him at will and kicked him with more force each time. He was beaten, kicked and stomped by his unknown assailants repeatedly. His face was bloody all over, and his body was on fire with pain.

"Deezo said you better stop talking to the cops," one of Ben's assailants growled in his ear.

Ben laid limp and moaning in the fetal position. He couldn't get up even if he wanted to. The posse of attackers finally let his arms and legs go, but Ben was too weak and injured to fight back.

"Yeah, you can't snitch on Deezo and get away with it," another of the assailants said.

"Deezo wants his shit or his money back. If you don't come up with it, you a dead nigga," another boy gritted, as he lifted his foot and stomped Ben in the head one more time. That was it. Ben's already injured skull could not withstand another blow like that. His world suddenly went black.

"That nigga look dead," one of the attackers whispered.

"Let's get the fuck outta here," they all agreed.

The group home residents Deezo had paid carried out their deed as instructed. They unlocked the room door and furtively scattered.

Ben laid unconscious and bloody on the floor for almost two hours before Ms. Tori came to check on him. "Help! Somebody call 911!" she screamed at the top of her lungs.

Chapter 12

Brooklyn, New York
August 2010

Celeste sat next to her public defender in court, rocking her legs back and forth. She turned around nervously in her seat and looked out at all the people, including the media, that had showed up for her trial. She had heard herself referred to as the drug-murdering mother and she had read headlines about herself that read, *Mother Feeds Baby Heroin to Shut Him Up.*

She had learned to ignore the lies that the media put out. It had gotten so bad she had to be housed in the protective custody cellblock at the Rose M. Singer Center on Riker's Island. Primarily, because the women in the general population had threatened her life so many times. In female prisons or lock-ups, crimes against children were the worst. Many of the women in general population, who were away from their own children, despised and sometimes tried to kill inmates that were in jail for abusing or killing their kids.

Celeste kept looking out into the crowd, until the court officer finally stood up in front of the courtroom and announced the judge. She stood when she was instructed to stand. She bunched her toes up inside her shoes nervously. She didn't know what to expect from the trial and she was starting to regret even taking her case to trial.

She had seen Drake in the courtroom, but his presence had not made her feel better. He had completely turned on her. He had bought into all of the media accusations against Celeste and he believed she had the drugs in the house that caused Keon to overdose. The judge's voice broke up her thoughts.

"We will hear from the prosecutor first in this case. Counselor, you may begin," the judge announced to the assistant district attorney on the case. Celeste sat upright in her seat when the prosecutor stood up to start his opening arguments.

"Ladies and gentlemen of the jury, I am here today to prove to you that the defendant, who is sitting in this courtroom, who tried to call herself a mother," the prosecutor began, "let her two-year-old son get hold of her illicit heroin stash and overdose. That poor baby was probably so hungry he thought his mother's drugs were food. I will take you on a journey into the defendant's life and show you the conditions this poor baby had to live under. I will also show you evidence found in the home that proves the defendant had heroin in her possession that was so pure, it could have killed all twelve of you with just a very small amount," the prosecutor announced loudly.

The prosecutor hesitated long enough for the jury to take in his comments, and then he walked over and picked up a plastic, sealed evidence bag. He held it up, and then continued his oration. "I will show you State's exhibit number one A, the Baggie that the defendant kept her pure, uncut heroin in, which she carelessly tried to hide in her teenage son's mail delivery bag while her baby lay dying in the hospital. His little body convulsing from ingesting so much drugs."

Celeste's eyes popped open when she saw the bag and when the prosecutor said where it came from. She started rocking her legs back and forth even faster now. She leaned into her public defender. She started to tell him that she had found those bags in Ben's room and that the bags must have belonged to her son. Now it all made sense to Celeste. Ben had been bringing drugs into her home.

Celeste's attorney turned to listen to what she had to say. But she sat back in her seat and fell silent. She let the prosecutor continue to berate her and portray her as the worst mother on the planet. She listened to the prosecutor drag her sex life into court. He talked about all of the men that had come forward to give testimony. Supposedly, they'd slept with her over the years while her son was sometimes in the same room with them. Celeste listened to the prosecutor announce she had had Ben when she was just fifteen years old and that his father had never been involved in his life.

The prosecutor continued to tell the jury that Celeste had to sell heroin to take care of her kids.

She wanted to just disappear. She was being dragged through the mud in front of a public audience. She hung her head and listened as her entire life was recounted in a twisted way. It was very clear to her now that the drug Baggie had definitely belonged to Ben.

As she sat there, Celeste began blaming herself for everything. She realized she had been so caught up in men and so money hungry that she had totally lost sight of Ben and how much money he was bringing into the house. Of course it all made sense to Celeste. And the truth was hitting her hard. She had purposely turned a blind eye to what her son was doing, because she had enjoyed the money he was giving her. Tears welled up in her eyes as she thought about how she had caused Ben to lose his innocence to the streets.

The prosecutor finished his remarks. Celeste couldn't be sure, but she thought he smiled at her after his opening remarks. It was time for the defense to try to clean up the horrible picture that had been painted of Celeste. Her lawyer was gathering his papers and about to stand up. Celeste grabbed her lawyer's arm and kept him from getting up. The young public defender looked at Celeste with furrowed eyebrows as if she was crazy. He was confused and a little annoyed at her. He sat back down.

"Counselor, is there a problem?" the judge asked when she noticed the exchange.

"I wanna plead guilty," Celeste whispered to her lawyer.

"Counselor, you want to tell us what your client is saying?" the judge urged strongly.

The young lawyer was frazzled. He was stammering and confused. "Um . . . your honor, I need a minute with my client," he stated, his words coming out awkward and choppy.

The judge rolled her eyes in disgust. However, she knew the young attorney was fresh out of law school and not really experienced. She granted him five minutes to speak with Celeste.

"I just want to plead guilty," Celeste told the lawyer forcefully. He looked perplexed. "I'm guilty, the drugs were mine," she lied. "I'm not a good mother. I let my son get to the drugs and I failed my other son too." Celeste had tears welling up in her eyes. She had a lump in her throat.

"I thought you said you had no idea where the drugs came from?" her lawyer asked in a gruff tone.

"Look, I wanna fucking plead guilty, I said! What the fuck don't you understand? Get it through your head, I'm guilty!" Celeste whispered excitedly and harshly.

The young attorney finally accepted what she was saying, although he thought she was crazy. Celeste watched him stand up. The attorney's hands were shaking as he nervously fumbled with his papers.

She was waiting for him to make the announcement. She swiped at the tears that were running down her face now. She had made up her mind. She wasn't going to sacrifice her other child to save herself. Celeste had resolved that she wouldn't tell anyone that Ben had been selling drugs and bringing it in the house. She felt she had failed and this was her redemption. She felt she was really the guilty party for not paying better attention to her kids, all over a man and her selfish greed.

"Your honor, my client has informed me that she would like to waive this trial and plead guilty in this case," the young attorney announced, his schoolboy voice wavering. "I have not had an opportunity to discuss this with the prosecution and to allow them to put together a plea deal, your honor. Therefore, I am asking for a continuance at a later date."

The prosecutor stood up in shock. The judge opened her eyes wide with shock as well. The courtroom erupted in murmurs and gasps of ohhs and ahhhs. Some of the media reporters ran out of the courtroom so they could try to be the first to break the news on TV. The judge banged her gavel and screamed, "Order! Order in this court!"

Ms. Tori looked down at Ben as she stood next to his hospital bed. She smiled. "You are being so brave, Ben. I'm so glad you have gotten up the courage," she soothed.

She looked over at the other side of Ben's bed

and nodded at the detective standing there. It was one of the detectives that had arrested Celeste. The detective Ben had dubbed the good cop.

"Yeah, Ben, it takes a real man to own up to his crimes," the detective agreed.

Ben just nodded. He wasn't able to speak because his left jaw was wired shut. He had almost lost part of the bone in his jaw due to his injuries from the beating. He had been in the hospital almost two months for the amount of injuries he had sustained during the incident. Although his jaw was wired shut, his broken arms had healed enough that he could write on a pad to communicate with Ms. Tori and the detective.

"So you're saying he wants to confess and tell us what happened to his brother?" the detective asked Ms. Tori, to confirm why he was there. The detective was looking at Ben as he asked Ms. Tori the question. Ms. Tori had called the detective and asked him to come to the center because Benjamin Early wanted to confess to inadvertently killing his baby brother, Keon.

"Ask him," Ms. Tori replied.

In big letters, Ben scribbled YES onto the pad that sat on the small rolling hospital tray in front of him.

"Why do you wanna confess now? You think it's gonna get your mother out of jail and since you're a juvenile you'll get a short two year sentence and go free?" the detective asked suspiciously. He had to be sure. People put kids up to confessing to serious crimes all the time. It was a well-known fact that juveniles got shorter sentences in most cases.

Ben shook his head no. He made his face into a frown to show his displeasure with the detective's conclusion. He started writing fiercely on his pad again. I want to confess because the drugs that my brother got into his system were mine. I was selling drugs and I brought them into the house. I meant to hide them, but I was careless that one time. My mother always said not to bring drugs in the house or to sell them. She doesn't deserve to sit in jail.

"In order for us to believe that you . . . a sixteen-year-old kid, had that high a grade of heroin, you will have to tell us who your supplier is and where you got the drugs from," the detective informed Ben. "I'm sure you don't know any Colombian cartel members, so you had to get it from somewhere. We will have to investigate before we even consider withdrawing the charges against your mother."

Ben closed his eyes in defeat. He had already anticipated the detective would tell him he had to give up Deezo in order to free his mother. He had already made it up in his mind that it was a sacrifice he was willing to make. I will tell you everything you need to know for my mother to go free, Ben scribbled on the paper. The detective nodded and pulled up a seat. He was all ears. In this case, all eyes.

"Early! Let's go," the court officer called out to Celeste. She was in a courthouse cell waiting to go into court for her plea hearing. She stood up with confidence. She had already made it up in her mind that she would not feel ashamed of herself anymore. She was ready to throw herself into the fire to save Ben, her only living son.

The court officer opened the cell and Celeste moved out. She was led into the packed courtroom. She looked out into the glaring crowd and she could feel the heat of eyes on her. She didn't feel nervous. The time for nervousness was over. She had already lost everything that mattered to her, so to her this was nothing.

The court officer announced the judge as she entered the courtroom. The judge folded her robe under her and motioned for everyone to take their seats. The sound of clothes rustling signaled to Celeste that everybody had sat back down and it was about to be on.

"Counselor, I take it you've had a chance to discuss this matter with your client and she is in agreement," the judge said to Celeste's lawyer.

"Yes, your honor," he replied. Celeste gnawed on her lip nervously.

"OK, would the defendant Celeste Early please rise," the judge instructed.

The courtroom was eerily silent and a cold chill passed down Celeste's back. She did as she was told and stood up.

"Ms. Early, has your attorney explained this proceeding to you?" the judge asked.

"Yes, your honor," Celeste said in a low whisper.

"Are you prepared to render your plea to this court today as to the charges against you? Those charges which have been reduced to just one charge of involuntary manslaughter?" the judge asked, looking at Celeste over the rim of her wire framed glasses.

Celeste answered yes.

"OK, Ms. Early, I will read off the charge and ask you how you plead. At that time you will tell the court how you plead," the judge instructed. Celeste nodded.

"Ms. Early, as to the charge of involuntary manslaughter in the case of the City of New York versus Celeste Early for the involuntary death of one Keon Drake Early, how do you plead?" the judge asked.

Celeste swallowed hard and closed her eyes for a second. She could see both of her kids' faces. Celeste began, her voice cracking, "Your honor, I, Celeste Early, plead gu—" Before she could get her complete statement out, she was interrupted.

"Wait!" a voice called out from the back door of the courtroom. The courtroom began to buzz with murmurs of shock and disbelief. Almost everyone turned around to see where and who the loud, crazy sounding voice was coming from, including Celeste. A few of the court officers began racing towards the voice as well.

"Your honor, I am the lead detective on this case," the detective stated. "At this time it is not necessary for Ms. Early to plead guilty. We are prepared to withdraw our case. We have developed new evidence that completely vindicates Ms. Early."

Celeste noticed it was the lead detective from her case, the one who pretended to be the good guy to his partner's bad guy. He was out of breath from running up to the courtroom. Celeste's legs got weak and a feeling of relief washed over her entire body. She had to sit down. Gripping the edge of the defendant's table, she eased down into the hardwood chair. She closed her eyes and exhaled. She felt like an angel had just come into the courtroom and given her an entirely new life.

The courtroom was alit with talking and movement. The judge banged her gavel several times to get everybody to simmer down. "Detective, I need to see you and both counselors in my chambers now!" the judge boomed. "This court will take a fifteen minute recess," she said, banging her gavel again as she rushed off the bench and stormed into her chambers.

The courtroom came alive like a third grade classroom without a teacher when the judge left. The media was buzzing and so was everybody in the courtroom. People had whipped out cell phones and were making calls, others were screaming across the aisles. The court officers couldn't control everyone. Including the people Deezo had hired to sit in on the case and report the play-by-play to him.

Deezo had decided to let Ben live when he found out Celeste was the one in jail for the drugs. He figured Ben couldn't have possibly talked to the cops. Too bad Ben had already suffered that horrible beatdown before Deezo realized Celeste was in jail. But things had changed. Deezo would be getting different information now, which would change up the game totally.

When the court recess was over the judge asked Celeste to stand up again. She held onto the table and pulled herself up. She was so nervous her eye was twitching, but she stood up straight and confident nonetheless.

"Ms. Early, after consulting with the prosecutor and your attorney, and based on some new evidence presented in the case, I have no choice but to dismiss the city's case against you," the judge told Celeste.

Celeste bent over at the waist and she cried tears of joy. "Thank you!" she said to the detective.

"You need to thank your son. He is a brave kid and he really cares about you," the detective told Celeste.

More buzzing erupted in the courtroom. Celeste knew she would be on the news again that night like so many other nights. She wondered if the media would be apologizing to her for calling her all sorts of nasty names. It didn't even matter if they didn't, Celeste was a free woman.

"Congratulations, Ms. Early. I hope everything works out for you and your son," Celeste's attorney said to her, patting her on the shoulder.

Celeste nodded at him. "I am going to make sure I take care of my son like I never did before," she told him with a big smile on her face.

Celeste was still led away by the court officers to a cell in the back of the courtroom. She had to be transported back to Riker's Island and have a proper release from the Department of Corrections. She didn't care. All she wanted to do was see Ben. She wanted to hug him, which is something she had failed to do over the years. When she had heard about Ben being jumped at the juvenile center and the condition he was in, she stayed up three nights in a row worried about him. She had been getting updates and that was how she knew Ben had made a great recovery from his injuries.

She thanked God that Ben didn't have permanent brain damage, because she had been told that he had suffered horrible head injuries. She wanted to tell him that she forgave him for bringing the drugs into the house and that they would grieve for baby Keon together.

She was released from Riker's Island and when the prison bus crossed the bridge, Ben and Ms. Tori were waiting for Celeste on the other side. She rushed over to her son and grabbed him into a tight embrace. Ben was still a wiry teenager and he wasn't big on public displays of affection, but he wrapped one of his arms around his mother and returned her hug.

Celeste and Ben climbed back into Ms. Tori's car and drove off. Celeste thanked Ben repeatedly for finally telling the truth about what happened. Additionally, Ben said he was sorry repeatedly for disobeying his mother's wishes and having the drugs in the house. They had one place to go before they headed home.

* * *

"Five–O, five–O!" a boy, the lookout, yelled. Everybody on the corner started to scatter. It was too late. There were ten black police vans all over the neighborhood. Every single one of Deezo's spots was being raided. The jump-out boys threw Quan up against the corner store wall and slapped handcuffs on him.

"I ain't do nothin', man!" Quan whined. The cops didn't have to say anything. They weren't looking for evidence against him. They already had all that they needed.

All of Deezo's workers at all of his spots were rounded up and hauled off in police vans. It was a good day for the narcotics teams in Brooklyn. They had received great insider information from a reliable source. But there was a problem. They had not found Deezo at any of his spots nor was he out in his car monitoring like he usually was. The narcotics detectives tried to get several of the corner boys to tell them where Deezo might be located, but none of the boys would cooperate. It seemed like Deezo had had a heads up before the raids.

Ms. Tori wheeled her car through the narrow path in the cemetery. Finally, she pulled up on the side of some newly laid graves. Celeste put her hand over her mouth as she stared out the window. Ben put his arm around her shoulder.

"C'mon Ma, you have to go say a proper goodbye to him," Ben said solemnly. He felt like he needed to do the same thing. He opened the car door and helped his mother out of the car. Slowly, they walked together through the overturned, red earth.

Celeste looked down and saw a small white cross that read KEON D. EARLY. She turned into Ben's chest and began sobbing.

"Shhh," he tried comforting her. "We have to do this together. He deserves us to come pay our respects," Ben said, sounding like a wise, mature, older man.

He moved Celeste from his chest and grabbed hold of her hand. They walked together and stopped at baby Keon's gravesite. Ben bent down and held his head down. Celeste did the same. She lifted her shaking hand and brushed some dirt off of the little white cross that the cemetery had placed on the grave.

"I'm so sorry baby. If I was a better mother this would not have happened to you. Please forgive me for everything. Keon, I love you so much," Celeste said through sobs.

"Keon, my little nigga, this was all my fault. I will always live with the fact that I was the one that caused your death. I know you are in heaven and I know you will look down on us forever," Ben said, his voice quivering a little bit.

They were silent for a few minutes.

Ben felt a presence behind them. He just assumed it was Ms. Tori. He stood up so that he could tell Ms. Tori a proper thank you for all of the things she had done for him while he was at the group home. When he turned around to face Ms. Tori, his mouth dropped open and all of the color drained from his face. Ben could not move. It was like his feet had planted roots in the dirt.

"What happened, you ain't happy to see a nigga?" Deezo said evilly.

Celeste jumped up when she heard the familiar voice. Her eyes hooded over with ill intent. She despised Deezo.

"How dare you disrespect the grave of my son when it was your drugs that killed him!" Celeste screeched.

Deezo started to laugh. It was an evil, shrill, maniacal laugh. "My drugs or this punk ass boy's stupidity?" Deezo replied. Ben bit down into his jaw.

"What do you want?" Celeste asked.

"I want what belongs to me," Deezo told her.

"Nothing here belongs to you. We don't have nothing for you!" Celeste spat.

"This boy of yours . . . he belongs to me! You ain't never tell 'em that I was his daddy?" Deezo said cruelly.

"Shut up! Get away from us! Leave us alone!" Celeste screamed.

Ben looked at his mother in disbelief. He couldn't believe his ears. All the years his mother let him struggle, working hard and all along she knew damn well who his father was.

"Now, I tried to be nice to him just because he was mine. But see, he ain't got no loyalty. The one thing I always told you lil nigga was never to cross me," Deezo said to Ben.

Ben balled up his fists and he was rocking on his heels. He wanted to kill both Deezo and Celeste for lying to him all these years.

"He didn't do anything to you. Get away from us!" Celeste cried out. She grabbed for Ben's hand to pull him away, but Ben yanked his hand away from her.

"Now your boy gonna face the consequences," Deezo said to her. "I can't go back to my house, all of my money done got seized, all my spots shut down . . . all because this boy you got here ran his mouth. I can't let it get out that no punk muthfucka like you is my son."

"Fuck you! I hate you!" Ben finally erupted. He started moving towards Deezo angrily.

"Naw Shorty, fuck you!" Deezo boomed. He lifted his hand that he had hidden behind his back and leveled a gun at Ben. Ben stopped dead in his tracks.

"Oh my God! No!" Celeste screamed at the top of her lungs when she saw the gun.

Ben could see Ms. Tori running from the car towards them. Everything seemed to be going in slow motion to Ben.

"Snitches don't deserve to live," Deezo said with finality.

BOOM! BOOM! BOOM!

Deezo shot three times.

Ben's eyes popped open as he looked down at all of the blood.

"I'll see you in hell," Deezo said, lifting the same gun to his own head and BOOM! He got off one more shot.

"Ma!" Ben screamed as his mother blocked him with her own body. The shots caused Celeste's body to lurch forward and she hit the dirt on top of baby Keon's grave.

"Ben!" Ms. Tori screamed as she finally reached them. It was too late. Ben was on his knees cradling his mother's head. Celeste's blood soaked his hands as she pressed down on her wounds, trying to get the bleeding to subside.

"Help! Help!" Ben screamed so loud and hard the veins in his neck were protruding through his skin. There was nobody around but them.

Ms. Tori began frantically dialing 911 on her cell phone.

Celeste looked up into Ben's face as blood spilled from her lips. She creased her face into a painful smile.

"Stay with me . . . just stay with me," Ben begged her as he rocked her.

Celeste moved her head side to side as she coughed up blood.

"Ma! Just please stay with me!" he cried.

"I'm s . . . s . . . sorry Ben. I . . . I . . . didn't me . . . mean to hur . . . hurt you," Celeste rasped.

"I know! I'm sorry too. You're gonna live, just hold on," Ben cried. He could hear the wailing of the ambulance and police sirens in the distance now.

"I will see K . . . Ke . . . Keon in heaven," Celeste managed to say.

The ambulance came to a screeching halt on the side of the path near the gravesite. Ben looked out of his tear-filled eyes and saw the EMTs running towards him. He shook his head. He knew they were too late. He reached down before they made it to where Celeste lay and closed her eyelids. He placed her head on the bloodied, wet earth right on top of his brother's grave. The EMTs finally made it over and started to feel Celeste for a pulse. One EMT held up his hand to signal to the others that she was gone.

"Oh my God, Ben . . . I am so sorry," Ms. Tori said, trying to grab Ben for a hug. He shoved her away. He started walking down the hill towards the path they had all parked on. Just as he made it down, the cop cars began pulling up. The uniformed and plainclothes cops came rushing past Ben, but he just kept on walking. He walked and walked with no destination in mind. He needed to clear his head. He had just lost his entire family all because he'd been a sucker for candy.

Available wherever books and ebooks are sold

Exposed **by Naomi Chase**
On the brink of a major promotion, Tamia Luke is within reach of the glitzy life she's always dreamed of—until her client, Dominic Archer, blackmails her into becoming his mistress, threatening to reveal her scandalous past. Tamia has no choice but to submit to his demands. But the tables turn when her hostility towards Dominic is replaced with insatiable lust. No man—including her boyfriend—has ever satisfied her the way he does. And as her infatuation grows, the closer she comes to losing everything—including her life . . .

Most Wanted **by Kiki Swinson and Nikki Turner**
Gigi Costner needs four million dollars she doesn't have and time she hasn't got. Her ex-con ex-lover swears to make her pay for the multimillion-dollar stash of diamonds she stole as she ditched him for a new life as a suburban wife. With time running out, will Gigi's new plan get her in front of the drama or drag her back into hood madness?

Heist **by Kiki Swinson and De'nesha Diamond**
Accustomed to a life of luxury, Shannon Marshall is devastated to lose everything after her husband, Todd, is sent to prison for gun running. So when Todd plans the ultimate stickup from behind bars, Shannon's ready to put her neck on the line. But she'll have to pull off the hustle of a lifetime and play one dangerous gangster who always gets what he wants . . .

Turn the page for an excerpt from
each of these exciting stories. . . .

From *Exposed*

"Your nine o'clock appointment is waiting in the conference room. I offered him coffee, but he declined."

"Thanks, Marjorie." Tamia rushed past the receptionist, barely sparing the woman a glance. She was ten minutes late to a meeting with a new client. Not exactly the best first impression to make. Thank God her boss was out of town this week, or she'd be in a shitload of trouble. Hell, if the client decided to go with another agency after today's consultation, Tamia could pretty much kiss her promotion good-bye.

Reaching her sleek glass cubicle, she stowed her Coach handbag in the bottom drawer of her desk and grabbed her OneNote tablet. Out of habit, she inspected her appearance in the hand mirror she kept hidden under a tray on her desk. Her MAC makeup was flawless, perfectly accentuating her dark, slanted eyes and full, juicy lips. Her lustrous black hair was cut in a stylishly layered, Rihannainspired bob that drew compliments wherever she went. Her silk button-down blouse molded large C-cup breasts, while her black pencil skirt showed off a round, healthy ass and long, toned legs.

As she hurried from the nest of cubicles that housed the agency's brand creative team, one of the copywriters popped his head up.

"Hey, Tamia, I need the final mock-up—"

"Not now," she said, cutting him off. "I'm meeting with a client. We'll talk later."

She headed quickly down the corridor, passing walls that were covered with framed awards, plaques, and press clippings the firm had garnered over the years, establishing it as one of Houston's top advertising agencies. Tamia had worked there for seven years, diligently climbing her way up the ranks. As an account executive, she'd spearheaded several successful ad campaigns and now boasted an impressive client list.

She loved her job. More important, she was damn good at it. So she had as good a shot as anyone else to land the coveted promotion to assistant brand manager of advertising.

Reaching the end of the corridor, Tamia strode briskly into the large conference room. A tall, broad-shouldered man stood at the huge picture window that overlooked the glistening downtown skyline. Dominic Archer, a Crucian-born businessman who'd made his fortune selling prepackaged Caribbean food products.

"Good morning, Mr. Archer. I apologize for keeping you wait—"

As he turned from the window, Tamia promptly

lost her train of thought. The man was at least six-four and copper brown, with sleepy dark eyes and a manicured goatee that framed full, sexy lips. Beneath his expensively tailored Gucci suit, his body looked well-toned and muscular. Solid as a rock.

Oh dayum, Tamia thought. *This brotha is foine!*

Recovering her professionalism, she stepped forward with an outstretched hand. "Tamia Luke," she introduced herself.

He clasped her hand, his eyes roaming her face. "Dominic Archer." His deep voice held a hint of a lazy island lilt. The scent of his expensive cologne wafted up her nostrils, subtle yet intoxicating.

Tamia smiled at him. "It's a pleasure to meet you, Mr. Archer. Are you sure you don't want any coffee, tea, or juice?"

He smiled, revealing a set of straight, white teeth. "No, thank you. I'm fine."

Yes, you are. Clearing her throat, Tamia motioned to the long glass conference table. "Please have a seat."

Once they were both settled at the table, she got right down to business. "I understand that you want a memorable advertising campaign to launch your first Caribbean-style restaurant."

"That's right." As Dominic leaned back in his chair and casually crossed his legs, Tamia's gaze was drawn to his Dolce & Gabbana black calfskin leather loafers. The man had style, which boded well for their collaborative partnership.

"I want something that's gonna grab people's attention," he explained to her. "Something that'll lure customers who've never even *thought* about trying Caribbean food. And I want something that'll drive as much traffic as possible to my restaurant."

Tamia smiled at him. "Then you've definitely come to the right agency. We have a proven track record of satisfying our clients' needs."

"So I've heard." Dominic's eyes gleamed. "I've been a fan of your work for years."

"Really? I'm so glad to hear that." Tamia was thoroughly stoked. "Now, before my team gets started on developing the creative concept for your ad campaign, I need to familiarize myself with your restaurant so that I can decide on an effective target market. So let's talk about—"

"You're even more beautiful than I'd imagined," Dominic interrupted softly.

Her cheeks warmed from the unexpected compliment. "Thank you."

"No, for real. I mean it." He held her gaze. "I always wondered what you looked like behind that black mask."

It took a delayed moment for his words to register. When they did, Tamia's blood ran cold and she stared at Dominic, stunned. "W-what did you just say?" she whispered.

A slow, knowing grin spread across his face. "Does anyone still call you Mystique?"

The room swayed. Tamia swallowed hard as a clammy sweat broke out over her skin. "When . . . how . . ." Her throat tightened, choking off the rest of her question.

Dominic grinned harder. "Like I said, I've been a fan of your work for years."

Tamia got unsteadily to her feet, crossed the room, and closed the door. She couldn't risk any of her coworkers overhearing the conversation she was about to have.

As she made her way back to the table, Dominic's eyes traveled over her body as if he were picturing her naked. When he licked his lips, Tamia felt dirty in a way she hadn't felt in years.

She stood behind her high-backed chair in an attempt to shield her body from his view. "What do you want?" She forced out the words past dry lips.

Dominic reluctantly lifted his eyes from her cleavage to meet her accusing gaze. "Why did you stop acting? You were a natural, Mystique."

"My name is Tamia."

He smiled, slowly shaking his head. "To me, you'll always be Mystique."

Tamia's manicured fingernails dug into the soft leather of the chair. "Again I ask. *What do you want?*"

His smile widened. "I want you to come out of retirement. Become Mystique again."

"That's not gonna happen."

"You misunderstand me." Dominic leaned forward in his seat. "I don't want you to perform for strangers. This time around, I want you all to myself."

Incredulous, Tamia stared at him. "You're out of your damn mind!"

He chuckled quietly. "If I am, Mystique, it's your fault."

"Don't call me—"

"I own every last one of your movies. I can't tell

you how many times I've watched them, wishing *I* was the lucky man you were fucking so enthusiastically. It never seemed like you were just acting. Like I said, you were a natural."

Tamia felt sick to her stomach. "Look," she said, darting a furtive glance toward the door, "I don't know who the hell put you up to this, but you wasted your time coming here. I stopped doing those movies a long time ago, and I have no intention of coming out of retirement for you or anyone else. Now you need to leave before I call security."

Dominic laughed softly, unfazed by the threat. "You won't call security."

"Think I won't?" Livid, Tamia spun away from him, rounded the conference table, and marched toward the phone at the opposite end.

"Do your colleagues know about your past life as a porn star?"

That stopped her dead in her tracks.

She stared across the table at Dominic. The wicked gleam in his eyes chilled her to the bone.

"Do they know about your alter ego Mystique, the submissive with a sublime pussy?" he taunted. "Do they know how much you enjoyed being spanked and fucked in the ass? Do they know how much you loved sucking your master's big, black—"

"Stop," Tamia whispered, feeling faint. "Just *stop*."

But he ignored her. "What about your boss? When I contacted the agency and specifically asked to work with you, he couldn't stop singing your praises. But does he know how *truly* talented you are? Would he risk the company's outstanding reputation by promoting an employee with a . . . checkered past?"

Tamia gaped at him in horror. "Are you *blackmailing* me?"

Dominic smiled narrowly. "Blackmail is such an ugly word, you know? I prefer to think of this as a business transaction, one that can be mutually beneficial."

"How?" Tamia hissed. "*You're* the only one who'd get something out of this damn deal."

"That's not true," he countered mildly. "In exchange for your cooperation, you'd get my sworn promise to keep your dirty little secret."

Tamia glared at him. "And if I don't 'cooperate'?"

"You will," he said with certainty.

Panic gripped her chest. "You can't make me do anything!"

"No?" he challenged, raising a thick brow. "Tell me, Mystique. Does the lieutenant governor's son know that you used to be a porn star?"

At the reference to Brandon, the blood drained from Tamia's head.

Dominic smiled, slow and satisfied. "I didn't think so."

"Why the hell are you doing this to me?" she cried.

"I already told you. I'm one of your biggest fans. I couldn't pass up the opportunity to meet you in person, to see if reality lives up to the fantasy." He looked her up and down slowly, visually peeling away each article of clothing. "So far I haven't been disappointed."

Nausea churned in Tamia's stomach. "It's time for you to leave."

He raised a brow. "But we haven't discussed my ad campaign yet."

Is he serious? Tamia wondered incredulously. "Under the circumstances, I'm sure you can understand why I'd have a problem working with you."

"You're up for a promotion," he smugly reminded her. "Can you really afford to turn away clients?"

Tamia didn't reply, but she knew he was right. Landing another major account would bolster her chances of receiving the promotion and give her an edge over her competition.

But at what cost?

"Why don't you give it some more thought?" Dominic suggested mildly. "I'd hate to have to tell your boss that you forced me to take my business to another ad agency."

Tamia glared at him, her jaw tightly clenched. The bastard knew how to play dirty. "You need to go."

He smiled, then unhurriedly rose to his feet, smoothing a hand over his silk tie.

As he rounded the table and came toward her, Tamia didn't know whether to bolt or grab the first sharp object she could get her hands on. She had time for neither before Dominic reached her. She folded her arms across her chest, a protective gesture that had the unintended effect of drawing even more attention to her cleavage.

Dominic stared at her bulging breasts, then licked his lips and gave her one of those lascivious smiles that made her feel violated. Powerless.

She closed her eyes and averted her face as he leaned close, his warm breath fanning her cheek. "You have twenty-four hours to consider my offer," he whispered in her ear. "Don't keep me waiting, or I promise you'll regret it."

Tamia swallowed hard, shaking from the inside out.

When she opened her eyes again he was gone, leaving behind a white business card on the table and a subtle trace of his cologne.

From *Most Wanted*

"Hey, baby?" I sang into my cell phone as soon as I heard Sidney's sexy voice come through the line. I could actually picture my husband smiling on the other end of the phone. He always smiled when it came to me.

"Guess where I am? No, silly, I'm not at home butt naked waiting for you." I laughed at his joke. "Seriously, I'm two minutes from the lot. Thought I would surprise you with lunch and a quick midday kitty call," I said seductively.

Sidney sounded excited to hear my voice. He just loved when I did little impromptu things like this. It wasn't always easy finding time to be spontaneous with him being such a busy businessman. He was much older than me, and I guess his previous relationships weren't as much fun. Sometimes I had to pull him out of his shell. It was nothing for me to try to keep him happy, so long as he kept making money.

"Don't worry about what I'm wearing . . . you'll

see when I get there," I cooed. He was saying something when my phone line beeped with another call interrupting our sexy talk. I pulled the phone away from my ear and saw that it was my mother. I blew out an exasperated breath. She always knew how to interfere at the wrong times. Sidney was saying something dirty, acting like the dirty old man that he was, but I had to cut him short.

"Look, baby, that's my mother on the other line. Let me holla at her and see what she wants. I'll see you in a few. Be ready for me," I told Sidney. He sounded excited as shit as we hung up.

I clicked over and put on my mental suit of armor. I loved my mother, but she could be a nag and annoying as hell too. It didn't make things easy that she basically lived off of me . . . well, my husband, really. The days of living off of me were long gone. I had come into some money, but I'd burned through it just as fast as I had gotten it. My mother had been right there burning up my little windfall with me. I had done some nice things for her because she raised me as a single mother in the rough streets of DC when most mothers were leaving their kids to go smoke crack and shit. Still, my money was gone, and she and I were basically dependents right now. Sidney took care of me, and in return I took care of my mother.

"Yes, Ma. What's up?" I answered the line, my voice dull and lifeless. Nothing like how I'd just spoken to Sidney. I wanted her to know I was busy and didn't have a lot of time to yak it up on the phone with her.

"Gigi?!" my mother belted out, damn near busting my eardrum. I pulled the phone away from my ear for a few seconds and frowned. She was bugging! I could hear her yelling my name again. "Gigi!"

"Slow down, lady . . . is everything all right? Why are you yelling?" I asked, concerned. I hadn't heard her all loud like this since she thought she'd hit the lottery a couple of months back. Long story. "You okay?" I asked again.

"Yeah! Yeah . . . everything is just fine. I got some news, baby!" she shrieked excitedly. *You got a damn job and no longer need to live off of us,* was what I was thinking, but I didn't dare say that. Once I realized her high-pitched voice wasn't caused by someone kicking her ass, I calmed down for a few seconds. I let out a long breath waiting to hear some crazy story of hers.

"Okay?" I said expectantly. "What is the news?"

"You will never guess who I spoke to today!" my mother yelped. Before I could even ask who, she volunteered the information. "Warren! I spoke to Warren! Your Warren, baby! He said he is coming home in less than a month and he wants to see us . . . well, really, he wants to see you the most," she said excitedly.

I felt like someone had just punched me in the side of my head. An immediate pain crashed into my skull like I'd been hit. "Warren?" I mumbled, my eyebrows immediately dipping on my forehead. I wished my ears had deceived me. A cold feeling shot through my veins and I almost dropped the phone and crashed the car. My heart immediately began thumping wildly, and cramps invaded my stomach like an army going in for the kill.

"Yes! Warren! He is getting out early on some kind of deal or good behavior . . . something like that! Isn't that good, Gigi?!" my mother continued.

I was speechless. I couldn't even think. Flashes of Warren's face started playing out in front of me. The last time I saw him haunted me now.

"You there, Gigi?" my mother inquired, her voice changing as she must've realized her news wasn't so good. I swallowed hard before I could get the words to come out of my mouth. I cleared my throat because the lump sitting in the back of it made it hard for me to talk. I could feel anger rising from my feet, climbing up to my head.

"How the hell did Warren get your new number?!" I asked through clenched teeth. My voice had no problems now. My nostrils flared and I gripped the steering wheel so hard veins erupted to the surface of the skin on the back of my hand.

"When I moved you from the fucking hood in Southeast DC, I told you to leave that shit behind altogether!" I chastised. "What is wrong with you?! You just couldn't leave well enough alone!" I barked some more. I was full on sweating now. My head was spinning a mile a minute. She had no fucking idea what she had done. "Whose side are you on?!" I screamed.

My mother was quiet at first. I'm sure she was looking at the phone like it was an alien from outer space. I guess she didn't know how to process my anger. She also didn't know the details of my history with Warren after our arrests, which probably confused her even more. It really wasn't her fault. My mother had always liked Warren for me. I mean, he had scooped me up out of the hood and given me a life my mother knew she could never give me. He didn't spare a dime when it came to her either. Sometimes my mother had seemed more enamored with Warren than me.

It was understandable given her history with men. As a kid, I had watched my mother go from one no-good bastard to another. My father had left as soon as I was born . . . typical hood story. My mother had always tried to find that perfect man, so most of my life her bedroom was like a revolving door. There would be one dude this month and another dude the next month. She would always come to me and say, "Gianna, I think this one is going to be your step daddy for sure this time. Baby, we gonna have a good life if it's the last thing I do." Pretty sad when I think back on how desperate my mother had been to find real love. I had watched niggas beat my mother, take her money, steal our TVs, and leave her so depressed she wouldn't get out of bed for weeks.

I was determined to be better than that when I grew up. I wanted to finally give my mother that good life, but school and hard work weren't in my DNA.

When I met Warren, he became my security blanket. He bought me food, clothes, and eventually, shelter. My mother was love struck herself. I would even catch her blushing sometimes when Warren would come to the house and joke around with her. I don't know why her staying in touch with Warren came as such a shock to me now. I always knew she'd probably pick him over me in a close call situation anyway. Plus, I had never told her what I'd done to him after he and I got knocked riding dirty. After Warren went to federal prison, I played the whole distraught girlfriend role in front of my mother, never letting on to the truth of the situation. She had seemed torn even then.

The news my mother had just dropped on me had me reeling. I started calculating shit in my head. I had been given a false sense of security thinking Warren was going to do much longer in prison. I didn't think he would be getting out so soon. . . . It had only been four years and according to the information I got, Warren had been charged with all types of gun charges, RICO shit, and the whole nine yards. I was under the impression from the feds that Warren would have the book thrown at his ass when he got sentenced.

Someone had fucking lied to me. This was definitely not part of the plan I had hatched back then. Even still, I thought for sure I had made provisions where Warren would never find me. I had changed my name slightly—no longer going by Gianna, I was now simply Gigi. I had moved out of DC, finally settling in country-ass Virginia, and started living the quiet, kept life as the wife of a fucking old rich dude, who technically could be my father. It would take my mother to fuck that all up!

"Ma . . . how did Warren get your phone number?" I asked again, finally able to calm myself down. My jaw rocked feverishly waiting for her answer. I was praying it wasn't her. I was hoping deep inside Warren had just paid a private investigator or some other Lifetime movie type shit.

"Gigi, when we moved from DC, I stayed in touch with Warren. I thought you would get over being mad at him one day and get back with him. I didn't know you were going to marry so fast. Warren was the only man who had ever done anything good for us and I felt obligated to him. He didn't have any family, so I wrote him letters and sent him packages. Not like you . . . you just got a new man and moved on," she replied.

All of my hopes of my mother NOT being the culprit who blew my cover were dashed. I wanted to scream at the top of my lungs. What a dumb bitch! How fucking stupid can you be?! I couldn't say those words, but I sure as hell was thinking them. Panic hit me like a wrecking ball going into a building at top speed. Warren was the last person on earth I wanted to see or hear from right fucking now. I had to breathe slowly through my mouth to calm down enough to keep talking to my mother. I also had to pay attention to the road.

"What have you told him about me?!" I inquired loudly. My voice quavered just thinking about ever seeing Warren again. This was definitely not what I had planned. Again, I silently hoped that my mother had never discussed me with Warren.

"Everything. He knows you're married. He said he is happy for you. He knows you are doing well living here in Virginia Beach with your new husband. I didn't see the problem. The man is locked up and he was still asking about you. I think he always loved you, Gianna. All I can say is sorry, but Warren seemed very happy for you," my mother said apologetically. Something like a cord just snapped inside of me. I was literally coming apart at the seams listening to her.

"You are stupid! You had no right telling him my business! He is my ex and you don't know what the fuck I went through with him because I never told you! Just because you would do any fucking thing just to say you had a man doesn't mean I grew up to be like you!" I boomed, the cruel words hurling from my mouth like hard rocks. I breathed out a long, hard windstorm of breath.

"Did you also tell him who I am married to? Anything about where I live? Or maybe you gave him my fucking social security number while you were at it?" I asked, trying to sound as calm as I could. It wasn't working; the base in my voice was deep and intimidating.

"Well, excuse me! I thought you would want him to know how well you were doing now, seeing that he almost caused you to go to prison right along with him. He didn't even sound like he was interested in getting back with you at all. His questions were all general . . . seemed to just want to know you were all right. I'm sorry if you feel like I did something wrong, but the last time I checked I don't have anything to hide," my mother retorted.

I immediately felt guilty for calling her stupid. I had to try and pull myself together. It wasn't her fault.

She was right. She had no idea what had happened, and maybe she just wanted Warren to know that despite the jeopardy he'd put me in four years earlier, I was doing just fine. There were a few minutes of awkward, eerie silence on the phone line. My mother wasn't the quiet type, so I knew the silence meant she was truly at a loss for words.

"I gotta go," I said. I didn't give her a chance to say a word. I just hung up the phone. A loud horn blaring behind me almost caused me to drive off the road. I swerved my car a little bit to keep from hitting others.

"What the fuck?!" I screamed, looking into my rearview mirror. I swerved onto the shoulder of the road. The string of cars behind me passed by, drivers cursing at me and laying on their horns. I was shaken up. I clutched my chest. I had been so distracted by what she was telling me that I was driving slow as hell, holding up traffic. The news from my mother had fucked me up so badly I couldn't even drive. I put my car in Park and sat there for a few minutes.

"Warren is coming home early and knows where I am," I said out loud as if I had to convince myself that what I'd heard was true. My insides churned and I felt like I had to throw up. My legs rocked in and out feverishly. I could see the snarl on Warren's face as clear as day in my mind's eye. I knew him so well. I knew how he was when it came to shit like loyalty too. I had made a promise to him that I hadn't kept. I had also seen Warren's wrath firsthand. There was no way he would just let go of what I had done to him. I could hear him speaking to me now. "No matter what, just never cross me. I can live with everything else. Just never betray me." Warren had said those words to me on several occasions. The same words over and over, he never changed it up. Each time he had said them, in return I promised him that I'd always be loyal, never cross him. I had sworn. I had pledged my allegiance to him. But then I'd turned around and committed the worst Judas act of treason against him.

"Fuck!" I screamed, slamming my fists on my steering wheel until they hurt. "Fuck! Gigi! What the fuck have you done?! What the fuck are you going to do now?!" I yelled out loud. Where Warren and I came from, what I had done was a cardinal sin. In any hood I knew of, snitching and stealing were both acts as heinous as raping a child or killing your own parents. That is how seriously street niggas took it. Most of the niggas I knew, Warren included, lived by the death before disloyalty creed. I was terrified just thinking about the consequences. Maybe he'd shoot me execution style right in front of my mother. Maybe Warren would torture me with battery acid and jumper cables before finally putting me out of my misery. I could only imagine. I closed my eyes and all I could do was think back to how things had gone so wrong. How we'd gone from being so happy—the hood's Prince William and Kate—to being the hunter and the hunted. I kept thinking. Thinking. Something I had tried to avoid doing for four years now. I couldn't help it. My mind went back.

From *Heist*

CRASH! BANG! "What the fuck?!" I was out of bed and on my feet with one big jump when I heard the sounds of crashing glass and wood smashing. I immediately started searching the side of my bed for my ratchet. I felt down around on the floor in the place I usually kept it.

Nothing.

"Fuck," I cursed as the sounds grew louder and louder. Shannon had moved my shit. I told her not to ever move my shit without telling me. She was always so worried about guns being around Lil Todd.

"What the fuck!" I exclaimed as I heard feet thundering in my direction. My heart pounded through my wife-beater like the shit was going to jump loose of my chest bones. My mind was not foggy with sleep anymore; I was wide awake and on alert.

I didn't know if it was jealous motherfuckers from the hood or those hating-ass five-o bastards who had a vendetta against me, banging up my fucking minimansion doors. The shit sounded like a fucking earthquake was happening right there in my crib. At first I didn't hear them say "POLICE!" but as soon as I was facing down the end of an MP5, I knew what the fuck was up.

"Get on the floor! Get the fuck on the floor!"

Those commands were very familiar. I put my hands up, folded them behind my head, and assumed the position. I was pushed down to the floor roughly, and about five of those bastards dropped knees in my back and legs. My arms were yanked behind my back, and I was cuffed and made to lie facedown on my own fucking floor. Those fucking pigs were swarming my crib like flies around a pile of freshly dropped shit. It seemed like there were a million of them. All of them against just me.

"Punk bitches," I grumbled under my breath. I recognized one of them—a big-headed white boy who thought he was the shit. A snake motherfucker named Labeckie. He was the sergeant of the Norfolk Police Department's narcotics and gun unit, and he hated my ass.

"Take out that wall! Tear this fucking place up until we find some shit!" I heard that bastard yell as he looked down at me and smiled.

I closed my eyes when I heard them axing down walls and cabinets. Didn't they fucking know they could've just opened that shit up? My mind was racing, and I immediately hoped that Shannon didn't walk in on this shit with Lil Todd.

I lay there, facedown, knowing right away that

somebody in my camp had snitched. I knew my gun-running shit and five-o radar were airtight. There was no fucking way they could have known about my operation unless somebody told them. It had been three years since I had done my last bid on a drug charge, and when I got home, I had gone into a different line of work. Before I got knocked on the trumped-up drug charges, I was one of the biggest kingpins in the Norfolk area. I had all of Tidewater on lock, and I was bringing in at least fifty thousand a week. Almost all of the trap boys in the area were employed by me. I ran a tight ship, and the narcos found it hard to get my ass. The cops who arrested me the last time weren't gonna rest until they got my ass. I had beat so many charges because of my high-paid attorney, and those fucking pigs were mad as hell, so when they finally got me on some ol' caught-slipping shit, they was happy as hell.

When I came home, I promised my wife I was leaving the drug game behind me—the money, the bitches, and the fucking five-o too. I knew she was tired of riding with me through all this bullshit, so I told her I was going legit, and that is exactly what I did . . . at first. I opened my own short-distance trucking company. That shit was all good, but it wasn't enough money for me. Shannon was used to living a certain lifestyle, and I was going to provide it. I got into the gun-running shit by coincidence, and it was all up from there. I was bringing in cake, and my wife and kid were fucking happy. I was sure I was careful, and I surrounded myself with only a few cats who I thought were real.

It seemed one of those motherfuckers wasn't a real cat but a fucking snake-ass rat.

These bastard-ass cops had me facedown on the floor for mad long. The circulation in my hands felt like it was completely cut off. All I could hear was them destroying my beautiful home and rummaging through my shit. I bit into my cheek until I drew blood when I heard one of them whistle and say, "Hmm, the missus must be a pretty bitch—look at these pretty-ass panties." Then the bastard took a long sniff and said, "Ahhhh, pretty pussy smell. Think I could fuck his wife while he does his life sentence?" and then he started laughing. I squirmed around with the handcuffs biting into my skin. He was so lucky I was shackled like an animal or else I would've fucked his ass up. Shannon was my world, and I didn't want a nigga, especially a bitch-ass pig, even looking in her direction.

"Yo, these cuffs is tight!" I called out while they continued going through my shit.

"I don't give a fuck! You lucky we don't hog-tie you like the animal you are," the pig guarding me barked in my ear. His punk ass knew if I could get out of the fucking handcuffs, his wig would be twisted back.

It seemed like they were searching for days when one of them yelled, "Jackpot! I knew we would find something!" I just shut my eyes and thought about Shannon and our little man. I was a three striker, and my ass was going down. I had always made it a practice not to bring my shit where I live, but Jock—one of my boys—had met up with me the night before with a military-grade AK47 left over from his sales meeting. Apparently the cats he met up with had gotten cold feet on that shit and didn't buy it, leaving Jock to drive around with the shit on his way back to Norfolk. Jock was shook and didn't know where to take the shit, so being the man I am, I met up with Jock and took that load off of him. My intention had been to get that shit sold today. Either I was a few hours short or I was set the fuck up.

"Yo, I get a phone call, right?" I asked as two cops hauled me up off the floor.

"Don't ask for shit!" one of them barked.